This book should be returned to any branch of the
Lancashire County Library on or before the date

25 NOV
11. JAN 21

D0766116

LANCASHIRE COUNTY LIBRARY

3011813435151 3

Praise for *In the Family*

'It has the feel of a literary novel with the constant disquiet of a sinister undercurrent. *In the Family* is a book that I would read again, not only because of the rich tapestry of images, dialogue and internal landscapes, but also the thoughtful use of the written word. I can't wait to read the next Tim Yates novel.'

—ELAINE ALDRED

'The first thing you notice about the book is how well written it is. It has the feel of literary fiction.'

—SARAH WARD, *Crime Pieces*

'The slow-reveal of the Atkins' history is reminiscent of Ruth Rendell/Barbara Vine, forming a counterpoint to the brisk detective work of the police. The two stories – and two styles – are successfully brought together in the final chapters.'

—RICH WESTWOOD, *Euro Crime*

'An atmospheric and compelling psychological crime thriller set in the South Lincolnshire Fens. A "cold case" from 30 years ago is re-opened after the discovery of the skeleton of a young woman but even after all this time it is clear the family are hiding something. We think this is a really exciting addition to the UK crime writing scene and look forward to reading DI Tim Yates' next case.'

—*Lovereading*

Praise for *Almost Love*

'A book that I would read again, not only because of the rich tapestry of images, dialogue and internal landscapes, but also the thoughtful use of the written word. I can't wait to read the next Tim Yates novel.'
—ELAINE ALDRED

'Christina James has given me back my taste for good, gripping crime fiction.'
—VALERIE POORE

'A compelling read, holding the suspension and intrigue all the way through . . .'
—MARK MAJUREY

'With a well-written and cleverly plotted story and, above all, rich characterisation, this new piece of crime fiction is both believable and addictive from the start.'
—BLANDINE BASTIE

Praise for *Sausage Hall*

'If you're after a complex plot with some political and illegal undertones, plenty of suspicious circumstances and some interesting historical content, then give this a try.'
—*Mean Streets*

'James specialises in mixing suspense-flavoured first-person and historical narratives in with the police-procedural. In *Sausage Hall* she uses Kevan's voice to narrate events from the point of view of a troubled family man. This time, the tireless Juliet gets a richly-deserved romantic sub-plot.'
—RICH WESTWOOD, *Euro Crime*

★★★★☆ 'A police procedural with a depth and some mischievous twists that go beyond the average procedural. Yes, DI Tim Yates is back in a third outing, investigating skeletons in the cellar and a body in the woods; great stuff that just gets better.'
—ANI JOHNSON, *The Bookbag*

'I love the unfolding of a good mystery and *Sausage Hall* is certainly one.' —DIANE CHALLENOR, *Artuccion*

★★★★ 'Had me fairly engrossed at all times . . . Serious issues are touched upon regarding people trafficking, prostitution and exploitation.' —*Crimespace*

Praise for *The Crossing*

★★★★★ 'A seemingly straightforward case upends a termites' nest for DI Tim Yates. Riveting, thrilling and with that trademark Christina James shock at the end. Cracking crime writing at its best.'
—ANI JOHNSON, *The Bookbag*

'It's not the accident itself however that is the focus of the novel, but the events that it sparks off, as the wreckage is checked and the families of those involved contacted. More and more characters join the jigsaw which grows increasingly dark as the deeper and creepier element of the plot begins to emerge.'
—*Shots Crime and Thriller eZine*

CHRISTINA JAMES

ROOTED IN DISHONOUR

CROMER

PUBLISHED BY SALT PUBLISHING 2016

2 4 6 8 10 9 7 5 3 1

Copyright © Christina James 2016

Christina James has asserted her right under the Copyright, Designs
and Patents Act 1988 to be identified as the author of this work.

*This book is sold subject to the condition that it shall not, by way of
trade or otherwise, be lent, resold, hired out, or otherwise circulated
without the publisher's prior consent in any form of binding or cover
other than that in which it is published and without a similar condition
including this condition being imposed on the subsequent publisher.*

This book is a work of fiction. Any references to historical events, real
people or real places are used fictitiously. Other names, characters, places
and events are products of the author's imagination, and any resemblance to
actual events or places or persons, living or dead, is entirely coincidental.

First published in Great Britain in 2016 by
Salt Publishing Ltd
12 Norwich Road, Cromer, Norfolk NR27 0AX United Kingdom

www.saltpublishing.com

Salt Publishing Limited Reg. No. 5293401

A CIP catalogue record for this book is available from the British Library

ISBN 978 1 78463 089 8 (Paperback edition)
ISBN 978 1 78463 090 4 (Electronic edition)

Typeset in Neacademia by Salt Publishing

Printed and bound in Great Britain by Clays Ltd, St Ives plc

Salt Publishing Limited is committed to responsible forest management.
This book is made from Forest Stewardship Council™ certified paper.

For James, brave and humorous as
ever in an extraordinary year

LANCASHIRE COUNTY LIBRARY	
3011813435151 3	
Askews & Holts	24-Nov-2016
AF CRM	£8.99
HAC	

'His honour rooted in dishonour stood, And
faith unfaithful kept him falsely true'
—TENNYSON, *Lancelot and Elaine*

Chapter 1

DETECTIVE INSPECTOR TIM Yates stepped off the train at King's Cross and joined the throng of fellow passengers heading for the exit. It was a hot day and he was sweating. He slackened his pace and wiped his face with his handkerchief. He was halfway through a course of malaria tablets and, although he'd been told the side-effects would be negligible, was feeling decidedly unwell. He put down his briefcase for a moment and leaned uncomfortably against a pillar, taking a swig from the bottle of water he was carrying as he did so.

"Are you all right, sir?"

Tim was startled to find one of the stewardesses from the train standing at his elbow. He smiled wanly.

"Yes, I think so. It's just the heat. It's getting to me a bit."

"London does take some getting used to," she said sympathetically, putting Tim's back up straight away. Did he look like a country bumpkin?

"I'm just on my way to see my sister in Surbiton, so I should be all right," he replied haughtily. "I'll be able to relax today. Still here on business tomorrow, unfortunately." He gave her a challenging look.

"Well, take care." She smiled uncertainly. Tim abandoned his slouch, stooped to pick up the briefcase, adjusted the straps of his rucksack and walked briskly on.

As he passed through the barrier into the departures hall,

he gazed with mixed approval at the backlit latticed roof which was the most spectacular of the many features that made up the costly renovation the station had undergone a couple of years previously. Mostly he admired the brilliant transformation that had turned a grimy Victorian station in a suspect part of London into a twenty-first century cosmopolitan destination, but part of him still mourned its grubby predecessor, especially the insanitary old pub adjacent to Platform 6 where he'd often taken his life into his hands by buying a microbe-rich breakfast.

The brisk walk to the barrier turned out to have been unwise. By the time Tim had passed through it, swearing as he forced his crumpled ticket into the slot, he was sweating again and his vision was blurred. He tried to focus on a group of people standing on the concourse in front of him and noticed that each of them seemed to be ringed with a hazy yellow line, a bit like the line Forensics drew around corpses to show their exact position in death. Not good.

He glanced at his watch. It was 11.30 a.m. He'd arranged to meet his sister for lunch at 1 p.m., partly to thank her in advance for her hospitality, partly so that he could pick up the key and not have to hang around waiting in London until she left work that evening. As they'd agreed to meet at the restaurant at the British Museum, he knew he had ample time to buy himself some tea, sit down for a while and revive.

On a previous journey he'd familiarised himself with the various catering establishments on offer at the refurbished station, and much preferred the smaller bars and cafes on the mezzanine floor. Today, however, he could be bothered with neither the escalator nor the stairs, and settled instead for a seat at one of the tables at the large Pret-a-Manger that abutted the concourse. He claimed one of only two free two-seater tables next to the railings, leaving his rucksack there to 'bag' it while reflecting ruefully that he should know better than to leave his possessions unattended in a public place. He'd keep an eye on the rucksack while he bought the tea and rush over if anyone tried to remove it or eyed it suspiciously: it would be embarrassing if it were seized by the railway police as a potential security threat.

The tea came quickly, its production having caused much less of a palaver than if he'd demanded a coffee from the steaming Gaggia machine, and he regained the table without mishap. He lifted the plastic lid on his tea and peered at it without enthusiasm. The teabag, already coagulating with scummy milk, was floating in the slowly-browning liquid like a small indolent sea-creature tethered by a string to the rim of the cup. Tim yanked at the string, taking the teabag between his thumb and forefinger and squeezing it inelegantly. He inspected the beverage again. It still looked insipid, prompting an unexpected pang of nostalgia for the generously mahogany-coloured tea always available at Spalding police station. Another wave of faintness swept over him, this time accompanied by some slight nausea. The sweat was running down his face.

He was wearing a light raincoat and thought he'd feel better without it. He was about to peel it off when he heard a familiar voice rise to a crescendo very close to him. Resisting the urge to turn round to observe its owner, he now decided to keep the raincoat on, debating with himself whether to turn up the collar would draw unwanted attention or help him to retain his anonymity. He'd recognised the voice at once.

"Yes, yes, darling, I quite agree, but we all have to take a few roughs with the smooth, don't we? And the financial benefits are *so* great. Believe me, I wouldn't want to expose you to *any* sordid little enterprise. This one's the real deal, as I believe one says these days when in a colloquial frame of mind."

"It's not what I was promised." To Tim's surprise, the man had been talking to a woman. He itched to turn round and take a look at her. "Jas said he had a string of boutiques for me to find staff for. He didn't mention anything about having to look after his friends."

"Yes, but you will, won't you, dear?" The airy voice was darkening, the speaker now muttering through his teeth.

"I don't know . . ."

"Yes, you bloody well do know. And you'll do as Jas says. As we both say. That is, if you know what's good for you." There was a silence before the flute-like tone returned. "Now, do finish your tea, darling. I'm dying for a proper drink and we certainly aren't going to get one here."

Tim picked up his phone and speed-dialled Juliet Armstrong's number. It rang eight times and went to message. There was a scraping of chairs as the couple behind him prepared to leave. Tim stood up, intending to turn at the last minute and confront the male speaker. He was assaulted by a searing headache as an overpowering wave of nausea swept over him. He stumbled against the table, vomiting as discreetly as he could into a small trough of plants on the other side of the railings. He sat down again, heavily.

"How disgusting!" piped the voice. "Come along, darling. We've got to run."

Chapter 2

TIM TRIED TO apologise to one of the cheerful Pret-a-Manger baristas, but she brushed the incident off with a knowing smile. She probably thought he'd simply had one too many the previous evening. He was acutely embarrassed by the episode, aware that most of his fellow patrons were staring at him. With his head still pounding, he picked up his belongings and hurried away from the refreshment area and out of the station. Though he had intended to walk to the British Museum, the alarming dizzy feeling was returning and he decided he would have to queue at the taxi rank.

Despite his malaise, he was furious that he'd been unable to confirm identification of the familiar-sounding speaker who'd been sitting at the table behind him. He knew who it was, of course - that voice was unmistakable - but no-one would believe him unless he could actually have claimed to have seen the man's face. Half-heartedly, he scanned the long line of people standing at the rank, but none remotely resembled the man he was looking for. He wasn't surprised: the queue was moving quickly and even if his suspect had joined it, he and the woman accompanying him would have ridden away by now. The question that really concerned him was whether he had himself been recognised. If so, he knew that man would effect a disappearing trick long before Tim could muster a search for him.

The taxi that picked him up was bright pink and covered

in slogans about breast cancer awareness. Normally he would have preferred a more anonymous-looking vehicle, but in his present state he was grateful for any haven and sank back with a sigh against the leather seats.

"'Avin a tough day, are you, gov?" said the driver, meeting his eye in the mirror. Tim guessed his affability would vanish if he'd known that his fare had just thrown up in a public place.

"Sort of," he replied cautiously. "Had to get up too early and I don't think it agreed with me."

The driver eyed him suspiciously.

"Didn't 'ave one too many last night, did you?" he asked, meaningfully.

"Certainly not," said Tim. "I'm a police officer here on business," he added somewhat primly.

The driver barked a short, hoarse laugh.

"Fat difference that makes," he said. "I've seen coppers as paralytic as the next bloke. Where to?" he added, becoming business-like.

"The British Museum, please." He'd barely spoken the words when his mobile began to ring. He turned his attention from the driver with some relief.

"Hello, Juliet. Everything ok?"

"Yes, I think so. You called me a little while ago?"

"Did I?"

"Yes." Juliet paused for a moment. "Sorry I didn't answer. I was in a meeting. What was it about?"

The pain in Tim's head had driven away all recollection of the call, but he knew what he must have wanted to ask her.

"Do you remember Peter Prance?"

"How could I forget him! Why do you ask?"

"I think I saw him in a café just now. Or rather, I didn't see him."

"I'm sorry, Tim, I must be a bit slow today. How did you manage to see and not see him at the same time?"

"To put it more accurately, I heard him. He was sitting at the table behind me, talking to a woman. I'm sure it was him: as you know, his voice is unmistakable. I didn't want him to see me, so I didn't look round. I meant to follow him discreetly after he left the café."

"But you lost him?"

"No, I . . . yes," said Tim wearily. He had neither the energy nor the will to describe to Juliet the little vignette in which he'd just starred.

"You must have seen him leave the café, though. You confirmed that it *was* him?"

"No. No, I didn't. He . . . he managed to give me the slip. I don't think he recognised me, though, which is important. You know as well as I do he'll go to ground straight away if he thinks we're on to him."

"So what do you want me to do? Alert the London police? It might be tricky if you can't say you positively identified him."

"No, I don't want you to do that. I'm seeing Derry Hacker tomorrow and I'll discuss it with him then. It's his patch – he can decide on the best course of action. What I'd like you to do is check the records to see if there have been any sightings of him, confirmed or otherwise, in the London area since he disappeared after he was given bail. And find out from his file if he has any known connections in London."

"Ok, I can do that. Are you all right?"

"Yes, I'm fine. Why do you ask?"

"You just sound a bit strange, that's all."

"I've got a humdinger of a headache. I'm on my way to meet Freya for lunch. I'm hoping some food might help to get rid of it."

"A glass of red wine's good for knocking out a headache. Unless it's hair of the dog." Tim could hear Juliet's smile.

"Don't you start!" he said.

"What do you mean..?"

"Here we are, mate," said the driver. "Seven pounds, please."

"Sorry, Juliet, I've got to go. If you could do that work for me, I'd be grateful."

"Sure. When do you want it by?"

"I don't want to push you, but if you can make a bit of headway before I see Derry tomorrow, that would be brilliant."

"What time is your meeting?"

"We're going to have breakfast together at 8 a.m."

Juliet laughed. "No pressure, then."

Tim was fiddling with his wallet and trying to think of a witty quip in reply when the hammering in his head increased. He felt the vomit rise in his throat. Precipitately cutting his call with Juliet and flinging open the cab door, he retched copiously into the gutter.

When it was over, he climbed out of the taxi, his eyes still watering, a foul taste in his mouth. He took ten pounds from the wallet and passed it through the passenger window to the driver, who took it gingerly by one corner with a moue of intense disgust.

"Keep the change," said Tim.

"Thanks, I will. Listen, mate, if my cab had copped it with that lot, it would've cost you a lot more than three quid. You want to get a grip, you do. Shut the door, will you?"

Tim slammed shut the rear cab door and the taxi driver roared away, leaving him overcome with a guilt that, deep down, he knew he didn't deserve to feel.

Chapter 3

THE LUNCH WITH Freya was pleasant enough. After she had gone back to work, Tim debated briefly whether to take a look at an exhibition about the Raj while he was at the museum. His headache had almost gone and he was reluctant to pass up the opportunity, but he still felt very fragile and decided that the wisest course of action would be to leave straight away for his sister's house. He skirted the huge ceramic elephant standing sentry at the entrance to the exhibition and emerged once more into the sunlight.

Under normal circumstances, he'd have enjoyed the walk to Waterloo, but today it was out of the question. He knew his legs wouldn't carry him that far; he didn't think they'd even get him to the Underground. As he'd noted more than once, the BM was quite a distance from its nearest tube station and he didn't fancy trudging to either Russell Square or Tottenham Court Road. London buses were a mystery to him: apart from not understanding their timetables, he was chary of being unable to recognise the landmarks near his destination and mistakenly remaining on board until he ended up in some God-forsaken place like Gunnersbury or West Ruislip. Despite the bad experience of a couple of hours earlier, he decided to hail a taxi. They always circled the BM like sharks and he spotted one immediately. Thankfully it was black and anonymous.

Tim hauled himself into the cab. The driver was a Sikh who sported a magnificent red turban.

"Where to, mate?" he asked, using the classless lingo that Derry Hacker called 'London multicultural English'.

"King's Cross, please," Tim replied. The cab shot off towards Southampton Row. It took Tim a minute or so to realise that he'd meant to say Waterloo. He met the cabbie's eye and decided to live with his mistake. He could get to Waterloo from King's Cross quite easily on the Tube.

His driver had decided that making eye contact indicated a desire to chat.

"Had a right wasterman in here this morning. One of them immigrants."

"Oh?"

"Yeah. He wasn't gonna pay until I told 'im a few 'ome trufes."

"Oh," said Tim again. He had no energy for arguing the toss with the guy, much less having to admonish him for issuing threats if it transpired that was what he'd been doing.

Taking the hint, the driver flashed him a withering look and fell silent. Tim usually enjoyed friendly banter with cabbies, but he was getting nowhere with them today. The taxi bumped along sullenly until Tim was deposited outside the sliding glass doors of the station. He paid the cabbie and dawdled along until he reached the Underground. He remembered looking at a tube map and feeling bewildered by the choices.

Somehow, he lost the next thirty minutes. When he became aware of his surroundings again, he was getting off the train at Stratford. As if he'd been doing it all his life, he boarded another train and stayed on it for fifteen minutes before leaving it at Ilford. He walked briskly out of Ilford station and took a short walk unerringly, as if it was his daily routine, to a residential street called Belgrave Road. His malaise had vanished completely, as had the depressed, defeated feeling that had accompanied it. Now he was on a high, ebullient and ready for anything.

He marched along the street, a pleasant road of double-fronted terraced houses, until he'd covered a third of its length. Then he stopped outside a yellow-clad brick house with a gable and two bay windows and waited.

He didn't know what he was waiting for, but he stood there for some time. The street was fairly deserted, but eventually a man came along and eyed him suspiciously. The man walked past Tim, turned round to look at him, changed his mind and walked back again.

"You looking for someone?" he asked.

Tim snapped out of his reverie.

"I'm . . . not sure," he said.

"Well, if I was you, friend, I'd piss off back to where I came from. We don't like loiterers round here. We've got a good neighbourhood watch outfit. I belong to it and we don't miss much. Believe me, if you try anything on, you'll wish you hadn't of."

Another threat, Tim thought dimly, though he couldn't quite remember what the first one had been. He felt confused and lost. He had no idea what he was doing in this alien place.

"I'm sorry," he said. "I'm a bit disorientated. Can you tell me where I am, please?"

"Don't try to pull that stunt. It's obvious you was casing Number Forty-One. Now clear off, before I call the cops."

Tim turned to head back up the street. He glanced once more at the house as he went and thought he saw something reflected in the windows, swinging heavily. He couldn't quite make it out, but it looked like the hanging body of a woman. He stared again, more intently, but the image had evaporated.

"I said 'op it," said the man pugnaciously.

Tim hopped it. He couldn't remember the way to Ilford station – could barely remember that he had arrived in Belgrave Road via the station – and had to ask the way of a postman further up the street. He pointed Tim in the right direction, but as grudgingly and laconically as possible.

"What is it with these people?" Tim thought to himself. He had the strange sensation of having stepped through the looking glass or finding himself, against his will, in a parallel universe.

Once at the station, he decided not to ask for more help. He didn't like the look of the clerk in the booking office and thought that he'd likely get short shrift there once again. He spent some time working out how to get to Surbiton from Ilford, as much to reassure himself that he still had command of all his faculties as because he disliked the clerk.

By the time he reached Surbiton station his physical strength was completely restored. It was not yet 5 p.m. and the rush hour crowds had still to come sweeping through. He decided to walk to Freya's house, only stopping en route to enter one of the several off-licences on Ewell Road to buy a bottle of wine.

When he arrived at Freya's, the door was flung open. Freya was standing there, hands on hips, her frown of worry morphing instantly to one of exasperation.

"Where on earth have you been?"

"I decided to walk from the station. I'm sorry, I didn't think you'd be back so early."

"I told you there'd been a change of plan and I wasn't going to work all afternoon. I said I'd just got a few things to clear up at work and then I'd come straight here to meet you. Don't you remember?"

"No. But you could have called the mobile."

"I *have* been calling the mobile. Constantly. So has Katrin. You must have switched it off."

"Well, come off it, Freya, it's not such a big deal, is it? It's not as if I've turned up at midnight or been missing for days."

"No. But you were so strange at lunch that I've been really worried. Where have you been, anyway? It hasn't taken you all this time just to walk here from the station."

"I've been to Ilford," said Tim, in a voice that sounded as surprised as his sister looked.

"Ilford? But why?"

"I don't have the faintest idea."

Chapter 4

"I DESPAIR OF you, Tim, really I do," said Freya. It was fifteen minutes after he'd turned up on her doorstep and he was now seated on one of her comfortable but elegant sofas, sipping green tea. He pulled a face.

"You may well look like that . . ."

"Sorry," he said. "It's this tea. Bit of an acquired taste, isn't it?"

"You'd do well to drink it. I think you must have swallowed something toxic and it's made you hallucinate. It's probably those malaria tablets you're taking. The tea will help to cleanse your system."

"If you say so," said Tim, grimacing again.

"Have you called Katrin?"

"No. I thought I'd do it later. When Sophia's in bed."

"Don't you think you'd better do it now? She's worried about you."

"She wouldn't be if you hadn't alarmed her for no reason," Tim grumbled, getting to his feet. He wandered off into the kitchen to gain some privacy. Freya and Katrin were always very civil and sometimes, as on this occasion, presented a united front of sisterly solidarity, but he knew that they didn't really hit it off. He wasn't sure why, because to him they seemed to have many qualities in common. He took the opportunity to pour away the rest of the green tea, holding the cup as close to the plug-hole in the sink as he could so that

Freya wouldn't hear. He had just completed this manoeuvre when the phone started ringing in the other room. He almost jumped out of his skin.

"Hello?" Freya's carefully-modulated, cut-glass voice carried well, though she rarely raised it. "Oh, hello, Katrin. Yes, he's here. I'm sorry, I thought he'd called you when he went upstairs. I've just reminded him. No, I don't know what he's doing now. He was supposed to have gone into the kitchen to phone you."

Tim could hear Freya's voice coming closer. Swiftly he moved towards the patio doors at the end of her kitchen and stood gazing nonchalantly out at her small, pretty garden and the high fence beyond it.

"Tim? It's Katrin. I thought you were supposed to be ringing her." Freya advanced towards him, holding the phone in her outstretched hand.

"Sorry, I got sidetracked," he said, wondering why his sister so frequently made him feel like an erring schoolboy. She raised one eyebrow as he took the phone from her.

"Well, I'll leave you to it. I need to buy some milk from the convenience shop. I won't be gone more than a few minutes."

"Katrin, I'm sorry. I've had a weird sort of day. I did mean to call you earlier."

"Freya said. But where have you been? And what happened earlier? Freya said you were quite ill when she met you for lunch."

"I'd just had some kind of dizzy spell. And I was sick, but that was before I saw Freya. I didn't think she'd noticed I was under the weather and I don't think it's anything to worry about. Probably something to do with the malaria tablets."

"If they're having that sort of effect on you, perhaps you

should stop taking them. There must be some alternative the doctor could prescribe."

"I'm halfway through the course now. Besides, I don't have time to start the treatment again. I'll be leaving for India any day now."

"Do you know when, exactly?"

"No. I'm seeing Derry Hacker tomorrow. I'll probably have a better idea then."

"You'll come home first, won't you?"

"Yes, of course I will. What on earth makes you ask that?"

"No particular reason. It's just that your behaviour has been a bit . . . well, impulsive, recently."

"Honestly, between you, you and Freya'll be giving me a complex. I'm not aware that I'm behaving any differently from usual, but if I am, it's because I'm a bit preoccupied with this case. Anyway, let's just drop it, shall we? How are you? How's Sophia? Did she have a good day?"

"I think so. She did go to Mrs Sims' for her settling-in session, so she's tired now. She'll be there for her first full day tomorrow, so probably better if we Skype you late afternoon."

"Did you see Thornton?"

"Yes, we had a good meeting. He's quite happy with my suggestion. I'm going to start working three days a week from now on."

Chapter 5

T HE NEXT MORNING Tim rose early and left the house before Freya was up. He'd agreed to meet Derry Hacker for breakfast at a café near Victoria Station before they headed for Hacker's office, which Hacker described as 'like a bear garden at the moment', as he and colleagues prepared to move to their new location. Tim was feeling weak and washed-out. Although he was no longer suffering from nausea or giddiness, he hadn't slept well, having been woken on several occasions by vivid and violent dreams of intense cruelty. The details were already slipping away from him, but still he could recollect scenes of physical torture and sadomasochistic human vivisection that, as products of his imagination, appalled him. He had no direct experience of such perversions and was alarmed at how proficient his subconscious seemed to be at inventing them. The hazy image of the hanging woman was a constant that continued to haunt his waking hours.

Groggily he retraced the route to the station that he'd taken the day before, on the look-out for taxis as he went, but seeing none. He failed to get a seat on the Surbiton to Waterloo train and had to stand the whole distance, unable to divert himself with reading the paper because he'd discovered to his chagrin that the news-stand at Surbiton had closed. Arrived at Waterloo Station, he was searching his pocket for his Oyster card and bracing himself for the double descent to the Jubilee line when some sixth sense made him look up. He was just in time to see a dapper little man with a bald pate fringed by snow white hair darting across the concourse in the direction of the cab rank. Tim ran after him, having no time to try to conceal himself. The little man didn't look round, but, once outside, sprinted smartly across the road and hailed a cab as it was about to enter the station. Once his fare was aboard, the driver turned the vehicle round and headed in the direction of Waterloo Bridge. Tim debated briefly whether to jump into a cab himself and try to follow, but one glance at the taxi rank told him this would be hopeless: at least twenty people were waiting there. If the little man had indeed spotted him, he'd outwitted him very smartly.

Wearily, Tim turned back into the station and headed for the Jubilee line. He changed at Westminster to the District line and arrived at the café at Victoria at 7.40 a.m., a good twenty minutes before he was expecting Derry Hacker to appear. He wondered if it was too early to phone Juliet, and decided to risk it. She could always ignore the call if she found it inconvenient.

She answered almost immediately.

"Hello, Tim. I would have called you a bit later. You said you were seeing Derry at eight?"

"Yes, but it might be difficult to speak after he's got here. I'm not breathing down your neck. If you'd prefer to call me a bit later, that's fine."

"No, no, it's ok. I don't have much to tell you, so it won't take long. As you know, Peter Prance's description was passed on to the Fraud Squad. They've had a number of reported sightings of him, all over the place, and followed them up, but either he's very good at making himself scarce or their informants have been mistaken. There's a reward being offered by one of the banks for information leading to his arrest, but I'm inclined to agree with you about rewards. They can be more of a hindrance than a help."

"Quite. But when you say 'all over the place', where do you mean, exactly?"

"Well, apparently he's been seen in Hull, Truro and Carmarthen. The most recent sighting was the Welsh one."

"What about Liverpool, where he comes from, or London?"

"Not in Liverpool. The Fraud Squad have been to see his sister twice and she swears she hasn't seen him since his disappearance. She's probably telling the truth. She's a professional woman – a dentist – and struck me as being quite straight when we met her. And not very enamoured of Prance, either."

"Yes, I remember her. Had her head screwed on, hadn't she? Didn't want the family inheritance to slip through Prance's fingers. What about London?"

"Nothing on record. Though he does know London: it's where he committed the fraud that he served time for. A financial services scam. I've read the trial report. It was complicated: something to do with price fixing."

"Yes, I read it when we were after him, too. But that was a long time ago: must be getting on for ten years. Where was he living when he was caught? Does it say?"

"Yes. It was a Wimbledon address: 15 Rosemount Gardens. He didn't own the house. It belonged to one of his cronies – actually, William Jennings, the banker who helped him set up the scam. Jennings got a much longer sentence – seven years to Prance's three – because he abused a position of trust."

"Typical of Prance! I know he served less than three years, after getting the sentence reduced for good behaviour.

Jennings will be out now, though. It might be worth tracking him down. My guess is that Prance would be the last person he'd want back in his life, but you can never tell. His capacity for inveigling himself in where he wants to be is uncanny."

"I can check on the address that Jennings was using when he was released from prison. It won't be the Wimbledon house. The judge ordered it to be sold to pay back some of the money."

"Thanks. I'd be grateful if you'd do that, but don't go to the trouble of taking it further than that. If Jennings has turned into a wanderer, he's going to be hard to find and Prance won't be interested in him anyway, if he can't cadge a reasonable standard of living from him. I may be wrong in any case: there was certainly someone after Prance when he was living with Hedley Atkins and I had a feeling it was connected with the fraud: one of Jennings' buddies, maybe. Where did Jennings do his time?"

"He was moved around a bit, but it was mostly Wormwood Scrubs and Brixton."

"As you'd expect. Odd that Prance managed to get himself sent to Liverpool – nicely out of the way of the London mob, if they were after him."

"He pleaded hardship. Said that he had an ancient mother and she wouldn't be able to travel far to visit him."

"It was true he had an ancient mother. Whether she wanted to visit him is another matter. Probably another instance of him getting round authority to suit his own ends, making the very best of a bad job. Do me a favour, Juliet, and just get in touch with the Fraud Squad. Tell them that I think I've seen him twice now, both times at London stations – King's Cross and Waterloo – and suggest they keep an eye out."

"Yes, sir. You didn't say you'd seen him again. When was that?"

"Earlier this morning, about half an hour ago."

"Should I tell Superintendent Thornton?"

"Up to you. He may not be interested in Prance if he's not in South Lincolnshire. But it might be diplomatic to mention it. Has he got you working on the Verma case?"

"Yes, mainly to support you. We have the Verma family under surveillance. They're adamant that the cousin in India is innocent but they have no explanation for Ayesha's disappearance. The mother seems very upset."

"I know. There could be a variety of reasons for that, though."

"Do you really think that you'll be able to arrest the cousin if you go to India?"

"The police in Delhi have agreed to help. And apparently the cousin, although insisting that we fit in with his travel arrangements, isn't trying to hide or run away."

"I just don't understand this honour killing idea. It seems to be a contradiction in terms."

"I don't, either. The Met's dealt with more cases than anywhere else. That's why I need Derry Hacker's help."

"Taking my name in vain again, Yates?" said a cheerful voice. Tim looked up to see a tall, thickset man standing in front of him. He rose to his feet to shake the man's hand.

"Derry! Good to see you."

"Hi, Tim. How's tricks? You're looking a bit washed out."

"Just a minute, Derry. I've got Juliet on the phone. Juliet, Derry's here now. Thanks for all that. I'll call you again later."

"Love and kisses!" Derry Hacker shouted at the phone. Juliet terminated the call without replying.

"Now," said Derry, "we've got a lot of catching up to do. We'll have a good dinner tonight. I've invited someone else you know, as a surprise. But first things first: breakfast, and then work. You look as if you could do with some breakfast. Are you sure you're all right?"

Tim flinched a little under his old comrade's scrutiny.

"I *have* been a bit under the weather, but nothing to worry about, I think. It's the malaria pills the quack gave me: they've made me feel a bit rough."

"You want to watch that stuff. It can really fuck you up."

"You've been to India, though, haven't you? Didn't you take the pills?"

"Did the first time. They made me feel dreadful. Since then, I've just chanced it."

"I don't think Katrin would like me to do that."

"I suppose not. It would be out of character, wouldn't it? A mismatch with her prudent Teutonic roots."

Tim laughed uneasily.

"It's a pity you and Katrin don't get on better. I'd see more of you then. The same goes for Freya: she's never quite seen eye to eye with Katrin, either. Why don't you like her?"

"It's not a case of not liking her: she was a good-enough worker when she was in London. Not my type, but that's beside the point. I've just always felt sad on Patti's account, that's all."

"I'd forgotten you knew Patti. But she and I were over before I met Katrin. I didn't two-time her."

"No, but you'd probably have got back together if Katrin hadn't turned up."

Tim shrugged. "That's conjecture. It was quite a stormy relationship: nothing like what I have with Katrin."

23

"Nothing wrong with a few storms. Keeps the interest going, I'd say."

"Well, you and I have to agree to differ over that. Besides, I'm tickled that you're sitting here preaching fidelity. You must have had scores of girlfriends over the past ten years."

"Ah, but never a little gem like Patti."

"If you're so keen on her, why don't you . . . ?"

"Do you think I didn't try?"

A spivvish waiter arrived and thrust a spotty menu at each of them. Derry returned his with alacrity.

"No need to look," he said. "Full English, and a pot of tea. Always have the same when I come here," he added to Tim. "Place doesn't look much, but they understand fry-ups."

The thought of a greasy spoon breakfast made Tim queasy.

"I think I'll just have a couple of slices of toast. And a pot of tea as well."

"Christ! You are feeling peaky, aren't you? I hope you'll be able to tackle the strange grub in Delhi."

Chapter 6

BREAKFAST WAS OVER. Derry Hacker poured the last dregs of tea into his cup and, thrusting back his chair, drew a packet of cigarettes from his pocket.

"Mind if I smoke?"

"Go ahead," said Tim, although his stomach was churning. "I assume they won't mind, as we're sitting outside?"

"Nah. That's another good thing about this place. Wouldn't mind if we were sitting *inside*, probably." He took out a cigarette and lit it, drawing the smoke deep into his lungs. "That's better," he said as he exhaled. "Can't beat the first one of the day. Now, tell me about this case of yours."

"As I said on the phone, an Indian girl has disappeared. A teenager. We think she might have been the victim of an honour killing."

"How old?"

"Seventeen, nearly eighteen."

"Why do you think it's an honour killing?"

"Her cousin came from India to marry her. An arranged marriage, agreed by both sets of parents. It didn't happen, because the girl disappeared. The cousin's gone back to India."

"How did you find out the girl was missing?"

"The father reported it."

"That's not typical. Not unheard of, but often the family just waits for us to discover that the girl's gone. Often we don't. It's hard to keep track of girls once they're past the school leaving age, especially if the family doesn't want them to get a job. How well educated are the parents?"

"Reasonably. The father works as a clerk for a local housing association. Mother works part-time, as well, at a florist's. He's a first generation immigrant. So is she, but she grew up in Sweden."

"Any other children?"

"Two other girls, both younger. No sons."

"Again, not typical, though every case is different. But often it's the girl's older brothers who carry out these honour killings. The father's usually complicit, of course, sometimes the mother, too, but it's more likely that she just has to go along with what they decide. From what you've told me so far, I think you've only got half a case. What's to say the girl didn't just bugger off because she didn't like the look of the cousin?"

"That's not what the family is suggesting. And you know as well as I do, it's difficult to disappear without trace in this country. They've still got her birth certificate and passport. And she has a National Insurance number, which hasn't been used."

"Bank account?"

"Yes, but virtually empty. And again, not touched."

"I agree that it *could* be an honour killing, but you seem to have come to that conclusion quite quickly, considering it's South Lincolnshire. No other evidence of honour killings in your part of the world, is there?"

"No. We don't have any proper Indian communities: just the odd family, like this one. But Superintendent Thornton's taken on board all the recent government stuff about forced marriages, etcetera."

Derry Hacker's broad face split into a grin.

"I should have guessed! Thornton's seen a chance of being flavour of the month, has he? A rare opportunity, I'd say, in his little backwater."

"It's not as far-fetched as all that," said Tim huffily. "If I didn't think he was on to something, I'd have told him so."

"Ah, yes," said Derry teasingly, wagging his forefinger, "but not averse to a small jolly to India, are you?"

"I've no intention of wasting my time or taxpayers' money," said Tim with more than a hint of priggishness. "That's why I'm here. To benefit from your experience, see if you can put me on the right track."

"All right, old son, only joking. And in bad taste, because this isn't a funny subject. I'll tell you about the cases I've been involved in, so you can see if yours makes sense. As a possible honour killing, I mean. For a start, they're not just Indian. They take place in countries all over the world, though mainly in Southern Asia and the Middle East or families who've settled elsewhere whose ethnic origins are in those places. They're not associated with a single religion, either, though the people carrying them out often claim they're rooted in their faith. Sometimes they just say whatever the victim's doing is going against their customs. For the record, there's no religion in the world that officially condones honour killing, though that doesn't stop extreme and some not-so-extreme religious leaders from encouraging it. And the victims aren't always female, though most of them are."

"But it's usually the relatives of the person who do it?"

"Yes, although there's some evidence that wealthier families have hired hit men, to distance themselves from the actual act."

"I've never really understood the term 'honour killing', I

suppose because it attempts to dignify sordid murders. Is the motive always disapproval of the victim's sexual behaviour?"

"Usually, but not always. There was a case in Canada where a husband and wife arranged the 'accidental' death of three of their daughters because they'd been seeing men unsupervised. This couple took the opportunity to dispatch the husband's first wife at the same time, not because of the way she was behaving, but simply to get rid of her. And it's not necessarily the victim's actual sexual behaviour that is being disapproved of: it can just be what the relatives think or suspect."

"Sounds paranoid."

"You may have hit the nail on the head there. Apparently there's a psychiatrist who's carried out a study of some perpetrators of so-called honour killings and come to the conclusion that they were all mentally ill at the time. Two caveats there, though: in the first place, he was judging them by Western standards; secondly, we come back to the hoary old chestnut of whether any murderer is entirely sane. From the cases I've worked on, all I can say is that often the person who carries out this kind of murder has been pressured by someone else to do it: if not the head of the family, then a religious leader or some other person in authority, which raises the further question of exactly who is insane."

"I'd like to study your cases."

"Yes, you said so when we spoke. I've had someone dig the files out for you. We've got electronic versions of most of them. I've also looked out a couple of accounts of foreign cases that I asked for when I was boning up on it. Two more things you need to remember: one is that we're fairly new to honour killings in the UK, but they've been going on for centuries in some places. And there've only been a handful of convictions in this country, but I strongly suspect that other cases have gone undetected, as we know they have elsewhere."

"Thornton won't let this one go undetected, if he's right about it. He's buzzing with it. It's the second case we've worked on recently where he's got really involved."

"Not after a gong of some kind, is he?"

"That hadn't occurred to me, but you could be right."

"Let's go to the office and get started, shall we? I'd hate to disappoint him!"

Chapter 7

A S I GET Sophia ready for her first proper day with Mrs Sims, I'm less apprehensive about leaving her than I thought I'd be. I suppose all working mothers do some soul-searching, but I've worked through most of it already. It's Tim who's worrying me. Not just this sickness episode in London – though that sounds as if it was bad enough – but his behaviour generally over the past few weeks. I know he's preoccupied with his latest case – he always is when they're new – but he won't talk to me about it. I have a general idea of what it's about – Superintendent Thornton's said he wants me to do some background work for it – but I don't know what Tim thinks. I've tried talking to him, but he just clams up. We haven't had a proper conversation for weeks, not about the case or anything else. I feel as if a shutter has come down between us.

Sophia is looking pretty in a green dress with a black dog on the front. There are little black dogs on her tights, too. I set her down on the floor, allow her to choose a toy. Her favourite is the Postman Pat figure that one of Tim's colleagues has re-dressed as a policeman. I pack it into her small bag with spare clothes and her milk.

Mrs Sims is a registered childminder. We can't get Sophia into a nursery until later in the year, but I'm happy with the Sims set-up. She has a couple of girls helping her and the house is safe and cosier than the nursery. At the moment, there are four children there besides Sophia. Mrs Sims has space for one other. I've promised to keep my ear to the ground for her.

She's waiting on the doorstep for us when we arrive. She's in her thirties and has bright yellow hair cut in a pageboy. She's buxom rather than dumpy and dresses in Breton tops and jeans. She holds out her arms; Sophia goes to her straight away.

"Come in for a moment," she says. The house is a Victorian end terrace in Havelock Street. I follow her into the spacious front room, which is set out as a children's playroom. One of the girls is seated on the wooden floor, helping a small boy to build a tower of bricks. She looks up when she hears us.

"This is Margie," says Mrs Sims. "I think you met her when you came with your husband."

Margie has a pinched little face. Her hair is very dark and cut short in a jagged asymmetrical style. She looks cross, almost sulky, until she smiles, when she is transformed.

"Hi," she says. She carries on with the bricks.

"Cup of tea?" says Mrs Sims, depositing Sophia on the floor next to the boy. Evidently the other babies have yet to arrive.

"I'll get it," says Margie, springing to her feet. "If you don't mind watching Thomas, that is."

I notice as she walks to the door how thin she is. Her legs, encased in the skinniest of jeans, are like matchsticks.

"Nice girl," I say. "How old is she?"

"She's eighteen. Older than she looks, I know." Mrs Sims gives an uneasy little laugh. I recognise policeman's wife syndrome kicking in. Its message: you're always be a bit of an outsider, to be treated warily in case you let something slip to the law.

"I wasn't implying that she's under age for the job," I say quickly. "She just looks very fragile, that's all."

"Fragile's probably right," says Mrs Sims grimly. "Her parents are splitting up and she's taking it hard. Her father's left her mother for a younger woman and more or less kicked over the traces, from what she tells me. The upshot is that she won't be able to go to university this year, as she'd planned. She's going to have to save some money first. I'm hoping she'll stay all year – she's a good little worker – but I know I'll lose her if she can find something that pays better."

It's on the tip of my tongue to say that if Mrs Sims is getting what she's asked us to pay for four other children besides Sophia, she should be able to afford decent wages for her staff. Not a good start to Sophia's career chez Sims, I realise! I bite back the words.

Margie returns with the tea. She hands me mine with the same radiant smile, but I think I spot conflict in her eyes: a mixture, perhaps, of defiance and sorrow. I wonder what sort of man her father is, to abandon his daughter at such a vulnerable stage of her life. I look at Sophia, content and safe, clapping two red bricks together, and hope that we'll be able to give her what she needs to make her confident, fearless and happy when she's growing up. Suddenly the anguish that I thought I'd mastered creeps in sideways and I have to contort my face to stop it crumpling. I down the tea with haste and stand up.

I'm sure that Mrs Sims has noticed, but she's too discreet to mention it directly.

"She'll have a lovely day, don't you worry," she says, patting my arm, "and four o'clock will come round in no time. Are you working today, or just taking a bit of time for yourself?"

"I'm working for some of the day. Just going back to the office to get myself used to it again. There's a project lined up for me, I think."

"I expect they'll be glad to have you back. What is it that you do, exactly?"

"I'm a police researcher."

"Lovely!" says Mrs Sims, in a tone of voice that indicates little understanding and no interest. "You take care, now. And don't worry."

I nod and head for the door. I look back just once, to see Sophia still engrossed with the bricks. Margie has gone back to building her tower. Thomas is hovering nearby, his arm outstretched. As I leave, I hear the bricks come crashing down and Thomas's peal of laughter.

Chapter 8

JULIET PAUSED FOR a moment outside the house in Hannam Boulevard and had not unfastened the gate latch when the door was flung open. A small plump woman emerged. She was wearing a dark green sari with gold borders. A broad silver strip rippled through her otherwise jet black hair, which was swept back off her forehead and fastened in an elaborate chignon at the back of her neck. Juliet thought she was pretty in a sad sort of way. She had very fine skin, entirely uncreased by wrinkles. Her age was hard to guess. She might have been forty, perhaps a few years younger.

The woman advanced down the short path to meet her.

"Mrs Verma?" said Juliet. "I'm DC Armstrong. I phoned yesterday. Thank you for agreeing to see me."

The woman clasped her hands together as if in prayer.

"I am so happy to meet you," she said. "Please, come in." Her voice was cultured, with just the faintest trace of inflection. Juliet opened the gate and held out her hand. Mrs Verma's own hand was as soft and as plump as the rest of her. Juliet saw that she wore the vermilion dot on her forehead.

Mrs Verma turned and led the way into the house, glancing once at her neighbour's windows before entering. Juliet guessed that Ayesha Verma's disappearance was the talk of the street. It was hard not to feel sympathy for the small woman she'd just met, though she knew it might well be misplaced.

34

It was nevertheless difficult to envisage Mrs Verma involved in the act of murder.

Inside, the house was immaculate.

"Please, sit down," said Mrs Verma. "Would you like some tea?"

"Thank you. Yes."

It was an ordinary sitting room, containing a velour three-piece suite and several small tables. There were a few nice arte-facts from India: a brass gong mounted on an elephant's back, decorated in brilliant enamels, and some intricate wooden boxes – but apart from these and an abundance of cushions in jewelled colours, the room was in all probability furnished very similarly to its counterparts in the other houses in the street.

Several silver-framed photographs stood on one of the tables. Juliet picked up the largest of them and was examining it when Mrs Verma returned, bearing a tray set out with two delicate porcelain cups containing milky tea. Two biscuits had been arranged in the saucers of each. She set the tray down carefully.

"These are your daughters?"

"Yes. Ayesha, Pia and Geya."

"Ayesha is much older than her sisters?"

Mrs Verma looked down at the tea tray.

"Yes. Unfortunately, we lost two boys. Miscarriages. Then Pia and Geya came quickly afterwards. They're out with some friends today. I didn't want them to be here when you came. Do you have anything to tell me?" Mrs Verma was apprehensive.

"I'm afraid not. You'll have seen the appeals for information on the local and national news. Her description has been sent to police forces throughout the country. I know DI Yates has asked you this already, but is there anywhere else you can think of where she could have gone? Friends or relatives in a big city, say?"

"DI Yates did ask me and my husband that question and our answer was no. We have virtually no family here. Bahir, my husband, grew up in Birmingham. His parents are dead now. He has a brother, but he has returned to India. It was his son, Zayed, that Ayesha was to have married."

"And yourself, Mrs Verma? Do you have other relatives here?"

"I was brought up in Stockholm. I was adopted. My adoptive family is still there, but I haven't seen them for many years. The girls don't know them."

"You don't think Ayesha could have tried to find them?"

"I have been in touch with my stepsister in Sweden, of course, but she doesn't know anything. She was obviously upset to hear of Ayesha's disappearance. I myself did not think she would be there. We still have her passport, you see."

"Yes, of course. Forgive me for asking this, but why are you and your husband living in Spalding? You both come from cities. It seems an odd place for you to have made your home in."

"We have been happy here. In Birmingham, Bahir worked for a housing association and he was offered a similar job here. Similar, but less hassle. We thought it would be a nice place to bring the girls up. And the housing is cheap."

"Did either of you go to university?"

"No. Bahir has a management diploma. From college. And I have a certificate from the British Floristry Association. We both studied for A level."

"So you want your daughters to be well educated?"

"Yes, within our traditions. Ayesha is clever. She has studied A levels. The results will come soon. I think she will have done well."

"Has she applied for university?"

"No. The marriage was to come first. Afterwards her father and Zayed agreed that she could study if she still wanted to."

Juliet thought this sounded unpromising and wondered what Ayesha's own view had been, but Mrs Verma was clearly on edge and quite defensive, so she decided not to push it. She replaced the photograph on the table and, sitting down, helped herself to one of the cups of tea. It was strong as well as milky, and very sweet. Juliet tried not to grimace.

Mrs Verma had perched herself uncomfortably on a wooden chair at the very edge of the room.

"Should I pass your tea?"

She shook her head, then suddenly burst out vehemently.

"I know you suspect Bahir and Zayed of hurting Ayesha, but you are quite wrong. Honour killing is not something we understand. Bahir loves his daughters; he would never do them harm. I don't know Zayed well, but I trusted my husband's judgment. So did Ayesha. And all the time you are following up this honour killing idea, you are wasting time not trying to find her."

Mrs Verma was wringing her hands. Tears were pouring down her cheeks.

Juliet's instinct was to believe her, though this didn't mean that the woman's menfolk were as upright as she was asserting.

"I understand how you must be feeling, Mrs Verma. Please believe me when I say that the honour killing idea is only one line of enquiry that we're pursuing. I realise it must seem unfair, but it's something we have to do, mainly because of the circumstances of Ayesha's disappearance. Arranged marriages are not against the law, but forced marriages are. We have to consider the possibility that your daughter refused her father's chosen bridegroom and he punished her for it."

"No! Bahir is not that kind of man."

"What sort of mood was Ayesha in when you last saw her?"

"She was . . . happy. Enjoying the summer. And looking forward to spending more time with her cousin."

"How long had Zayed been here when she went missing?"

"About a week, I think." Mrs Verma looked away evasively.

"You don't know exactly how long?"

"No, I can't remember."

"I see." Tim had already asked Air India for the dates of Zayed's arrival at and departure from Heathrow and Juliet had verified them. There was always the chance that he hadn't spent the whole of the intervening time with the Verma family. It was odd that Mrs Verma claimed not to remember, even so. "Did Ayesha and Zayed seem to get on well?" she continued.

Mrs Verma hesitated.

"I think she was a bit surprised at first."

"Oh. Why was that?"

"Zayed is a bit older than she is."

"How old is he?"

"He is almost fifty, I think. Bahir's brother is a lot older than him. He's a half-brother, really."

"Did Ayesha discuss Zayed's age with you?"

"Not exactly, no. I could see she was surprised. But then he was very nice and she seemed to like him."

"And you say she was in a happy mood the last time you saw her?"

"Oh, yes. We'd been for a picnic on the banks of the Coronation cut. She was very happy. We walked back here afterwards, then Ayesha said she wanted to go into town to buy some things for her hair. Zayed said he would go with her, but she said she'd rather go on her own. He didn't insist," Mrs Verma concluded meaningfully, as if to illustrate what a reasonable man he was.

"So she went out again on her own. This was last Wednesday? At about what time was it?"

"Wednesday, yes. Mid-afternoon, I'd say. Quite some time before Bahir came home. He and Zayed went out to look for her later. But Bahir has told you this already."

"Yes, I know, Mrs Verma, but I wanted to hear your own account. In case you remember something that hasn't been mentioned so far. When did you start to worry about her?"

"I was worried by the time her father came home. I'd tried calling her mobile and found she had left it here."

"Yes, I noticed that in DI Yates's report. Was that unlike her?"

"Usually she took it everywhere. But she'd left it charging, so maybe she just forgot it. I don't know."

"So what did she have with her?"

"Just her handbag. And her purse."

"How much money did she have?"

"I don't know. Not very much. Thirty pounds, perhaps. And her banker's card. But the account hasn't been touched."

"So I understand. Did she have anything besides the debit card? A credit card? Or retailers' cards of any kind?"

"Not credit or other cards like that, no. We don't approve of them. She had a young person's railcard."

"Thank you," said Juliet. "That's very interesting. I don't think your husband mentioned that to DI Yates."

"Bahir must have forgotten about it," said Mrs Verma uncomfortably.

"Yes, I suppose he did. Could we have something of Ayesha's? So that we can get a DNA match?"

"DI Yates already took her hairbrush. He asked Bahir for it."

Juliet frowned. Tim hadn't included that in his report. And what had he done with the hairbrush? She'd have to ask him. Not like him not to have found out about the railcard, either. That could yield a very promising lead.

"Of course. I'm sorry, I was forgetting. I think you've helped me as much as you can for the moment, Mrs Verma. I shall probably want to come again. I understand that you have a part-time job?"

"Yes. It's just at Hardy's in Winsover Road. The flower shop. Usually I work on Thursdays, Fridays and Saturdays only. Sometimes on other days if we're really busy. I mostly make up the flowers for weddings: bouquets and table settings."

"And your husband?"

"He has a normal nine-to-five job."

"You're not planning to go away any time soon?"

"No. How could we, with Ayesha missing?" Mrs Verma's eyes filled with tears. "Please find her."

Juliet resisted the impulse to place a comforting hand on the woman's arm.

"We'll do our best," she said.

Chapter 9

TIM HAD ACCOMPANIED Derry Hacker to New Scotland Yard. All around him people were busy moving stuff, but he'd been allocated a temporary office which was relatively peaceful, and a detective constable, DC Nancy Chappell, to help him. He hadn't hit it off with DC Chappell from the word go. She was the most alternative policewoman he'd ever met, and he found her 'otherness' disconcerting. Petite and wiry, she had jet black hair cut in a Goth style and sported a row of studs in each of her ears. In the lobes of one of them had been affixed an inch-long object resembling a paper clip. Her eyelids were dusted with some kind of plum-coloured powder and her lipstick was blackish. She was dressed completely in black; neatly enough, it was true, but her feet were shod in oxblood-coloured Doc Martens. Her fingernails were best described as talons, painted silver. She spoke with an ugly London drawl. Quite frankly, he was astonished that Derry rated her so highly.

DC Chappell patently didn't think much of Tim, either. She spoke to him abruptly and with scant respect. She made it quite clear that she had plenty of work to do without being side-tracked by the importunate training requirements of a copper up from the provinces.

"DI Hacker's downloaded all the files on to this computer," she said to Tim. "There's the four cases we've worked on, and a couple from the States and Canada that we asked for. Derry told you about them, did 'e?"

"Yes," said Tim. "Thank you." He met her eye, tried to provoke a smile. She looked away quickly. Tim's own smile sickened and died on his lips. He was beginning to feel queasy again.

"You all right?" She scrutinised him suspiciously.

"Yes, I think so. It's a bit warm in here, isn't it?"

"'Aven't noticed, myself, but I can turn up the air-con." She rose and twiddled the switch on the wall. "Yer'll 'ave to turn it dahn again when it's cool enough. Otherwise you'll freeze to death!"

She was smiling now, evidently pleased by the thought of his stiffening corpse.

"You need me for anyfing? If not, I'll be getting on."

"I'd hoped you'd stay awhile, if you've got time. Talk me through some of these cases, tell me if you've seen any similarities between them."

"Well, there's one obvious 'similarity', isn't there? All done by blokes to young girls and all of the blokes 'eartless bastards."

"DI Hacker told me that sometimes the victims could be young men, and sometimes female perpetrators were also involved."

"Yes, well, he's getting too PC for words, i'n't he? Tell you what," she said more brightly, "you have a read of these, write down any questions you 'ave, and I'll go fru them with you later. 'ow does that sound? Better use of bofe our time, I fink."

"That sounds great," said Tim, relieved that she'd suggested a solution to spare both from the passive hostility they'd already managed to create.

"OK, I'll come back in a couple of ahrs, then. There's a

water cooler by the door, if you ain't feeling too good. And don't forget about the air con. It's vicious if you overdo it."

"Thanks," said Tim, forcing another smile. He received a measured one in return, before DC Chappell exited as silently and lithely as a cat, despite her clumpy boots.

Tim took her advice and poured himself a plastic cup of water. He was sipping it slowly as he clicked on the computer screen to open the first file. Suddenly the screen exploded into colour. Instead of opening the Word document that he'd selected, he was confronted with a nightmarish frame of reds, oranges and yellows all bleeding into each other. His eyes were transfixed by the small square window that now opened in the middle of the frame. At first the outline was fuzzy, almost nondescript, but second by second it grew clearer until he could be in no doubt about what the blackening shadow depicted: it was the outline of a woman swinging from a gibbet.

Tim felt the bile rise in his throat. Just in time, he seized the waste paper bin and vomited into it copiously, his stomach heaving and retching for long minutes after it had emptied. He took a long draught from the cup of water and forced himself to look at the screen again. The Word document was sitting there, pristine in its dullness. Tim splashed some water on his face and smoothed his hair with his hands. He'd found the episodes he'd experienced yesterday unnerving. Now he was frankly scared.

His mobile rang. Taking it out of its pouch, he saw that the caller was Juliet. He pressed the green button with alacrity.

"Juliet! Am I glad to talk to you!"

"Hello, Tim. Why do you say that?"

Tim thought for a few seconds. How could he explain to her what he thought he'd just seen?

"No reason. It's just that things are a little strange here. Out of my comfort zone, I suppose. But they're being very helpful. I think I'm making progress. What about you?"

"I've just come back from interviewing Mrs Verma. She told me a couple of things I need to check with you. First of all, did you know that Ayesha Verma has a student railcard? It was probably in her purse when she disappeared."

"No. And when I asked her father if there was anything she could have with her that might help her to get away, he said only the cash, and he didn't think she could have very much."

"That's interesting. Mrs Verma also said that she didn't have much money with her. I must admit that she was a bit shifty when she mentioned the railcard. Perhaps the father didn't know about it."

"I think that's highly likely, don't you? Because if we can prove that she used the railcard, it doesn't rule out the possibility that she's been murdered, but it does make it less likely."

"That's what I thought. I'm not sure how to raise it with Bahir Verma without making him annoyed with his wife, if she gave Ayesha the railcard without telling him."

"I'll leave it to you to ponder that. You're better at tact than I am."

Juliet laughed. She might have felt flattered if the statement had not been incontestable.

"What was the other thing you wanted to mention?"

"What? Oh, yes. Mrs Verma told me that you'd taken Ayesha's hairbrush for DNA testing. There's no record of that in your report. Did you really take it? And if so, where is it?"

"Oh God," said Tim.

"Tim? Are you all right?"

"Yes, I think so. But I did take the hairbrush, and I've

44

forgotten to have it processed. It's still in the top drawer of my desk. Would you mind having it sent to the lab for me?"

"Of course not," said Juliet. "I'll do it straight away." Her voice was taut with disapproval. Tim wasn't surprised.

"Thanks. I'd better get on now. I've got a load of files to read before DC Chappell comes back."

"Who?"

"The DC I'm working with. Don't worry, she wouldn't interest you. A very difficult woman."

"Goodbye, then. I'll keep you posted."

"Thanks. Goodbye, Juliet."

Tim put down the phone. The call hadn't been at all satisfactory. First he'd annoyed Freya, then Katrin, and now Juliet. Not to mention assorted taxi drivers, residents of Ilford and DC Chappell. What was wrong with him?

He glanced down at the waste paper basket. Perhaps he was suffering from a virus. The next task he had to negotiate was how to dispose discreetly of a waste basket full of vomit. He sighed, and recoiled at the smell of his own breath.

Chapter 10

THE HOTEL RECEPTION area was vast and glittering. Trees had been planted in beds of earth let into the floor and trained to grow straight and tall until they reached the two-storey-high ceiling. White leather chairs and sofas were arranged around a central fountain which flung out leaps of water that increased in size by degrees until, after an extravagant crescendo, they subsided, then began to grow again from tiny jets. Outside the temperature was 27 degrees, but here the noiseless air conditioning kept the ambience fashionably chilly.

A phalanx of reception desks had been installed, sunray fashion, around three walls, each serviced by two mannequin-like young women to minimise the chance that any guest might be kept waiting. Each of these young women was presented as exactly like her counterparts as possible: long dark hair entwined in a perfect French pleat on which sat a small taupe-coloured pillbox hat, dramatic, skilfully-applied kohl and mascara, cherry-red lips and fingernails. They wore tailored skirt-suits in taupe with discreet dashes of red, the single-breasted jackets emphasising high breasts and small waists as snugly as if the flesh of their owners had been poured into a mould. The pencil skirts were also skin-tight, their little kick pleats revealing a tantalising flash of red lining as the women walked cautiously on their five-inch-high scarlet stilettos.

The small man entered this wealth-infused atrium with considerable aplomb. He was neatly dressed in a blazer and flannels, his shirt fastidiously adorned with a highly-starched detachable collar, his feet Church's-shod. To the casual observer he was on home territory, belonging as much to this milieu as the French millionaire seated on one of the white leather thrones playing with his iPad or the gaggle of rich young Arabs drinking coffee and chattering excitedly next to the fountain. A closer inspection would have indicated he was not as affluent as at first he appeared: the elbows of the blazer were shiny, the shoes in some need of repair. However, the cosmopolitan clients of the hotel were not disposed to scrutinise, much less judge, their fellow guests. They were too bound up in contemplation of their own superiority, for one thing; and the presence of an eccentric Englishman merely served to enhance their appreciation of the place, for another.

The small man walked up to the counter nearest the back wall, having flicked his gaze quickly at the two desks most adjacent to it, perhaps to check that he wasn't being watched or overheard. He disregarded the two young women stationed there and they as studiously ignored him. Deftly, he pressed a buzzer fixed to the edge of the counter and so near the back of it that he would have been unlikely to spot it if he hadn't already known it was there.

A middle-aged woman appeared as if by magic and stepped to one side of the desk. She, too, was dressed in a taupe uniform, though her figure was much more buxom than those of the many receptionists and her more generously cut skirt was long enough to brush her ankles. She wore cherry-red loafers on her feet. She had wide, almond-shaped eyes. She might have been of mixed race descent.

"Hello, darling," said the small man. "I'm rather early, I'm afraid, so glad that you're here. And looking lovely, if I may say so."

The woman regarded him impassively. Undeterred, he continued as animatedly as if she'd been more encouraging.

"I've come to see Jas. He said we could meet this afternoon."

"He isn't here yet."

"No matter, I can wait. Is there somewhere comfortable for me to sit down?"

The woman gestured towards the white leather furniture.

"You can buy coffee here. Or a drink, if you'd rather. One of the girls will send a waiter over."

"Yes, but that will cost me an arm and a leg, won't it darling? I'm sure Jas wouldn't expect me to pay for my own refreshments. Besides, he hasn't paid me yet and the expenses are totting up. To tell you the truth, it's leaving me a bit short."

The woman scowled.

"You can start an account, pay later."

"I suppose I'll have to, darling, won't I, if you're in that frame of mind? As you know, I'm the last person to try to cause any kind of disturbance."

"Is he bothering you, Moura?" The tone of the speaker's voice was teasing, not menacing.

The small man did not spin round to confront this unexpected intruder into his conversation, but instead gave an adroit bird-like flick of his head which served the same purpose and simultaneously made a good stab at conveying his nonchalance.

"Ah, Jas, I was just saying that I didn't think you'd begrudge me a few refreshments."

The newcomer was quite tall and rather thick-set. Like the

woman, he could have been of mixed race, but his English was perfect. Though it was a warm day, he was conservatively clad in a charcoal grey suit and blindingly white shirt. He held out one arm expansively and pointed at the furthermost sofa, shooting his cuff as he did so to reveal a discreetly opulent gold cufflink adorned with a small crescent of diamonds.

"Certainly. If you'd care to sit over there, I'll join you shortly. What would you like? I always think that iced tea is excellent on a day such as this."

The small man grimaced.

"You are joking, darling, aren't you? No? Well, all right then, I'll have an iced tea, but only if you'd be so good as to provide a whisky chaser to go with it. A large one, please: none of your penny-scrimping little optics."

The newcomer gave the woman called Moura a quick nod. They exchanged a momentary expression of distaste before she said to the mannequin standing nearest to her: "Please ask a waiter to serve the gentleman."

The newcomer clapped the small man briefly on the back.

"Order what you wish, Peter, with my compliments. Now go over to that sofa and wait for me there, otherwise the waiter will have arrived before you. I'll try not to leave you alone for too long."

Chapter 11

HAVING SURREPTITIOUSLY SMUGGLED the puke-filled waste-bin into the lavatories and cleaned it, Tim returned to his temporary office. He'd decided to read the files in chronological order, so he began with the Canadian case that Derry Hacker had mentioned when they were having breakfast.

His head was beginning to ache and he started to see a yellow rim around the page on the computer screen, for him a classic sign of impending migraine. Quickly he popped the Mogadon tablet that he produced from his rucksack, drank another cup of water and waited for the symptoms to subside. After a while, the effects of the drug kicked in and he was able to limp his way painfully through the first of the case reports.

It was the police account of the Canadian honour killing and much as Derry had described it, though the report provided more details. Mohammed Shafia, a Shi'a Muslim who'd made a fortune in real estate in Dubai and emigrated to Canada with his two wives and several children, had, along with his son and second wife, been convicted of murdering his first wife and three daughters. Shafia had himself reported the disappearance of the four women, which Tim noted: Bahir Verma had also reported that his daughter was missing. Shortly afterwards, a car was found submerged in a local lock. When it was hauled out, four female bodies were discovered inside. At first the Canadian police had thought that the deaths were accidental, but when they realised that the son had notified police that the family's other car had been damaged on the same morning as his father had reported the women missing, a detective put two and two together and decided there were grounds for suspicion. Forensic evidence proved that the second car had been used to ram the first into the lock. Shafia and his wife and son were convicted of first degree murder, which under Canadian law meant that they must serve at least twenty-five years without parole.

Tim made a few notes as he was going along, but although he found the case fascinating, he realised when he reached the end of the report that he only partly understood the motive. This concept of honour killing was puzzling, particularly as it had been applied here. One of the daughters had been suspected by her parents of becoming too friendly with a Pakistani youth, but as far as Tim could gather there was no suggestion that the other daughters or the first wife (who had brought up the children jointly with their mother: biologically they belonged to the second wife) had been behaving 'improperly'. It seemed to him it was glaringly obvious that the motive for the murders was to enable the husband and second wife to dispose of the first, though even this did not quite convince, as apparently she had relatives who were prepared to look after her. And why did all the girls have to die? He could just about comprehend that a warped logic might dictate a girl should be murdered for bringing her family into disrepute, unnatural though it was for both her father and her mother to collude in the crime, but how could it then impel them to get rid of all their daughters? If the reasoning was that the whole family was now contaminated by the eldest daughter's sin, why not kill the son as well? Indeed, why not end their own lives? Tim scribbled a few words to remind himself to ask Nancy Chappell if she could explain.

He turned to the first of the crimes that Derry himself had been involved in. This had taken place towards the end of 2012, the same year that the Shafias had been convicted. The victim in this case was of Punjabi descent. Her father, Naresh Kaul, had arrived in the UK as a child and his family had settled in Hounslow. He worked for a catering company that supplied in-flight meals to Heathrow Airport. He'd married young, to a bride chosen by his father, and they'd had two daughters and a son. The elder of the two daughters, Sahika, was a clever girl who'd won both a scholarship and a bursary for Kingston Grammar School. Apparently the parents were dubious about allowing her to travel so far to school and although she managed to persuade them, they subsequently refused to allow the younger daughter, Daivi, also to attend. Sahika was working for her A levels, intent upon studying Law at university, when she was sent to the Punjab, ostensibly for a holiday, but in reality to meet the man chosen by her extended family as her fiancé. She expressed dislike of the man and apparently reacted so extremely to any suggestion that she should stay in touch with him that she tried to kill herself by drinking bleach. She damaged her throat badly and returned to the UK early in order to receive medical treatment.

She hadn't been back in Hounslow for very long before the parents decided to remove her from the school. She was so distressed by this and such a promising pupil, that one of her teachers, a woman, offered to coach her in private so that she could still sit her A levels. The parents were persuaded to agree, but after some time discovered that she had also been receiving tuition alone from a male teacher introduced to her by the female teacher. Naresh Kaul confronted the man with such vicious threats that he felt obliged to resign. He was under police protection for a while and eventually relocated to another part of the country.

Sahika disappeared from view. Her old Kingston school friends weren't allowed to contact her. One of the Kauls' neighbours, a Scotswoman, later told police that it was more than two weeks since she'd seen Sahika, although apparently the rest of the family's comings and goings had been much as usual. Eventually the police were alerted because Sahika had failed to keep appointments at the hospital where her throat was being treated. The Kauls were evasive when questioned about her whereabouts. They said that she'd run away from home – the neighbour confirmed that she had done this before – and claimed that they thought she'd 'gone to wickedness' and therefore they'd disowned her, which was why they hadn't reported her missing.

Derry Hacker was put in charge of the case. His notes showed that he was extremely suspicious of the Kauls, especially Naresh, who seemed completely to dominate his wife and children, but he could find no proof that Sahika had been murdered. He was refused a warrant to search the house, but on one of his visits still managed to secrete a listening device in the main downstairs room. Later he was criticised for using this unorthodox method. Tim smiled when he reached this part of the account: 'unorthodox' described Derry to a T. The listening device didn't produce any conclusive results, though Naresh Kaul was heard on more than one occasion warning the other two children not to discuss their sister's disappearance.

Derry and his team made no progress until the body of a

young woman was found in the Thames at Richmond some four months later. It was partially dismembered and so badly decomposed that the pathologist could not establish the cause of death. However, it was possible to prove that the body had been deliberately wedged beneath some rocks. Police retrieved several items of jewellery, which upon being questioned the Kauls admitted had belonged to Sahika. That the corpse was hers was further confirmed from her dental records.

Though the coroner ruled that the death had been caused by 'unlawful killing', there was still not enough evidence to pin it on the family. Derry was again refused a search warrant, in all probability because the magistrate was wary of being accused of victimising members of an ethnic minority.

The case wasn't closed, though the police could make no progress. The breakthrough came when, out of the blue, Naresh Kaul decided to challenge the coroner's ruling and requested it should be changed to an open verdict. He could offer no sound reason for this – he claimed rather lamely that it would stop the neighbours suspecting him and his wife of murder. Derry concluded that Kaul's somewhat naïve reasoning was that if the coroner changed the verdict, the police would drop their investigation. He applied again for a search warrant, which was granted. Examination of the Kauls' living room showed that a large quantity of blood had seeped into the floorboards. Although the boards had been vigorously scrubbed with a detergent strong enough to destroy DNA evidence, the stains remained. Some tiny drops of blood had also fallen on to a rug, which was taken away for forensic examination. A match was found with Sahika's DNA. When questioned separately from her parents, Daivi Kaul said that she was almost certain that her parents had murdered her sister, though she had not actually witnessed it. She provided further details that suggested she was telling the truth. The police accepted that she'd been too afraid to reveal them before, as it would have meant putting her own life in danger. It was because of her evidence that her mother was convicted as well as her father. Both parents were serving jail sentences of twenty-five years.

Tim scribbled some more notes. This was much more like the Verma case. The family were Punjabi Hindus; they were of modest means and only the daughter who'd 'dishonoured' them had been targeted. Also common to both cases was a kind of ambivalence about educating girls. On the one hand the parents were proud of their clever daughters and encouraged them to pursue a good education; on the other hand, they did not want to support this to its logical conclusion, i.e., the prospect of the daughter getting the sort of job that would give her financial independence. Bahir Verma had said that his daughter's husband would allow her to study for her degree after their marriage, but how likely was that in practice? She'd probably have her first child within a year of the wedding.

Tim got up to pour himself more water and saw that Derry Hacker was peering through the glass in the door. "Can I come in?" he mouthed. Tim nodded.

"Christ!" said Derry as he entered, "it's bloody cold in here."

"I don't feel cold – in fact, I'm sweating – though DC Chappell did warn me that the air con was ferocious."

"If you're not cold, there must be something wrong with you," said Hacker suspiciously. "Are you sure you're all right?"

Tim briefly lost his temper.

"I wish people would stop asking me that! I'm just a bit

under the weather because of the malaria tablets, that's all."
He'd been debating whether to tell Derry about the strange
image on the computer screen, but abandoned the idea
immediately.

"Sorry I spoke! How're you getting on, old son, anyway?
Is Nancy being helpful? Where is she?"

"I've read through a couple of the files – the Canadian one
you told me about and the Kaul case. The Kaul case is interesting because the family was Hindu, like the Vermas. But
I admit that I'm finding all this honour killing stuff confus-
ing. It goes without saying that it's against nature for parents
and siblings to kill their womenfolk; but aside from that I'm
finding all sorts of inconsistencies that I'm struggling to get
my head around."

"I know what you mean," said Derry. "I've been involved
in four of these cases now, and each time I've really had to
fight my way into them. A couple of things that might help:
you need to remember that each case is different. Although
I hope that reading the files might help, you won't find a
blueprint or common pattern there. That's not surprising,
really, since both victims and murderers come from a range of
countries, religions and social backgrounds. And I think you
should forget about the word 'honour', except as shorthand
to help you identify the motive. To a Western mind, there's
nothing honourable about these murders, but, as you say, the
term causes confusion. That's been reflected in some of the
sentences that have been handed down, even in European
countries. Ask Nancy. She's an expert on it. You didn't say
where she was, by the way."

"She left me to work through the files. She said she'd come
back to deal with any questions I might have later."

"Good. OK with you, was she?"

"Reasonably. I found her a bit difficult to get on with, but I thought it might have been me. I seem to have developed a talent for rubbing people up the wrong way since I've been in London."

Derry Hacker grinned.

"Only since you've been here? Seriously, though, she's great when you get to know her. You can't blame her for being wary, given the circumstances."

"What circumstances?"

"Didn't she tell you? I thought she might have done, considering why you're here."

"Tell me what?"

"She was almost the victim of an honour killing herself. She's half Bangladeshi – looks European, I know, must have inherited her mother's looks."

"You mean her father tried to murder her?"

"Yep. The family wasn't even particularly religious – couldn't have been, otherwise he wouldn't have been allowed to marry the mother."

"So he chose his wife but his daughter wasn't allowed to choose her own boyfriend?"

"I think she'd have been allowed to choose a boyfriend all right. The point was, she wanted a girlfriend. Next to punishing young girls for daring to consort with men, the most common reason for honour killings is to get rid of anyone with LGBT tendencies. That's why some of the victims are men: they're almost always gay men."

"God," said Tim. "That *is* a surprise: and it explains a lot. Is her name really Nancy Chappell?"

"No. It's not even an Anglicisation of her real name. She

was given a new identity long before she joined the police. She was recruited especially to help us with honour killings. She knows what she's talking about. As I've said, she's boned up on international law on them, too."

"It's great that you've asked her to help me. Thanks!"

"You and I go back a long way. And you need friends in this game. I'm sure there'll be something I'll want help with one day. And talking of surprises, I have another small one up my sleeve."

"Oh?" said Tim cautiously. Derry's voice had taken on a laddish twang that Tim recognised of old.

"Yes. I didn't mention the specifics earlier because you weren't well, but you seem to be better now. Patti's up in London today and tomorrow, attending a Forensics conference. I've asked her to have dinner with us."

"Oh," said Tim again, in what he hoped was a neutral tone. A dozen thoughts shot through his head, foremost among which was that he would have to tell Freya a white lie to explain his absence. He couldn't have her getting wind of the fact that he was meeting Patti socially, however innocent the occasion.

Chapter 12

I HEAD FOR the office, which has now moved from Holbeach to Spalding. It's in New Road, just a street away from the police station. Being in the car without Sophia gives me an unexpected empty feeling, but I'm looking forward to getting my teeth into some work.

I haven't worked in the new office before, though I've dropped in on Janey a few times and I spent a couple of hours there rearranging my stuff after the move. It's in one of the old buildings with sturdy brass-plated doors that open straight off the pavement. Janey and I are sharing the building with traffic control – they've got most of it – because there's no longer room for them at the station. It's a venerable town house, at least two hundred years old; the wooden staircases are narrow and winding, the windows still have sashes and the ceilings are ornate, decorated with plaster roses and cornices. It was probably once the proudly-owned townhouse of a professional man and his family, but has now been half-transformed by some state-of-the-art fittings. Our office has simple stud walls with two work-stations separated by a low screen and an alcove for the hanging files that neither Janey nor I would part with, but the traffic crew are backed up by banks of computers and simulation units straight out of the Tardis. I think I'm going to like working with them: they're energetic and cheerful and give a buzz to the place.

Janey's on holiday this week. She's taken her son to stay

with relatives in Wales. She's a single mother. I've never asked her about her exact circumstances – she's been on her own as long as I've known her – but I can tell her wounds are still red raw. That's why I don't pry. I think she finds it tough, bringing up a boy on her own. His name's Gwillim: she says she's always been determined to show him his Welsh heritage. I can't remember how old he is now: fourteen, perhaps fifteen? She must have borne him very young; she's only a few years older than I am.

I'm sorry Janey's not here, although she said it would be for the best; that I'd get used to working in the new place more easily if I was there on my own at first. Already I'm beginning to think she's right. Janey may be brittle on the subject of her past, but she's wise about almost everything else.

I prowl a little, inspecting cupboards, loos and coffee-making facilities, before I settle down. There is a small stack of documents in my in-tray, but I know that most of the work will have been e-mailed to me. I boot up the computer.

There are several e-mails waiting, including a 'welcome back' message from Superintendent Thornton. Tim has taught me always to look beyond any generous gestures made by Thornton and try to work out what might have prompted them, but sometimes I think he's being too cynical. Thornton obviously wants to get the most he can from everyone, but I believe he has a real regard for both of us. There's a short e-mail from Juliet, also welcoming me back and saying she'll drop round later. There's also a note from Andy Carstairs, about a boundary dispute between two farmers that's led to blows. Not my favourite kind of project, but of a type that I've been involved in many times before. There's a fairly cut-and-dried set of steps to take to work out who's in the right. Quite a good thing to start back with.

I contact the land registry to ask for copies of the relevant documents and am just settling down to read Andy's account of the vicious physical attack made by one of the farmers on the other, when the phone rings.

"Police research office."

There's the sound of musical laughter.

"Juliet? Is that you? What's so funny?"

"Nothing. It's just that you sound so professional."

"Not sure how to take that! Don't I usually sound professional?"

"Yes, of course. It struck me as strange, that's all, probably because I've not seen you in the work context lately."

"If you mean you've come to define me as the mother of a small child, I can see I haven't come back a moment too soon!"

"Well, I'm glad you're back, anyway. We all are. And the work's stacking up, as usual."

"So you said when we last spoke, but all I've got so far is some pretty routine checking to do for Andy."

"That's great, because I have something more unusual that I'd like you to help with. I think Superintendent Thornton may have mentioned something about it to you. Have you got time to see me now?"

"Sure. It won't take me long to get as far as I can with Andy's job. I'll put the kettle on. I've just found out where it is."

"Excellent. I'll be there in ten minutes, tops."

Juliet arrives even sooner than she'd said. I notice the change in her immediately.

"You've had your hair cut! I'm sorry, that's such an inane

thing to say. It looks lovely. Have you lost some weight as well, or does that style just make your face look thinner?"

Juliet pulls a face.

"Just a few pounds, nothing drastic. Glad you like the hair. I thought it was time for a change. No milk or sugar in my tea, thanks," she adds, as I pour hot water on to the tea-bags. "When's Janey coming back?"

"Not until next week."

"You'll appreciate being on your own for a while."

"That's what she said. But we get on so well that I'd just as soon she was here."

"Well, I'd rather give this piece of work I have to you than her, even though I'm certain she'd want it if she knew about it, so the fact that she's on holiday solves a problem."

I carry the two mugs of tea over to the small table that separates my desk and Janey's.

"I'm intrigued. Will you tell me what it is?"

"Of course, but you'll have to be discreet. It's only semi-official. Superintendent Thornton knows what I want to ask you to do and he's ambivalent about it. He's more or less said that he's not sure about it, but he'll look the other way."

I laugh.

"If Tim were here, he'd say that was typical."

"Yes, well you might have to keep Tim a bit in the dark about it, too. He'll probably like it even less than Thornton."

"Now I'm really curious! Tim and Thornton don't often take the same view, not even at different points of the spectrum."

"Their reasons will be different. Thornton doesn't want us to do anything that'll make the force look bad and Tim will think of it as encroaching on his territory."

I stop smiling.

"Is it something to do with this suspected so-called 'honour killing'? Tim's hardly talked to me about it, but I can't help feeling that there's something about it that doesn't stack up. I understand that a girl's disappeared, but why are you all so determined to believe that she's been murdered?"

"That's the point, not all of us are. Her disappearance coincided with a dossier of stuff that Thornton received about honour killings and how to look out for them. Some of the signs fit her case and, in my opinion, others don't. I think Thornton's getting cold feet now, but despite what you think about him and Tim always being on opposite sides, Tim's gone overboard on this one. The main suspect's gone to India and Tim's determined to follow him there. He's with Derry Hacker this week, finding out more about some of the honour killings they've worked on at the Met."

"That much I knew. But who is the suspect? One of the girl's relatives?"

"Not one of her immediate family, and that's one of the anomalies as far as I'm concerned. You're right when you say it's usually the victim's kin who decide to murder her to avenge their honour, but in this case it's the fiancé - or putative fiancé, I should say, as my understanding is that the family chose him for her. He is her cousin, but she only met him recently. The girl's name's Ayesha Verma. She was - or is - clever, hoping to become a solicitor. The fiancé came here from India to meet her. I don't know much about him, except that he's nearer fifty than forty, so has almost certainly either been married before and divorced or has another wife living. Officially, Hindus can no longer practise polygamy, but there's evidence some still do. But according to Bahir Verma, Ayesha's father, the cousin is single."

"How old is she?"

"Seventeen. Nearly eighteen."

"So she rejected their choice of husband?"

"Neither her father nor her mother admits to that, but I'd say it's likely, wouldn't you?"

"Yes. But I'd also say it's as likely that she ran away as was murdered. If she's almost eighteen and has a bit of gumption, she could easily get a job."

"That's what I think - or thought. But neither her bank account nor her National Insurance number has been used. The parents still have her birth certificate and passport. And apparently she left her mobile phone behind."

"That makes it sound a lot more serious. She could be a runaway, but she could also be being held prisoner somewhere. Or have been murdered without it being an honour killing."

"Tim's convinced it is one, and so was Superintendent Thornton, at first. As I said, he's having second thoughts. I just don't think there's enough evidence to justify Tim going to India to interview the fiancé - who appears to be quite willing to co-operate, by the way. As do the parents. The father's a bit stiff and formal, but the mother's nice. If she's making up how worried she is about Ayesha and knows that the girl's already dead, she deserves an Oscar."

"Tim and Superintendent Thornton must have some reason for thinking that there's been an honour killing."

"From what I know, they've jumped to that conclusion mainly because the family is Hindu. And because Thornton got that dossier about honour killings around the same time. Thornton's now wondering if the girl's been murdered by someone outside the family. I still think she's probably a runaway."

"I'd say there's a fifty-fifty chance that any one of you may be right, but I don't see how I can be of much help. What do you want me to do?"

"I'd like you to meet some girls whose lives have been put at risk because they've defied their families' wishes. I'd like to know what you think makes them tick – how they reacted to authoritative parents and being coerced into something they didn't want to do."

"You mean, compile some case studies? Sounds fascinating. But you're the sociologist, not me. Why can't you do it?"

"I'd love to, but I'm a policewoman as well as a sociologist. I'm not allowed to waste time on conjecture. The sort of evidence I'm asking you to find won't stand up in a court, but if we're lucky it may help us to find Ayesha."

"Wow! Of course, the answer is yes. But I don't know where to start. I doubt if there are many Hindu girls in Spalding, and even if there were, I could hardly accost one in the street and ask her about her private life. Her parents would be down on me like a ton of bricks."

Juliet laughs.

"I wouldn't put it past you, but I agree the consequences would probably be dire. And you're right that there aren't many Hindus living here – another reason that I'm dubious about the honour killing theory, because frequently they take place in large communities where the families all know each other's business and influence each other's behaviour. The girls you speak to don't have to be Hindu, though. Honour killings have been carried out by people of many different nationalities and several religions. I've been in touch with social services at Peterborough, and I think they'll help. You'll have to be extremely discreet and not tell anyone about it. The girls' identities will have to be kept completely anonymous."

"What about Tim?"

"Up to you how much you tell him. Between you, you seem to have worked out a way to keep your professional lives separate from your private lives. I know that anything you tell him will be treated confidentially. It's really a question of whether he'll think that you – and I – are invading his patch."

"I'll have to tell him a certain amount, otherwise he'll be furious when he finds out. I think it's highly unlikely it'll dissuade him from going to India, though, even if I've completed the case studies before he plans to leave."

"You're probably right about that, but at least it'll help us to demonstrate that we didn't fail Ayesha Verma by blindly going down one single alleyway."

"Talking of Tim, how has he seemed to you lately?"

"I'd thought of asking you the same question and decided it would be rude of me. But since you ask, he's been a bit strange. He puts it down to the side effects of the malaria tablets he's taking, but I'd say there was more to it than that. He called me yesterday to say that he thought he'd seen Peter Prance, wanted me to check on any sightings since the Sheppard case."

"Peter who?"

"A conman who was blackmailing Hedley Atkins, the bloke who was finally convicted of killing his grandmother and sister about five years ago. It was all quite strange: it started out as a cold case enquiry into the murder of a woman called Kathryn Sheppard, whose remains were dumped at the side of the road many years before they were found. I don't know if you remember it?"

"Vaguely. I don't remember Peter Prance. Did I ever meet him?"

"I doubt it: otherwise, I'm sure you wouldn't have forgotten him! As I've said, it was a few years ago, probably not long after you and Tim got married."

"So why do you think it's odd that Tim says he saw him?"

Juliet shrugs.

"It just seems unlikely, that's all. And Tim was obsessed with the idea when he rang me."

I laugh.

"I'm sorry, you're not convincing me. Tim's always obsessed about whatever it is that's going on in his mind at any one time. I suppose everyone is, really," I add, feeling I should show some loyalty.

"I suppose you're right. And he is a larger-than-life character."

I don't answer. She's right, but what Sophia and I want from Tim at the moment is not flamboyance, but a little bit more TLC.

Chapter 13

"FREYA? IS THAT you?"

"Yes, of course it's me. Is something the matter, Tim?"

"No, not really. Derry's arranged for me to have dinner with him and someone who can probably help me with the case I'm working on. But I wanted to check if it's all right with you?"

Freya laughed.

"It sounds as if it's already settled! What would you do if I said I'd planned to cook a three-course meal accompanied by fine wines and am now mortally offended?"

"God, you haven't . . ."

"No, of course I haven't. I was going to cook for you, but probably something quick picked up from Waitrose on the way home. As it is, you've given me enough warning to change my plans and go to a lecture that's on at the V & A this evening instead."

"Thanks. If you're sure you don't mind. Sounds a bit of a heavy way of ending a working day."

"Not really. It's about early twentieth century fashions. As you know, clothes interest me."

"Well, I hope you enjoy it. And that you'll have something to eat."

"Don't worry, it's not like me to skip supper. I may buy something before it starts. I take it you'll be coming home eventually – not spending the whole night out, are you?"

Freya's question was studiedly casual.

"Of course not. I'll probably be quite late, though. If you're in bed, I'll be quiet."

"I should hope so. Don't forget to call Katrin, will you? Have fun!"

"Thanks. I . . ."

Freya had already rung off. Without being able to put his finger on quite why, Tim knew that she didn't believe him. She was right not to, but almost certainly for the wrong reason. Or was it the right reason? Tim felt both confused and guilty. He decided to call Katrin straight away.

He'd just placed the call when Derry Hacker came back. Tim put his hand over the phone.

"Give us a few minutes, Derry would you?"

"Sure," said Derry, shrugging. "I just wanted to say that the table's booked for 7.30. It'll take us half an hour to get there, so you've got more than an hour before we need to leave. I keep spare shirts here if you want to freshen up." He smiled knowingly.

Tim pretended not to notice the smile, but the offer was a tempting one. Although he'd managed not to vomit on his clothes, his shirt felt stale and sweaty. A quick wash and change would make him much more comfortable and in a better frame of mind for dinner. Although at first he'd been annoyed with Derry for inviting Patti, he'd come round to the idea. The relationship between them had been strained for too long. A relaxing evening with a few drinks would help them to clear the air, and Derry's presence would act as a safeguard – not that Tim thought Patti remotely capable of becoming a siren.

"Thanks," he said. "I'd appreciate it, if you don't mind."

"OK. I'll come back in a few minutes."

When Derry had gone, Tim realised that he was still holding the phone in his hand. He turned it round and looked at the screen. 'Call dropped', it said. Cursing, he pressed the speed-dial number again.

"What are you playing at, Tim?" said Katrin crossly when she answered. "You've just kept me on hold until I lost you."

"Sorry," he said. "I'd pressed the button when someone came in and disturbed me. I'm on my own again now. Did you have a good day?"

"Yes, thanks. We've just got in. Sophia's very tired and she hasn't eaten yet, so I won't be able to talk for long. But she seems to like it at Mrs Sims'."

"What about you? Good first day back? Anything interesting cropped up for you?"

"Mostly routine stuff. Helping Andy to settle a dispute between two farmers, and one or two other bits and pieces. But I'm going to have to go now. Can you call back in a couple of hours, after she's had her bath and gone to bed?"

"Umm . . ."

"Well, if you can't just say so," Katrin continued snappishly. "Has Freya got something planned?"

"No, she's going to a lecture at the V & A. I'm spending the evening with Derry and a colleague. He sends you his regards, by the way."

"Really?" said Katrin. "You'd better say I send mine back, then. Is the colleague anyone I know?"

"No, I don't think so." Tim couldn't think of anything else to add; he was appalled by the lie even as he said it. There was a long silence.

"OK, well, I hope you enjoy yourself. Perhaps we can

talk some more tomorrow? On Skype, so that you can see Sophia?"

"Yes, that would be great. Sorry about this evening. I love you."

"I love you, too," said Katrin perfunctorily, before ending the call.

Tim sighed. He'd now managed to lie to both Freya and Katrin, convincing neither, when he had no intention of doing anything that would upset either of them. All he was trying to do was to avoid giving either of them cause for concern - or disapproval, he was forced to admit. He'd been unwise to allow himself to be pushed into this situation by Derry. Perhaps he should back out of it now, go back to Freya's and have a quiet evening and an early night. He'd probably feel the better for it. He could call Katrin again then, too.

Derry returned, bearing a crisp blue shirt swathed in a polythene laundry cover.

"Here you are, old son. Collar size is probably a bit big for you, but presumably you'll leave it open."

"Derry, I'm not sure I can make it. I haven't been feeling too good, and . . ."

"Sure you can make it. You've stuck it here all day, haven't you? If you've got a touch of something, a couple of drinks'll do you the world of good. What's the matter? Has your sister been getting at you?"

"No. Actually, she's quite pleased, because there's something she wants to do this evening."

"Well, there you are. If you go back to hers on your own, you'll have to fend for yourself. Much better to have a decent meal with me and Patti. Besides, Patti will be really disappointed if you cry off now."

"That's what worries me. I was very fond of Patti at one time - still am, in a sort of way - but the real relationship between us has been over for years. I don't want her to think that I'm trying to kindle that spark again, because I've got no intention of doing so and I don't want to hurt her. I'd like you to take note of that, as well."

"Relax, Tim. You flatter yourself. It's just a dinner between three old friends. Nothing more. You seem to think I have some kind of ulterior motive, but I assure you I don't. Not where you're concerned, anyway. I admit that at the back of my mind there's a faint glimmer of hope that she might take more of an interest in me. You'd be helping me out in that respect. She probably won't agree to come if she finds out it's just the two of us."

Tim hesitated. He'd gone right off the idea of the dinner and wasn't convinced that Derry was telling the truth. And even if he was, Tim wasn't sure that he wanted to play the pander on Derry's behalf. Much as he liked his old colleague, he had no doubts about his fickleness where women were concerned. If Patti succumbed to his charms, she'd be bound to come to grief.

"Be careful with Patti, Derry. She doesn't deserve to get hurt."

Derry whistled.

"Look who's talking!" he said with a smile, though Tim didn't miss the hard edge that had crept into his voice. "Butter wouldn't melt! I suppose you've never done anything to hurt her. Anyway, if you're so worried about her feelings, you'd better come along as chaperone."

Tim returned the smile uncertainly. He didn't want to fall out with Derry: he was grateful to him for the trouble he'd taken to help with the Verma case. Eventually, though, he gave in because he couldn't summon the energy to resist further. His head was beginning to throb and he knew Derry's assertive nature could turn nasty if crossed. He stood up and took the shirt.

"OK, you win. I agree that it's unreasonable of me to back out now. But you know it's true that I'm not feeling well. I want to get back to Surbiton quite early – before Freya comes home, if possible. So just the restaurant, not a pub crawl afterwards. We can go out drinking on another evening, when I'm feeling better."

"Right you are," said Derry chirpily. "I can't say I'm much into pub crawls myself these days, not during the week, anyway. We're both getting old! If I were you, I'd barricade myself into the gents pretty swiftly," he added. "Once the cleaners get in there, they won't let you in. It's worse than trying to enter a nuclear exclusion zone."

"Thanks for the tip," said Tim. "And for the shirt. I'll try to make myself look presentable."

Chapter 14

TIM'S CALL HAS upset me and made me very angry. I don't know what's got into him recently. I know he's worried about the case he's working on - though his attitude to it seems odd. It's as if he's hell-bent on going to India, whatever the evidence indicates. Juliet's not the only one who's sceptical. I'd like to talk more to her and Superintendent Thornton about it, but I don't want to be disloyal. I suppose this is just a blip: Tim's always been impulsive and I'm certain those malaria pills he's taking are having an effect on his mind. But he doesn't seem to understand that I need his support now, just as I'm starting work again. He was so helpful with Sophia at first, sharing the chores as much as he could. Usually I can cope with him going off at a tangent occasionally, but this time it's going to be difficult. At the back of my mind I can't help wondering if he sees the trip to India as a way of escaping for a while. And I really don't know why he had to stay with Freya. It would have been much more convenient for him to check into a hotel in London. The force would have paid. I didn't protest at the time because I thought Derry Hacker might suggest Tim stayed with him, but it looks as if they're socialising together anyway. Derry's very bad news - how bad, I can't tell Tim without causing a row.

I've fed Sophia and am about to take her for her bath when the doorbell rings. Holding Sophia in my arms, I look out of the living room window to see who it is. I'm surprised to find that it's Margie standing there. She turns to look at me and gives a half-smile. Sophie waves both arms excitedly. It's clear that Margie's scored a hit with her.

I go to open the door, still holding Sophia, who stretches out her arms to Margie and plants a kiss on her cheek. I laugh. Margie seems pleased.

"Margie!" I say. "This is a surprise."

She stands in the doorway uncertainly. She's wearing a tight black T-shirt that clings to her rib cage and three-quarter length black leggings. She's painfully thin.

"I hope I'm not being a nuisance," she says. "I can come back."

"No, it's OK. I was just going to take Sophia for her bath. You can come with us if you like."

"I'll give her her bath if you'd like a rest, Mrs Yates."

I look at her again. Her face is thin and hollow, her skin almost transparent.

"Have you eaten?"

She looks down at her feet.

"I had lunch at Mrs Sims'," she says defensively.

"Would you like to bath Sophia while I make some supper for us both? Then we can talk in peace, after we've got her settled."

She nods, still hesitant.

"I'd like to give Sophia her bath. I don't eat much in the evenings."

"It'll just be a snack. Nothing fancy. And thank you for bathing her. I'll show you where everything is."

I head for the bathroom and Margie follows a few steps behind.

75

Chapter 15

JULIET ARMSTRONG, JUST home from work, sighed as she caught sight of her reflection in the hall mirror of her small flat. There were lines on her forehead and the beginnings of crinkly skin around her eyes. She'd chosen the new hairstyle to boost her confidence, while knowing deep down that nothing so trivial could have a lasting effect on her mood.

She'd be thirty-four next birthday and had been doing the same job for seven years, living in the same flat and working with the same colleagues. Despite two serious attempts to share her life with a 'significant other', she was still alone, and, if she was completely honest with herself, still uncertain about her sexuality. She had no close family: she'd been born in New Zealand and her few distant relatives, most of whom she'd never met, still lived there.

Entranced by Spalding and the magical fens and farmlands surrounding it when she'd first arrived, she was beginning to wonder if this was really the place where she wanted to spend the rest of her life. If there were any prospect of promotion, she might feel more upbeat, but she and Andy Carstairs and Ricky MacFadyen were all treated as exact equals by DI Yates and Superintendent Thornton. The South Lincolnshire CID Division needed a Detective Sergeant, but Juliet had overheard a conversation between Tim and Thornton that suggested that they'd be choosing someone from outside with the express purpose of preserving the equilibrium between these three colleagues. Juliet had raged inwardly at the knowledge that her two seniors believed they could manipulate the appointment so glibly, but knew there was nothing she could do about it. If she and Andy and Ricky all applied for the job, she knew they'd all be interviewed. Neither Tim nor Thornton would be stupid enough to do otherwise, even if they had no intention of appointing any of them. It was short-sighted of them, even so. Did they expect all the DCs to be content with staying in the same job forever?

Juliet sighed again and kicked off her shoes. She ought to cook something for supper – she'd had to skip lunch – but couldn't find the energy. Instead she fixed herself a stiff Bloody Mary and sat down with it and a packet of crisps. She'd flinched from sorting out her thoughts for too long. It had taken all her resilience to keep on an even keel after the split with Louise Butler and she'd been reluctant to delve deeper below the surface than she had strength for. Now she knew it was time to stop this emotional drifting and put more purpose into her life.

At the heart of the problem was her relationship with Tim Yates. It wasn't a sexual problem: she wasn't one of those deluded doormat women who fell in love with her boss and turned her whole existence into becoming his willing slave. She didn't remotely fancy Tim, for one thing, and she got on too well with his wife, for another. She had no intention of encroaching on their personal territory. But until recently she had believed that Tim held her in high esteem and appreciated her more than the others: that she was, in fact, a prima inter pares. Now she doubted it, which meant that she'd probably been wasting the past three years at least looking after Tim when she should have been focusing on developing her career.

She smiled wryly. If this was true, then she *had* been deluded; just not in the usual way.

Nevertheless, she was worried about Tim. He'd always been a bit bumptious, thoughtless rather than uncaring, but ready to admit when he was at fault and usually deeply sorry if he wounded feelings. Now, however, he was ploughing a furrow that was not only lonely but decidedly strange. There'd never been any doubt that he was the team leader – that was his job, after all – but during this last case he'd hardly consulted the team. The quality of his work was slipping, too. The old Tim Yates would not have called her mobile and then forgotten what he'd wanted when she'd got back to him; would never have forgotten to send samples of Ayesha Verma's hair to be tested.

He'd been so headstrong about how to tackle the Verma case that Juliet had more or less had to go behind his back when deciding to involve Katrin. Admittedly, Superintendent Thornton had encouraged Tim's approach at first, but now he'd definitely got cold feet, though he hadn't been honest enough to admit it. Perhaps Thornton was also part of the problem. Tim had been using him as a sparring partner for so long, allowing him just about enough deference not to get himself into trouble, that maybe it had warped his judgment. It was also possible that Tim was worried about his own career, his own future, though he was not much older than Juliet and had made much better progress. Like her, however, he'd been in the job for a long time.

Then there was this business about Peter Prance. Had Tim really spotted him twice in two days while he was in London? To Juliet it seemed unlikely, especially if it *had* been Prance on the first occasion and he'd noticed Tim: he'd have taken good care that Tim didn't see him again. No, the supposed Prance sightings must be a red herring. Had Tim's subconscious summoned them up as a cypher for all the crooks who'd got away? Did they indicate a profound lack of confidence in Tim in his ability to do his job?

Juliet's glass was empty. As she rose to refill it – one more wouldn't hurt – she realised that, once again, she'd allow her thoughts to be hijacked by Tim and his plans and problems. If she had another drink, she must take care to dedicate it to forging her own independence. Both methodical and introspective, Juliet had since childhood found it helpful to write things down. Taking an A4 pad from her briefcase and arming herself with a fresh drink, she settled down on her sofa again, this time intent upon an exhaustive SWOT analysis of her own career.

Chapter 16

As I heat up the remainder of the Bolognese sauce I made yesterday, I hear Margie singing to Sophia. She has a beautiful voice. She pauses, and there is laughter. Sophia is enjoying herself. It's going to be easy to get her to sleep this evening.

I've just put the spaghetti into the boiling water when Margie appears.

"She's sleepy now, Mrs Yates. I've laid her in her cot."

"Thank you. I'll go up and settle her. Help yourself to a Coke if you'd like one – there's some in the fridge. And give this pasta a bit of a whirl, if you would."

Sophia is almost asleep when I look into her cot. I lean over the side and smooth her curls, kiss her on the cheek and re-arrange her sleeping bag to make her more comfortable. She barely stirs.

I return to Margie. She's standing by the stove, methodically stirring the spaghetti with a wooden fork. She doesn't hear me come in. She's staring at the steam and swirling pasta as if she's in a trance.

"That'll do," I say to her gently. "It'll be another five minutes or so. You can leave it now."

She turns quickly, startled, splashing the back of hand with some drops of boiling water. She drops the fork into the pan, sucks her hand.

"Careful!" I say. I smile at her. "You didn't get yourself a drink. Would you like one now?"

"Yes, please. Just water."

I debate whether to pour myself a glass of wine and decide that I probably shouldn't. She's old enough to drink, but still it could make things awkward. I fill two glasses with sparkling water and take them to the kitchen table.

"Come and sit down," I say. "We can keep an eye on that from here."

Hesitantly, she obeys. She takes a sip from the water and plays with her thumb in the ridges made by the pattern on the glass.

"What did you want to see me about?"

She looks up, meets my eye and shrinks away again. She seems timid, yet I note again the streak of defiance in her manner which I first spotted at Mrs Sims'.

I smile.

"I won't eat you," I say.

"I don't suppose you will. I just don't know whether I can trust you."

"You've no reason not to trust me. But if you tell me something that I feel I can't help with, or that I don't think is right, I promise you I won't tell anyone else. Unless you're breaking the law," I add.

She grins and immediately looks her proper age again, instead of resembling an anxious young woman just this side of thirty.

"Mrs Sims said your husband is a copper."

"He is. And I work for the police as well."

She eyes me.

"I've been taught to look out for coppers."

I laugh.

"You wouldn't be the first. But I'm not one. I'm a police researcher. I don't have any legal powers."

She looks at me again, takes a deep breath and then shuts down, playing abstractedly with the glass, her eyes fixed to the table. The pan of spaghetti begins to boil over.

"God, I forgot it after all!" I say, jumping up and seizing the handle of the pan with a tea towel. I strain the spaghetti in a colander. I take out two plates and begin to ladle it onto them.

"Don't bother for me," says Margie gracelessly. "I'm not hungry."

"Please yourself," I reply, equally offhand, "But if you don't want to talk and you don't want to eat, I'd like you to tell me exactly why you're here."

Tears well up in her eyes.

"I'm sorry. I didn't mean to sound so rough." Immediately I'm repentant.

"It's not you. It's my Mum and Dad."

"Mrs Sims mentioned that they might be splitting up. I'm sorry," I say again.

"Not *might be*. They have. Dad's left her for some tart who works in his office. And she's going to pieces, drinking all the time, although there's no money."

"Are you very close to your Dad?"

"I was. I don't see much of him now."

"What about your Mum?"

"I'm living with her. That's what they agreed on. No-one's close to her any more. She's just a zombie."

"I can understand how upsetting it must be . . ."

"No, you don't understand. It's not about them. If they want to fuck up their lives, that's up to them. But there's no money now for me to go to university. I'm going to have to work until I've saved enough. And what I get at Mrs Sims' is barely enough to keep me."

"*Keep* you? Is your mother taking money from you?"

Margie shrugs, but I can tell she can hardly be bothered to defend her mother.

"Doesn't have much option, I suppose."

"I'll try to help you, but it might take a while. I could look into scholarships, foundations that help students suffering from hardship, that sort of thing."

She's silent. Evidently such a solution doesn't appeal. Perhaps it sounds too daunting.

"Did you have something else in mind?"

She scrabbles at the glass.

"I was wondering . . . you've seen me with Sophia; you know I'm good with her. And I know it's hard being out at work when you've got a baby. The other mothers are always dashing in late or asking Mrs Sims to take their kids when they're not really well enough to be there. I wondered if you'd like a live-in nanny? For a couple of years, maybe. Then I could save for university and Sophia would be well-looked-after until she goes to pre-school. And you wouldn't have to worry about her."

I'm speechless, not because I think the suggestion is out-rageous, but simply because it isn't something I've considered. My first reaction is that Tim and I wouldn't be able to afford it; my second, that we'd have to think very carefully about the implications of live-in help. The bungalow is small. What's more, Tim is implacably opposed to any kind of domestic service, which is why we don't have a cleaner. And Margie might be good with children, but as far as I know she's not been trained as a nanny.

"You don't like the idea, do you?"

"I wouldn't say I don't like it." She's fragile and I know I must choose my words carefully. "You've taken me by surprise, that's all. I'll talk to my husband about it when he comes home. He's working away at the moment."

She gets up suddenly, almost knocking the glass flying. She catches it emphatically, stands it foursquare again.

"Don't bother. There's other things I can do."

She's out of the kitchen and has crossed the hall before I can reply.

"Thanks for the water," she calls as she opens the door, "and for letting me put Sophia to bed."

She doesn't slam the door, but she's obviously desperate to get away. I don't call after her.

I sit at the table for a few minutes before I get up to confront the congealing spaghetti. I throw it away and contemplate cooking some more before I decide it's not worth the effort. I spoon the bolognaise sauce onto a soup plate and eat it with a hunk of bread. When I've finished eating, I pour a large glass of red wine.

I'm not sure whether I'll mention Margie's visit to Tim. He'll probably tear me off a strip for letting her into the house. Perhaps I shouldn't have trusted her with Sophia, though something tells me that, even if Margie's unstable, she would never harm a child.

Chapter 17

TIM AND DERRY emerged from the cool of the building into the warm evening air. There was a festive feel to the city as people finishing the working day dawdled and chatted.

"Only 6.50," said Derry, consulting his watch. "We've got time for a swift drink if we step on it."

"Where're we going?"

"To the Tube. St James's Park. We want to be in Tottenham Court Road, so there's a change at Embankment, but with a bit of luck we won't get held up."

"Why did you choose that part of town? Because it's cheaper than round here?" Tim smiled. He was feeling quite a lot better and had decided not to let Derry get the upper hand for once. Derry gave him a straight look.

"Not at all. It's because Patti's staying in a hotel nearby. St Giles. I thought it'd be better for her not to have to traipse around too much, as she doesn't know London well. And it'll be easy for you to get back to Waterloo afterwards."

"Thanks," said Tim dubiously. "Where's the restaurant?"

"In Charlotte Street. A French place I found some time ago. And, for your information, not at all cheap."

"I'm happy to pay my share . . ."

"Nonsense. It was my idea, so my shout."

Tim decided to say nothing but to play it by ear. It would be out of the question to charge a meal for three people in a fancy restaurant as subsistence (he winced inwardly as he imagined Thornton's enraged expression) and money had been tighter since Katrin took maternity leave. But it was equally unconscionable to allow Derry to foot a very large bill on his own.

They reached Tottenham Court Road quickly. It was still only 7.15 p.m..

"St Giles is at this end, isn't it? Are you planning to pick Patti up on the way?"

"No. She said she'd be out somewhere this afternoon: she's coming straight from wherever."

"We could have headed for Goodge Street, then. It would have been nearer."

"As I said, we'll have a swift drink along the way. There's a pub just by the station that serves drinks outside. It need only take a few minutes."

Again Tim felt dubious. He didn't really want a drink and he thought it would take them at least fifteen minutes to walk most of the length of Tottenham Court Road. Wearily, he followed Derry up the station steps.

The pub was only a few yards away. Inside, it was crowded and very noisy, but Derry was right: there were a few tables outside, one of them just being vacated as they arrived.

"Grab that," said Derry. "I'll get them in. What'll you have?"

"A glass of red wine, thanks. A small one."

"Bit of a girl's drink, that. What about a real ale? Sussex Mild?"

"Whatever you like. I'll leave it to you." Tim was too tired to argue. He sank down on one of the wrought iron chairs and rested his arms on the cockly table, drawing a rivulet of spilt beer towards him. He moved hastily and tried to shift the table to a more stable position.

Derry returned quickly, bearing two foaming pint glasses. He had started draining one before he handed the other to Tim.

"Just what I need," he said with satisfaction. "It's been a tough day."

"It certainly has," said Tim.

"Cheers, anyway," said Derry, raising his glass. "And now we're here, old son, there's a little favour I'd like to ask of you."

"Oh?"

"There's no need to look like that. You know what we were talking about earlier?"

"We talked about quite a lot. Which specific thing did you have in mind?"

"The conversation about Patti. As I said, I'd like to have another go. You'd help me out if you left a bit early, so I can walk her home on my own. Should fit in with your plans, from what you've been saying."

"But what if Patti..?"

"That's up to her, isn't it? She's a big girl. I'm sure she knows how to say no. Besides, you've given up any rights you might ever have had to look out for her."

"Don't keep going on about it. Yes, all right, then, as long as she doesn't seem upset when I start talking."

"Cheers," said Derry again, giving Tim's arm a punch. "Drink up, now, we're going to be late."

Tim downed about half of the beer and immediately began to feel nauseous.

"Let's just go, shall we? I can't drink this in a hurry on an empty stomach."

"As you wish. Waste of a good ale, but we're late already. Better get a cab."

Derry whirled into the road, his arm outstretched. A black cab stopped almost immediately. The driver didn't complain when he was asked to turn round and head back the way he'd come.

The traffic was heavy. It was 7.45 p.m. when they reached the restaurant in Charlotte Street. Tim tried to pay the driver, but Derry insisted that he would do it, so it was Tim who entered the restaurant first. It was dark inside, the gloom accentuated by oak-panelled walls. Patti must have seen him first, because by the time his eyes were accustomed to the change in light she was already staring at him, her face a picture of astonishment not exactly tempered with pleasure.

She had been seated at a square table near the back of the room, but stood as soon as she saw him. He noticed that she was wearing a pale dress of some floaty material: an unusual garb for the Patti he knew, who spent most of her life in trousers. She extended her hand.

"DI Yates," she said archly. "When DI Hacker said he'd like me to meet a colleague, I had no idea it would be you." She glanced over Tim's shoulder. "Rather disingenuous of you, really. You gave me to understand that it was someone I hadn't met before." The last sentence was addressed to Derry, who had just appeared behind Tim.

"I thought you'd be pleased!" Derry cackled brazenly. "Anyway, we're all here now, and we're going to have a bloody good evening. I'll see to that."

"Will you?" said Patti coolly. But Tim could see she was amused. She dropped the subject.

"Sorry we kept you waiting," Derry continued. "I hope you've ordered a drink?"

"I've asked for a big bottle of water. I thought we'd all want some of it."

"Possibly. But I meant a proper drink. What will it be? A gin and tonic?"

Chapter 18

JULIET RESISTED THE temptation to fix a third Bloody Mary. She remembered she'd meant to call Katrin and looked at her watch. 9 p.m. Not too late.

Katrin took a while to answer: so long that Juliet debated whether to abandon the call before she woke the baby.

"Hello?" The voice at the other end of the phone sounded hoarse and groggy.

"Katrin? Is that you? It doesn't sound like you." Juliet regretted this observation immediately. Katrin sounded as if she'd been crying.

"Yes, of course it's me." Katrin's false little laugh was unconvincing. "Who did you think it might be?"

"Are you OK?"

"Yes, just a bit tired after my first day back. And I had a rather strange visitor, which put me off my stroke a bit."

Juliet noted that she didn't mention Tim.

"Are *you* all right, anyway?" Katrin continued, making the question sound like a challenge. "You seemed pretty down when I saw you today."

"I'm fine. Just wondering what I'm doing with my life, that sort of thing," said Juliet lightly.

"Join the club!" said Katrin with feeling. As if afraid she'd been disloyal, she added, "Missing Tim, probably."

"He's such high maintenance, I'm surprised you aren't enjoying a few days without him."

They both laughed.

"Did you have a reason for calling? Not that it's not nice to talk with you."

"Yes. I meant to call you before you left the office this afternoon. I've spoken to the woman I mentioned in Peterborough, the one in social services who's helped girls whose families have tried to force them into arranged marriages. She says she can see you tomorrow morning. Apparently she's away for the rest of the week. I said I'd ask you. I realise it may be too short notice. Is tomorrow one of the days you're working?"

"Not supposed to be, but I agreed that I'd be flexible. Sophia can probably go to the childminder again tomorrow. I'll have to check, but the childminder's not fully booked up at the moment."

"Don't do anything you can't cope with. If you think Sophia needs to be at home tomorrow, I'll understand."

"Waiting until next week's not really on, is it? If this woman's going to give us some clues about Ayesha Verma's state of mind, I'll need to talk to her as soon as possible. Where does she want to meet? In Peterborough?"

"Actually, she said she could come to see you tomorrow. She's got a lunchtime meeting in Boston, apparently, and can make a detour."

"Even better. Let me call Mrs Sims. I'll let you know, either way. Shall I text you?"

"If you want to, but you can call again if you like. I'm completely at a loose end this evening."

Chapter 19

THE SMALL MAN, no longer dapper, was running. Without stopping, he looked fearfully behind him, his tie streaming over his shoulder. He could see them in the distance, distinctive in their brilliant white shirts. They were running, too, but seemingly effortlessly, their loping strides much longer than his own. They were tall, each of the three of them rising half a head above the milling sea of faces that made up the crowd. He knew they still had him in their sights, that he hadn't shaken them off. He was flagging. He had a stitch in his side and his breath was coming in ragged bursts.

He was frightened. More than frightened, shit scared. He'd been chased before, even beaten up before and he hadn't enjoyed it, but on those previous occasions he'd known that he'd survive. His assailants then had smacked him to teach him a lesson, but they hadn't planned to kill him. They weren't nutters. These three weren't even fucking nutters, they were worse: human automatons who obeyed orders with no attempt at compunction or mercy, no questions asked and no fear of the consequences. And if he stayed on the pavement he knew they'd catch up with him in minutes.

There was a crossroads up ahead. He dived to his right and entered a much smaller street. Here there were fewer crowds but many more cafés and pubs. The whole street was full of them. Summoning up a final spurt of energy, he passed the first two and flung himself through the doorway of the third, knowing he could get no further before his pursuers rounded the corner. Ahead of him he saw a bar. He hurtled towards it and grabbed hold of the brass rail set on the customer side of its counter, using it to support him as he edged to the furthest end of the bar, a dim little recess beside a grimy hardboard service door.

"Are you all right, sir?" The barman was of a type that he'd encountered many times before: florid and slightly overweight, thinning hair plastered flat against his scalp, studiously polite but ready to get heavy if he scented trouble.

"Yes, yes, just had to run for a bus, that's all. It's kind of you to ask," he gasped.

The barman eyed him sceptically.

"What would you like to drink, sir?"

"A double scotch. Better make it a treble . . ."

"We don't serve more than double measures here."

"Oh; well, a double, then. I can always have another," he said conspiratorially. The barman didn't share the joke. Turning his back, he seized a shots glass from the rack above his head and carefully pressed it against the optic of the giant bottle of Johnnie Walker suspended in front of him. He repeated the action and pushed the glass smoothly across the counter.

"Seven pounds, if you please, sir."

Although he was still recovering his breath, the small man blenched.

"But that's a preposterous price! I . . ."

"Seven pounds or I take it back," said the barman, enclosing the glass with a beefy fist.

The small man spluttered and searched his pockets. After some awkward fumbling, he managed to produce one two pound coin, three one pound coins, two fifty pence pieces and a handful of change. He spread it out on the counter. The barman scooped up the coins with practised deftness.

"Thank you, sir," he said, a tinge of irony spiking the politeness now.

The small man shot him a defiant look before re-focusing his darting brown eyes on the entrance. Picking up the drink, he swept the room with his anxious gaze before he selected a seat behind a one-person table adjacent to where he had been standing, but on the other side of the service door. From this vantage point he could sit with his back to the wall and observe the entrance. The barman resumed his activity of polishing glasses, but he, too, was now keeping an eye on the door to the street. He'd seen trouble too many times not to realise he was staring it in the face now. There had been other hunted men who'd sat at that table. Not all of them had vacated it of their own volition.

The small man nursed his drink as best he could, obviously making an effort not to gulp it down. The barman saw him search through his pockets forlornly, perhaps hoping for the miraculous discovery of a ten pound note. His eyes flicked across to a jovial group of tubby men drinking beer and watching the snooker on the giant television screen. The barman guessed he wouldn't be above scrounging a drink from them under normal circumstances, but on this occasion he evidently had more pressing concerns to worry about. The small man continued to sip his drink, hunching himself down in his chair so that he looked even smaller.

A series of deafening staccato cracks rent the air. Instinctively the barman ducked down. The men who had been watching the snooker match also dived for the floor like burly rugby players for the line. The small man remained where he was, his brown eyes blinking, petrified by fear.

The service door swung open so violently that one of its hinges was ripped from the flimsy hardboard. Three men sprang through it, agile as big cats stalking their prey. The first of them was waving a gun.

"No-one's going to get hurt," he shouted. "Just make sure you keep down."

The other two had seized the small man and roughly hauled him to his feet. His eyes were wild now, searching hopelessly for an ally.

"No!" He screamed. "No! Help me, somebody, please help me."

"Shut it," said the man with the gun. "You ain't got no friends here."

They dragged him through the service door and out to the alley beyond the kitchen. The barman and his customers listened to a succession of harrowing screams, followed, after about five minutes, by a jolting silence.

One of the snooker watchers was the first to get to his feet. He walked shakily across to the bar and peered over it, meeting the eye of the barman as he crouched there. Unwilling to compromise his dignity, he, too, stood up.

"You going to call the police, old cock?"

"In a bit," he said. "No hurry. I knew that bloke was trouble as soon as I clapped eyes on him."

Chapter 20

DERRY HACKER ASKED for another round of gin and tonics. Tim tried to refuse, but Derry just eyed him with amusement and went ahead anyway. They'd ordered dinner some time before, but the restaurant had swiftly become crowded after they'd greeted Patti and, as Derry said, none of the food would be arriving via the microwave or freezer: the wait would be worth it.

Patti seemed unperturbed by the prospect of another drink, surprising Tim, who remembered her as a very moderate drinker. Tim himself was feeling queasier by the minute. He resolved to try to dispose of his next drink, perhaps by simply leaving it until the waiter brought the food. He poured himself a glass of water.

The conversation had been a little stilted, but friendly enough. They'd kept to neutral topics. Tim wondered what Patti had been doing in London that day, wearing that dress, if she really hadn't been back to her hotel to change. She certainly wasn't dressed for her grisly trade, or for the conference that Derry had mentioned earlier and then seemed to forget about. He didn't ask her because he was afraid of overstepping the boundaries of professionalism. He'd resolved to show a polite interest in Patti's work while at the same time conveying that he knew that her personal life was off limits for him. She seemed to have adopted the same strategy, asking briefly after Katrin and Sophia but listening to his reply without showing too much interest.

The second round of gin and tonics arrived: evidently the bar staff could move a lot more swiftly than their colleagues in the kitchen. Derry scooped one of the glasses from the tray before the waiter could even set it down and took a large swig before hoisting it in the air.

"Cheers!" he said. "Here's to old times!"

He was always ebullient, but Tim noticed that his mood was becoming ever more boisterous. He'd drunk more than either of his companions, too. He was giving a good impression of a man with a drink problem, but perhaps he was just nervous, if what he'd said about wanting to get closer to Patti was true.

Patti herself was beginning to look uncomfortable. Derry's raised voice had attracted stares from people sitting at the adjacent tables: Tim knew that she hated drawing attention to herself in public. Derry took another gulp from his glass before setting it down noisily.

"Well, excuse me," he said. "I'm ready for a fag break, I think. I'm going to need one before the starter comes."

He stood up and brushed noisily past Tim's chair, patting his jacket pocket as he headed for the street.

"Same old Derry," Patti smiled, though Tim could see she felt awkward.

"Yes, I'd forgotten that he's best enjoyed in small doses." She laughed.

"How are you, Tim? I don't think I've seen you since you called me out to look at the remains of the baby at Sutterton Dowdyke. Weird case that one, wasn't it?"

"Yes," said Tim. "One of the weirdest. I don't think we ever got to the bottom of all that was going on there. And talking of getting to the bottom of things, do you remember a crook called Peter Prance?"

"The name vaguely rings a bell, but I'm not sure I ever met him. Remind me of why I should know him."

"It was the Kathryn Sheppard case, so quite a while ago now. He was the boyfriend of Hedley Atkins, who was eventually found guilty of the murder of his sister decades before. Unjustly, in my view."

"Do you think this Peter Prance was the murderer?"

"No. He's a confidence trickster. A plausible if unpleasant character, but without enough guts to kill. I mentioned him because I thought I saw him yesterday."

"Is he on the run?"

"He's still wanted for questioning about the Atkins case. He was blackmailing Atkins, and, from memory, I think he'd also broken the terms of his probation. He conveniently disappeared before we could nail him."

"Is it likely that he's in London? If he's used to operating in a place like Spalding, you'd think he'd be out of his depth here."

"He doesn't come from Spalding. He turned up there because he was lying low. He'd upset some thugs and was keeping out of their way. He's used to cities. He was born in Liverpool and has 'worked' in London. I think the thugs were based here, actually."

"He obviously made a big impression on you."

"He both annoyed me and fascinated me at the time. He's an unusual crook, but like most crooks in one respect: wherever he is, you can bet he's breaking the law in some way."

"I'm sure you're right, but from what I hear you've got your work cut out dealing with something rather more serious at the moment. Derry's on his way back," Patti added, as if in warning.

Tim quickly switched his untouched gin and tonic with Derry's half-finished one. Patti watched but said nothing. Her own drink was also untouched.

"Right, ready for anything now," Derry announced, squeezing past Tim a little more nimbly than when he'd made his exit. He looked around him. "Where is the bloody food? I know I said we should be patient, but this is getting ridiculous."

As if on cue, the waiter arrived with their starters. Tim hoped that his choice of melon would help to settle his stomach. Patti had also opted for melon. Derry was presented with a sizeable slab of chicken liver pate. Tim caught a whiff of it and almost gagged.

The wine waiter was also hovering.

"A nice Shiraz with this, I think," Derry boomed. "Or would you prefer white?" He looked at Patti. "If so, I'll get a bottle of white as well."

"Red's fine," she said. "I don't think we'll need more than one bottle."

"Let's wait and see, shall we? Tuck in, everyone. I'm starving."

Tim ate the melon slowly and carefully. He thought it was indeed helping to allay the nausea. He looked across at Patti and saw that she was merely toying with her food. He wondered why she'd agreed to come. The prospect of an evening with a man whom she'd rejected could hardly have been enticing, even with a third person present.

Derry had downed Tim's gin and tonic and was making inroads on his first glass of red wine when his mobile rang.

"Shit!" he said, inadvertently spitting pate and toast crumbs at Tim.

"Don't answer it."

"Got to, I'm afraid. Technically, I'm on call. And this may be a breakthrough in a case I'm working on."

Derry pulled the phone from his inside pocket and had already picked up the call as he was weaving his way back through the tables to the door. There was another awkward silence between Tim and Patti.

"We should start playing a game," Tim said. "Something along the lines of 'how many words of serious conversation can you get in during Hacker's absences'?" He grinned. It wasn't very funny, but Patti was grateful and smiled back at him.

"You were telling me about your ex-con," she said. "If he's in London he's no longer your responsibility, is he? More likely to be Derry's!"

"Depends what he's doing. My unfinished case is still on our books. He may very well have fitted in a few crimes on Derry's patch since then. I don't feel competitive about it. If Derry can nail him, that's fine by me."

Derry reappeared at that moment, once again jogging the adjacent table. The four diners glared at him in unison, but he appeared not to notice.

"Who do you want me to nail? I'll do my best but I'm afraid it won't be tonight. Sorry, but I've got to go. As I said, a breakthrough. A bunch of toughs I've been after for ages. It looks as if they've done something stupid."

"What kind of something stupid?"

"No time to tell you in detail, but they've pulled a gun on someone and then beaten him up, or worse. Petty criminal, probably, just some old bloke who's annoyed them. But now we know roughly where they are. With a bit of luck we might catch them tonight."

"Is the old bloke going to grass on them?"

"He can't, yet. They've taken him with them. Stupid move in some ways, as he'll be a liability, especially if he's hurt. Unless they choose the obvious solution, but as far as I know it would be their first murder."

"Do you want me to come and help?"

"Nah. You stay and look after Patti. We can't both walk out on her. I'll see you tomorrow."

He turned to Patti.

"I'm really sorry about all this. Will I see you tomorrow, as well?"

"I'm going home tomorrow, but I'll drop in briefly to say goodbye if I have time."

"Well, thanks for coming." A momentary look of sadness crossed Derry's face. He leaned across the table to kiss Patti on the cheek and gave Tim a clap on the back.

"Got to go! Don't do anything I wouldn't do!" he said, smirking and walking backwards into one of the diners at the next table as he did so. A portly man with a walrus moustache, rather incongruously dressed in a very short leather bomber jacket, rose to his feet.

"Excuse me," he said, "If you do that again I'm going to . . ." but Derry had already sailed past him. Tim met the man's eye and shrugged.

"I must apologise for the disruption," he said. "My friend's a police officer. He's on an important case."

The portly man sat down heavily.

"Let's hope it keeps him busy for the rest of the evening," he said. Tim looked at Patti. She was nodding in agreement, but whether this was because she was trying to mollify the man or really meant it was impossible to tell. Tim realised that, despite his original misgivings about dining with Patti, the evening was likely to be a great deal pleasanter now they were on their own. His stomach gave an unpredictable lurch. If only he could get rid of this bloody nausea.

Chapter 21

THE SMALL MAN'S mouth was bleeding. He licked his lips gingerly, felt for his teeth with his tongue. He didn't think any were broken, but the front ones felt loose and they were aching like hell. His ribcage had taken a pounding and it hurt when he breathed out. The skin had been scraped from his hand and shin as he'd been dragged along the pavement. The back of his hand was raw and embedded with an ugly swathe of grey grit particles which he knew from experience would have to be individually and excruciatingly removed with tweezers. His only pair of good grey flannels was ripped across the knee and his navy blue blazer dusty and spattered with something that looked like rotten banana. He wasn't a brave man. He perched apprehensively on the delicate pink and gold chair where they'd shoved him and tried not to cry.

Someone thumped him hard between the shoulder blades.

"Drink some water!" the voice behind him shouted.

Obediently he lifted the glass from the bijou table beside him and took a few sips. The water took on a pinkish hue.

"Keep drinking!"

He lifted the glass to his lips again, trying not to gag. The bloody water disgusted him.

"That'll do. Now answer the questions."

"Of course I will try . . ." he began, feebly attempting a stab at urbanity.

"Shut up until you're told to speak. You'll do more than fucking try. Got it?"

He nodded, triggering a burst of pain in his head. He clutched it with his uninjured hand.

"Put your hand down and listen. Put it down, I said!" The man behind him grabbed his hand and flung it roughly to his side.

"Now," said another voice. "Stay there like that. Don't look round. Just listen, and speak when you're spoken to. First of all, we want to know what you've been up to. *Exactly* what you've been up to. Then we're going to tell you what you're going to do next. And you'd better do it, if you know what's good for you. Understand?"

The man behind him poked him viciously in the back.

Chapter 22

DERRY HACKER HAD been feeling dejected during his short taxi ride to the bar. Uncharacteristically, he'd been mentally railing against fate, but by the time he'd paid the driver he'd shrugged off the blues and made himself focus entirely on the job at hand. Having to give up on the evening was a setback, not a disaster. Tim would still be around tomorrow and he might even see Patti again then. If not, he had other strings to his bow.

Two police cars were parked in the street outside the bar. The driver of one of them had remained in his vehicle. He'd noticed Derry's arrival and was watching him carefully. Derry thought about speaking to him first and decided not to bother. It wasn't someone he knew and he guessed the copper couldn't tell him much more than he knew already. Another was stationed by the door, but Derry didn't speak to him, either, beyond giving him a nod and a short "Evening!" by way of greeting. He squared his shoulders and strode into the bar in his usual rapid, decisive way, sucking on a mint.

Inside, the barman was standing stolidly behind his counter, answering as laconically as possible the questions being put to him by a uniformed policeman. Another policeman was questioning a burly man seated at a table opposite the television screen. The bar was otherwise deserted.

Derry moved closer to the policeman questioning the barman and listened for a while.

"So you didn't know the man who was dragged out of his seat?"

"Never seen him before."

"Could you describe him?"

"I didn't take much notice. He was a little guy."

"What did he have to drink?"

"A Scotch. A double."

"Did you notice anything particular about him? The way he was behaving, for example."

"Can't say I did. He seemed a bit hard up."

"Why do you say that?"

"Had to root around for the cash."

"Never mind all that," Derry butted in impatiently. "Who were the men who took him? Who fired the shots? Detective Inspector Hacker, in case you've forgotten, Siddy," he added.

"I've already said . . ." the barman began in an aggrieved tone.

"Don't bother with that stuff when you're talking to me, Siddy," said Derry. "I wasn't born yesterday and neither were you. You know damn well who it was, don't you?"

The barman looked belligerently into Derry's eyes for several long seconds before dropping his gaze.

"I said, you know who it was, don't you? And you'd better tell us, or I'll get you closed down."

"Could have been some of the Khans' lot," he muttered, looking at his feet.

"Could have been? Do you know them by sight?"

"I know some of them. I think there's a lot of 'em."

"How many came here?"

"I might not have seen . . ."

"There were three of them," the burly man shouted across.

"Thank you." Derry nodded at him. He turned back to the barman. "Three of them, Siddy. Did you recognise any of them?"

"Not personally. Like I said, they looked like they was from the Khans. Dressed in that way."

"Who else was in here?"

Siddy shrugged.

"A few people. Some punters sitting over by the door. They didn't see nuffin'. And the guy over there and his buddies, watching the snooker."

"What's happened to the buddies?"

"They had to go. He said he'd stay and tell you what he knows."

"I see. Did you try to persuade any of the others to stay?"

Siddy shrugged again.

"You know how it is. They don't want to get mixed up in any trouble. And no-one wants to cross the Khans."

"Did they all have guns?"

"No. Just the one. He fired it up at the ceiling." Siddy pointed upwards at the cracks in the plaster.

"How many times did he fire?"

"I don't know. A few times."

"Did you find any bullets?"

"Haven't looked for them."

"And you're sure he just fired at the ceiling? He didn't injure the man they took away with them?"

"I can't say whether they injured him. They didn't shoot him. Not in here, anyway."

"Did anyone try to help him?"

"You've got to be joking! What would you have done?"

"How long did you leave it before you dialled 999?"

"About five minutes. I wanted to make sure they weren't coming back. I didn't want no-one to get hurt," said Siddy guilelessly.

"Thank you for your help," said Derry abruptly. "We're going to have to ask you to stick around for a while yet. I'm going to talk to the gentleman over there for a minute, but I'll come back to you."

"Be my guest. Can I interest you in a little drink while you're working?" Siddy narrowed his eyes. "Or another packet of mints, maybe?"

Derry turned quickly away from him, but not, he knew, before the policeman standing next to him had got the barman's drift. The policeman gave the detective a curious look.

"Make sure we get his prints, will you?" Derry said to him curtly. "Probably have them on file already, I shouldn't wonder, but best to be on the safe side."

He joined the other policeman and the snooker enthusiast.

"Thank you for waiting, sir," he said. "Very good of you. You'll understand that we shall need the names and addresses of your friends?"

"I've already got them," said the second policeman. "Mobile numbers and e-mails, anyway."

"Let's hope those work. Otherwise we'll have to trouble you again," said Derry to the man, affably enough. "I'm sorry to ask you this again, as you've already given a statement, but could you tell me exactly what you saw?"

"Not much, to be honest with you. We was having a drink and watching the match. We got down when we were told to and didn't get up again until they'd gone."

"By 'they' you mean the men with the gun?"

"Yes."

"You said there were three of them. Are you sure of that?"

"I was sitting opposite the kitchen door. I was watching the match, but I heard a noise and turned to see them come in. There could have been more than three of them, but I don't think so."

"Did you know any of them?"

"No. I only work around the corner, but I don't come in here often. Didn't live round 'ere until recently."

"But you do now?"

"It's temporary. Me and me wife, we've split up. There's a flat over the office that isn't being used. I'm staying there for now. Mates came over to cheer me up and watch the match. That's why they had to go: they had trains to catch."

"I'm sure they did," said Derry, looking at his watch. The snooker match was over now, but only just.

"Can you describe the men?"

"All looked much the same to me. Tall, athletic, white shirts. I'd say they were foreign, but that's not done these days, is it? Could've been English, but 'of foreign extraction'? Isn't that what you're supposed to say?"

"Might be. It depends. Did you get a clear view of any of their faces? Enough to build up a picture for us, perhaps?"

The snooker enthusiast hesitated before shaking his head.

"No, I don't think so. They all looked much of a muchness to me. Besides, I wasn't looking at them. I was looking at the little guy. I'd certainly know him again if I saw him."

Chapter 23

THE SERVICE IN the restaurant continued to be slow, but now that Derry had gone Tim and Patti no longer noticed. They drank the bottle of wine very slowly, and gradually each of them relaxed. Tim told Patti about the day he'd just spent studying so-called honour murders and she gave him a few details about the new forensic techniques that had been discussed at the conference she'd attended.

"You don't look dressed for a conference," Tim ventured. "Especially a scientific conference."

She laughed.

"Do you imagine that scientists dress differently from other people?"

"Most of the scientists I've known have been wedded to their jobs and too earnest to care much about their appearance. The result can be quite grim."

Her laugh was more forced now.

"We don't all dress grimly. At least, I hope not."

"Sorry, I've put my foot in it again. I meant to compliment you on your dress and I've ended up insulting you! Typical of me, as you know."

She ignored his last sentence but responded brightly.

"I'm happy to accept the compliment! And I'm not going to say 'What, this old thing?' about my dress, because it wouldn't be true. I hadn't understood the conference would finish at lunchtime today. When I realised I had a few spare hours, I went shopping. I thought it was time I had some new clothes. And Derry said he had a surprise for me when he asked me to come to dinner."

"Oh, so you bought the dress for Derry!" Tim was flirting now, but he couldn't stop himself. He'd always enjoyed this kind of banter with women. He reflected with a pang that it had been missing from his life recently.

Patti picked up his teasing tone and instantly became more serious.

"No, I didn't buy it for Derry, but I didn't buy it for you, either. I thought I'd be meeting someone new and decided to make a bit of an effort."

"Derry still carries a torch for you. Did you know?"

"Now that is a back-handed compliment. Derry carries a torch for anything with a face and two legs, a far as I can see."

Tim smiled. Although, as Derry had already pointed out to him, he had no right to care about Patti's affections, he was glad that she'd got his friend's measure.

"I guess you're right, though it's disloyal of me to say so."

"You aren't asking me to respect that kind of Boys' Own loyalty? It's just an excuse for condoning bad behaviour!"

They'd nearly finished their main courses. There was still a drain of wine left in the bottle.

"Would you like a dessert?"

"I don't think so. I'll wait for you if you want one."

"No, let's just finish the wine and go. If we order anything else, we'll be here until midnight!"

"You don't need to walk me back to my hotel. It'll be quite safe walking up Tottenham Court Road. Or I can get a cab."

"It's a nice evening and not far out of my way to walk. I can catch the Tube to Waterloo easily after I've left you. Besides, I promised Derry!"

"Derry again! If that's your reason, I'll certainly get a cab."

"It's not really my reason. I'd like to walk and carry on talking for a while. If you're not too tired, that is."

"All right, if you let me pay my share of the bill. This is meant to be Derry's treat, but I see no prospect of his picking up the tab now. And it's probably not fair to let him."

"I agree it's not fair to let him," said Tim, with a pang. A rough calculation told him the bill would certainly be north of £150, perhaps more, given the bottle of wine Derry had chosen. "But I don't think you should pay, either. You were promised a treat and it's churlish to let you pay for it. Especially as it didn't turn out how you expected!"

"Don't fish for compliments, Tim! But if you insist, I'm not going to press the point. So, thank you."

"My pleasure. Did you bring a coat?"

"No, but I'd like to visit the Ladies. I think you have to go into that cubby-hole over there to pay. I'll meet you outside."

Patti was right. The restaurant didn't have facilities for allowing customers to pay at the table. Instead, they were accompanied by their waiter to a boxed-off alcove in one corner, where an ample, jovial woman totted up the damage. Tim had to wait for a few minutes for his waiter to appear. He saw Patti walk past the tables to the door and thought to himself that he only had a 50:50 chance she would be still be there when he'd finished. He was surprised by how sad this made him feel.

Including the automatically-charged twelve and a half per cent tip, Tim had to part with even more money than he'd anticipated. Shaking off the sting – he had enjoyed the evening, after all – he hurried to the open door and saw that Patti was standing under the street lamp outside. The light was shining on her hair, drawing out threads of auburn. He remembered that she'd looked just like this on a previous occasion, five – or was it six? – years ago, when they'd spent the day on a long, leisurely walk together and she'd returned to her flat briefly for a shower before meeting him again for dinner.

She smiled at him as he emerged and just for that moment it took all his self-control not to remind her of that shared experience. He wondered if she had thought of it, too. She may have done, because the smile faded rapidly and her next comment was quite brusque.

"We'd better step on it now. I don't know how late the trains to Surbiton run."

Tim looked at his watch. It was ten-thirty: later than he'd expected, but he was confident there'd be trains for at least another hour. He didn't want to give her the wrong idea, however.

"I think we've got time to walk, but we'll take a cab if you like."

She hesitated, as if trying to gauge his meaning. Finally, she shrugged.

"You decide. I shall get back all right either way."

"Let's walk, then."

He allowed her to make a start, then fell in beside her, matching her pace. They continued to the end of the street like this, chatting desultorily, until they reached Tottenham Court Road. They were about to cross it, and Patti had stepped off the pavement, when a cyclist came hurtling out of the dusk. Quickly Tim grabbed Patti's arm and hauled her back on to the pavement.

"Are you ok?"

"Yes," she said, rubbing her arm ruefully, "just a bit shaken. And you didn't have to pinch so hard!"

"Sorry," said Tim, stroking her arm lightly with the back of his hand. "Are you ready to cross now?"

She nodded and he took hold of her elbow. Gently, she released it, but then slid her arm through his. She didn't disengage herself when they reached the other side of the road.

"So you're going home tomorrow morning?"

"Yes. I've been away long enough. I have quite a large team to look after now. What about you?"

"I'm staying here a bit longer. Then I'm probably going to India, to interview the cousin of the girl I was telling you about."

"Is he a suspect?"

"Has to be, I think, though on the face of it he's co-operating."

"You'll be going home first?"

"Yes, of course. I've promised Katrin. Besides, I haven't quite finished the bloody malaria tablets yet. I shall be glad when they're done with. They've made me feel quite strange."

"Nauseous, you mean?"

"Mainly that. And a bit light in the head on occasions." Tim decided not to tell Patti about the strange episode in Ilford or the apocalyptic behaviour of his computer earlier that day. Nevertheless, she looked grave.

"You need to be careful. If it's Lariam you're taking, that stuff can really mess with your head."

"Not sure what the pills are made of. I don't recognise that name. But I suppose they're supplied under some kind of branding. I'm nearly through the course now, so I should be ok, but thanks for your concern."

They'd passed the larger shops now and were heading for the darker end of the road, nearer to the tube station, with its banks and bars and convenience stores. Tim was grateful to be embraced by the urban twilight. His head was beginning to spin and his stomach churned again. His mouth filled with saliva.

"You can leave me here," said Patti as they drew level with the narrow entrance to a cul-de-sac. "I'll be fine now. You can catch the tube from . . ." she turned to look at him. "Tim! Are you all right?"

He managed a sickly grin.

"Yes, of course I'm all right. And I'll walk you to the door. It's not far out of my way."

"Ok," said Patti abstractedly. She wasn't convinced that Tim was fit to go back to Surbiton by himself, but she was the last person to be able to help him. If she accompanied him to his sister's house, she'd have Freya's curiosity to contend with; if she offered him a bed on her sofa, Katrin would never believe it had been an act of innocent compassion.

Tim took her arm, but she felt that he'd done it more to maintain his balance than support her. The entrance to her hotel, a small bed-and-breakfast establishment, was at the centre of a curved Regency terrace. As they mounted the steps, Tim staggered like a drunk.

"You're going to have to come in for a few minutes," Patti said. "Whatever it is you've been suffering from has clearly come back. I'll make you some coffee, see if that helps."

"I've got to catch the last train," Tim murmured indistinctly. Patti guessed rather than heard what he was saying.

"If you don't feel better in a few minutes, you're going to have to go back to Freya's in a taxi."

"It'll cost . . ."

"It doesn't matter how much it costs. I'll pay for it myself if necessary."

Tim was leaning heavily on her now. Patti was quite strong, but it was still a hard burden for her to bear. She pushed open the glass-panelled door and half-dragged Tim inside.

The daytime receptionist had completed her shift and been replaced by a night porter, a stoutly-built Jamaican who could have doubled as a bouncer. He'd been sitting behind the counter reading the Evening Standard, but he got to his feet as Patti and Tim stumbled inelegantly into the foyer. She met his eye.

"Good evening, Ma'am. You ok there?"

"Yes, I'm fine, thanks, but my friend's . . . he's a little bit unwell."

"I can see that," said the porter with distaste. "He's not going to puke, is he, because . . ."

"No, he's just . . ."

At that moment, Tim wrenched himself from Patti's grasp and made a desperate dash back to the door. His legs buckled under him and he collapsed on the carpet, vomiting copiously on the dirt trapper mat that had been laid across the entrance.

The porter pushed open the hinged gate of the reception area and came bustling out.

"Will you get him out of here, please? Now! We don't want no drunks."

Tim groaned and wiped his mouth with his hand. He remained in a kneeling position.

"He isn't drunk," said Patti. "He's had a reaction to some medication he's taking. Please let him stay. I'll take him up to my room and he won't bother you again. I'll pay for the damage," she added.

The porter cast a critical eye over the dirt trapper.

"You're lucky it was only the mat. I might be able to throw that away, put another one down." He looked at her quizzically.

"I'm quite happy to pay for it."

The porter considered again.

"I guess that'll be all right. I'll get rid of this, we'll say no more about it." He looked at her again, obviously expecting her to take the hint.

Belatedly Patti divined that he was asking her for a tip. She fumbled in her handbag and extracted a £20 note. She held it out. The porter took it.

"Thank you, Ma'am."

"So he can stay?"

"He can stay. But no noise tonight and no mess left in the room tomorrow. Understood? Otherwise he'll have to leave now. And you'll pay for the mat."

"Of course. Thank you. Tim, you're going to have to get up now. Can you stand?"

Tim nodded, grimacing as he rose slowly to his feet by clinging shakily to the door lintel. Patti put her arm round his waist and guided him to the lift. They moved slowly, Tim shuffling like an old man.

Most of the hotel's guests had apparently already turned in for the night, so the lift was waiting for them, its doors already open. Patti hauled Tim inside and pressed the button.

"You take care, Miss," the porter called as they disappeared from view. Once they'd gone, he chuckled to himself.

"'Reaction to medication he's taking'," he mimicked in a high voice. "That's a good one, that is."

He'd almost forgotten about the soiled doormat until his nose alerted him to its continuing presence.

"Fucker!" he muttered.

Chapter 24

THE SMALL MAN was lying on his bed where they'd dumped him, afraid to close his eyes, motionless. He was so sore that the pain scared him when he tried to move. Two of them had brought him home to his shabby little studio flat, one hissing at him that if he made a sound it would be his last, and waited while he fumbled for the key. The other one had snatched it and eased open the door. They'd pushed him down onto the bed and disappeared, clicking the door to gently behind them. For a couple of seconds, he could hear them as they moved with stealth back down the stairs. Then all was quiet. As he lay in a vacuum of silence, it dawned on him that they'd stolen his key. He had another – they'd probably guessed he would have – but now they would be able to come and go as they pleased. He daren't ask the landlord to change the locks; he was already pissed off about the rent. Painfully, the small man understood that the innermost fabric of his life had been invaded by an evil over which he had no control.

He knew he ought to get up and bathe his wounds, then try to sleep. Somehow he couldn't summon the energy. The same words kept reverberating through him, as if a tape had been implanted in his brain.

"You'll do it if you know what's good for you."

"Do what?"

"I'll tell you. But first I want you to promise that you won't tell anyone. And, whatever it is, that you'll do it."

"Do what?" he'd repeated. His interrogator had smacked him across the face with the flat of his hand.

"Don't you get clever with me. Now, listen . . ."

He'd listened.

All his life he'd been a fraudster. He liked to think that he'd always carried his chosen profession with panache, even with an unconventional sort of honour. He'd been popular in prison, met men in there who'd appreciated him. Being an adventurous type, he'd always pushed at the boundaries and he'd have been the first to acknowledge that sometimes he'd come unstuck. Some of his lovers had turned out shadier than he'd suspected and he'd had people coming after him more than once. This wouldn't be the first time he'd discovered he was out of his depth, but it was the first time he'd had no clue about how to get back to dry land.

On previous occasions, if no other solution had presented itself, he'd put discretion before valour and simply scarpered, but he knew this time there was no hiding place. They would find him: their networks were too extensive and too enmeshed in his world for him to be able to find a safe haven in which to lie low. He knew, too, that they would kill him without a moment's pang if he ceased to be useful; and he would only be useful if he delivered.

He screwed up his dulled black eyes and rubbed them with grubby fingers. He let out a small sob at the enormity of it all. What was that atrocious American expression he was always hearing these days? 'It's not who I am' - that was it. He'd got involved in something that made him into a monster, but deep inside he knew he was only a likeable rogue.

He unclenched his eyes and stared at the drab wall of his room. He could always say no. He could refuse, go to the police, ask them for a new identity. He'd seen that policeman yesterday, the one he'd had a brush with a few years ago. He could ask him for help.

The small man smiled bitterly, flinching as the action caused liquid to ooze anew from his cut lip. The man had been quite a talented policeman, but was he really a match for *them*? There could be only one answer to that question.

He sighed. Would he continue to do as they demanded? There could be only one answer to that question, too.

Chapter 25

I'M NOT SURPRISED that Tim doesn't phone and after I've called Juliet back I decide to go to bed. I unhook the office phone from its cradle and take it with me, just in case. I'm tired and know I need to be in good shape for tomorrow, but I can't sleep. I lie awake for an hour, watching the red tip of the hand on the digital clock jerk from second to second until it's eleven-thirty and my mind has reached that state of frozen alertness that always heralds insomnia. My eyes ache. There's a burning behind them, as if they've been scrubbed with bleach. I consider turning on the light and trying to read, but I'm too exhausted. I lie there in a kind of waking stupor.

I'm desperately worried about Tim. It's not because he hasn't called - that's merely annoying - but because I don't understand what's happening to him. He seems to be falling apart. Juliet's too kind to say so, as well as being too discreet, but I know she believes his work is deteriorating. If she's right, and I trust her judgment, Superintendent Thornton must have noticed. He's lost interest in everything except this case and he doesn't even seem to be handling that well. As for Sophia, he's barely taken an interest in her for weeks. I've tried to talk to him about it but he says I'm imagining things. I'm going to have to make him open up before he goes to India. I'm inclined to agree with Juliet that the trip to India's a wild goose chase, anyway. I can't decide whether he's really hopeful of trapping a suspect or just looking forward to a bit of escapism.

I'm astonished that Superintendent Thornton has agreed to it.

I hear Sophia stir in the next room. She cries out once. I lie there, rigid, listening, until all falls quiet again. The second hand continues its futile circular walk.

I must have dropped into a doze. I'm suddenly snatched awake by the telephone. I fumble for the switch on my bedside lamp and stare blearily at the display panel. It's Freya's number. I look at the clock. Half past midnight.

"Hello? Tim?"

"It isn't Tim, it's me," comes Freya's clipped voice, not as well-modulated as usual. "But it's about Tim."

"What about him? Is he ill again?"

"I don't know. I was hoping he'd been in touch with you. I haven't seen him at all today. He left the house before I got up and called me later to say that he'd be out to dinner. He said he wouldn't be late, but if he ate in London he's missed the last train now."

"He did call late this afternoon. He said he was having dinner with Derry Hacker and someone."

"Yes, that's what he told me."

I wonder why Freya didn't mention Derry before I did. She probably knows I don't like him.

"Do you think he's decided to stay the night at Derry's?"

"I suppose that's the most likely explanation. I don't have a number for Derry, so I can't check. I'm sorry I've bothered you. I didn't mean to worry you. I wouldn't have called if he hadn't been ill yesterday."

"I think you were right to call me. I'm sure Tim'll explain it tomorrow," I say. I know better than to trust Freya's apologies. I congratulate myself on keeping my voice steady.

"I'll let you know if I hear from him."

"Likewise," I say. "I'm sorry he's not being a very good guest."

"Oh, I know my brother. I'm used to him!"

Freya produces one of her trilling little laughs. Running true to form, demonstrating her superiority despite her feigned anxiety.

"Good night, Freya," I say firmly.

"Good night."

"Cow!" I shout, hurling the phone to the floor. It lands with a crash. There's a burst of howling from the room next door.

I hurry to comfort Sophia. Her whole body is shaking with sobs; it takes fifteen minutes to settle her down again.

I creep back to bed. I try to fight back the tears, but they keep on coming.

Chapter 26

TIM WOKE WITH a searing pain in his head. For a moment he felt totally lost. He discovered that he was lying on the floor of a strange room, covered with a rough synthetic blanket. He was too hot. His head was resting awkwardly on a hard square cushion piped with cord: he could feel it digging into his neck. The room was in darkness but a dull orange light was vaguely penetrating the curtains, which had not been fully drawn, from outside. A street lamp, he guessed. He hoisted himself on to his right elbow and held up his wrist, squinting at his watch. It was 2.30 a.m. He guessed at rather than recognised his surroundings. Patti's hotel room.

"Christ!" he muttered to himself. "Freya will make hay of this."

He groaned and sat up, relieved to find that he was still fully clothed. The indignities and embarrassment of the previous evening came flooding back. His throat was dry and his mouth tasted as if he'd been chewing old newspaper. He'd thrown up in the foyer of Patti's hotel. What had happened next? He remembered being manhandled into the lift by her. Everything else was a blank.

But Christ, Freya! He hoped she hadn't gone tattling to Katrin. That they didn't like each other offered a glimmer of hope, but Freya's desire to make mischief would almost certainly outweigh her ability to remain aloof. His failure to turn up at her house as expected two days running would have provided her with the ideal opportunity to do a bit of stirring. Tim fumbled in his jacket pocket for his mobile and fished it out. The bill for last night's dinner slid out with it. He groaned again. He'd certainly have to keep that from Katrin, whatever else he told her.

He stood up shakily, holding on for support to the seat of a small sofa from which the cushions had evidently been removed. He pushed the curtain back a little further and leant against the sill while he typed his password into the mobile. There were five missed calls from Freya and one from Derry. Nothing from Katrin. Her silence alarmed him: were she and Sophia ok? He should try to get hold of her immediately. He would have called her if he hadn't glanced back at the bed and seen the outline of Patti's body, curled into the foetal position. His brain wasn't so addled that he didn't know that phoning Katrin from Patti's bedroom in the middle of the night would be tantamount to marital suicide. He groaned again.

"Tim?" Patti sat bolt upright in bed, holding the quilt up round her neck. Her voice was clear and incisive, as if she hadn't been sleeping at all. "You're not feeling sick again, are you?"

"No. Just dazed. I didn't know I'd stayed here. I must have been out cold."

She turned on the small lamp set into the garish padded plastic headboard that adorned the bed.

"You were. The night porter thought you were drunk. I couldn't blame him, really. You were behaving as if you were. How are you feeling now?"

"As if I've been hit over the head with a skillet. I don't know what you're laughing at. I wasn't drunk and I haven't done anything wrong – at least, I hope I haven't." Tim eyed her with foreboding. "But I'm certain I've succeeded in getting myself into trouble with just about everyone, you included, probably." He pushed back his hair with sweaty hands. "I seem to remember you saying something about getting a taxi back to Surbiton. Why didn't we do that?" His voice was petulant now.

Patti laughed again, but this time her voice rang with irony.

"You're not having the cheek to suggest that I tried to seduce you, are you? Get real, Tim. You passed out. It was all I could do to get you through the door and help you to lie down without hurting yourself. You were unconscious. There was no chance of getting you into a taxi, even if we could have persuaded one to take you. Do you think I wanted you to spend the night here?"

Tim was immediately contrite.

"I'm sorry, Pats, I'm just worried about Katrin, that's all. I can't trust Freya not to have put the wind up her when she realised I wasn't going home."

"Don't call me that," said Patti tensely.

"Call you what?"

"Pats. It's what you used to call me. I think you and I are long past trotting out the pet names, don't you?"

"Sorry," said Tim again. "Can you suggest anything that might help? With Katrin, I mean."

"I'm the last person to be able to help you. What do you expect me to do, call Katrin tomorrow and tell her you spent the night in my hotel room but it was all purely platonic? I don't like encouraging people to be deceitful, but on this occasion I think the only thing you can do is pretend you were somewhere else."

"Like where, for example?"

"I don't know. You could try telling Derry the truth, ask him to cover for you by pretending you stayed at his place. That's a bit of a risky strategy, though, as you can't rely on him to be discreet and he'll certainly think you owe him one if he agrees. Or you could say you missed the last train and had to stay in a hotel overnight."

"She'll think that's odd. She'll know that a taxi would be cheaper."

"You're right, she will. And if she's suspicious, she'll want to see the bill. Probably best not to ask me. I'm no good at lying, and it's true what they say: for every lie you tell, eventually you have to think up half a dozen more. I'll tell you what, though. Although it's against my better judgement, I'll go along with whatever story you come up with. I may not have to get involved at all, as only Derry knows we were together yesterday evening. But just in case."

"Thanks, Pats – Patti. I think you're great."

"I can't say the same for you. You look absolutely terrible. I suggest I make us both a cup of tea and then we try to get a few more hours sleep."

She leaned forward and reached across to the foot of the bed, where she'd draped the hotel's towelling dressing-gown. Seizing it, she threw it around her shoulders with a deft movement and eased her arms quickly into the sleeves before drawing the fabric across her chest.

Tim didn't try to look away. He caught a glimpse of two pale breasts, deeper and rounder than you'd expect for a woman of Patti's build. He remembered the first time he saw them and how he'd been surprised by the curviness of her figure when unclothed. Patti caught his eye and he had the grace to feel ashamed. She got out of the bed slowly and sat on the side of it for a moment before she stood up, brushing at her cheek. Tim was horrified to see that she was wiping away tears. His first impulse was to rush across the room and take her in his arms, but common sense prevailed.

"What's the matter?" he said in a low voice.

"I think you know," she answered. "I also think it would be very unwise to talk about it now. But one day, Tim, when we're both feeling a lot braver and stronger than we do at the moment, I'd like to sit down and have a frank discussion about what went wrong."

"With us, you mean?"

She'd lifted the doll-sized kettle from the tray on the vanity unit now and was heading for the bathroom to fill it. She gave him such a steadfast look that he felt like collapsing into tears himself.

"Yes. With us."

"OK," he said shakily. "I think that's a good idea. I should have suggested it myself, long ago. Too cowardly, I suppose."

She nodded and disappeared. Tim heard her snap open the lid of the kettle and switch on the tap. She'd be back in a minute or so. He sank down on the cushionless sofa and tried to think. What *had* happened to them? Was it just that Tim had met Katrin? That's what Derry believed, but Tim wasn't so sure. He'd thought that he and Patti had been drifting apart before that: he knew he'd been astonished by the depth of her grief when he'd broken the news. But right now he could remember few details about that summer. Had he edited them permanently from his mind, or was this bloody drug he was taking screwing up his mental processes again? He leaned forward and held his head in both hands as the pounding behind his eyes started again. When Patti came back with the kettle, he suddenly lurched to his feet and rushed past her, only just making it to the bathroom before he vomited copiously into the toilet.

Chapter 27

A FTER YET ANOTHER visit to Sophia to soothe her, I sit for a while watching her sleep before going back to bed myself. The night is warm, but I feel cold. My feet are blocks of ice and, however much I huddle under the quilt, my shoulders remain chilly. I'm unable either to sleep or read. I won't call Tim. I tell myself that it's up to him to call me, to explain to me what he thinks he's doing. A niggling voice at the back of my mind tells me to worry that he might have had an accident. A yet more insidious whisper suggests that a call from me might embarrass him, that perhaps he isn't spending the night alone.

I must have slept at last, or dozed at least, because I'm startled by the tinny scream of the alarm clock. It takes me a few seconds to recognise what it is. I swat at it with my hand, then peer at the clock face: 6.30 a.m. I wonder why I set it so early and remember that I've agreed to work today. I need to get up, now, if I'm to dress myself and dress and feed Sophia and take her to Mrs Sims before the office opens.

My head is throbbing, but I haul myself out of bed. Through the wall I hear Sophia's early morning babble: evidently last night's upset wasn't too traumatic. On non-working days I shall enjoy listening to her until the chatter gradually becomes more querulous, as she makes it clear that she's ready to start the day.

I pick up my mobile to look for texts and missed calls.

There aren't any. There's no time now to think about what that might mean. I throw on my dressing-gown and head for Sophia's room.

Despite my headache, the morning routine goes smoothly. We arrive at Mrs Sims' at 8.25 a.m. I'm glad: it means I won't have to dump Sophia at the door and rush off immediately. I'm unhooking Sophia from her car seat straps when I hear the door open behind me. Mrs Sims is standing on the doorstep, holding by the hand the small boy that Margie was playing with yesterday. I lift Sophia and her bag out of the car and smile as I walk towards the childminder. She smiles back, but she's looking worried.

"Is everything ok?" I ask. "You were expecting Sophia again today? I rang about it last night."

"I know. I haven't forgotten. I'm just a bit worried that Margie hasn't turned up."

I look at my watch, though I've just checked the time.

"It's early yet. She may be running a bit late."

"She's never late. She's always here by eight, often before then. I usually give her breakfast. I don't want to call her home number. She doesn't like me to, because of her mother."

"Doesn't her mother know she works here?"

"Technically she does. But she's off her face most of the time. I think that's why Margie doesn't like me calling there. She's embarrassed by it."

"Does she have a mobile?"

"Yes. I bought it for her when she started taking the pre-school children to their classes, in case she needed help when she was out with them. I've tried calling it, but I think she's switched it off. You'd better come in, anyway," she adds, noticing for the first time that I'm struggling to cope with Sophia, who is squirming expertly and is quite heavy now, and her bag of spare clothes. "Would you like some tea?"

"No, thanks, but a glass of water would be great. I've had a thudding headache ever since I got up. I think I need to take some paracetamol."

We're inside the house now. I sit Sophia on the rug with Thomas, who starts to bring her bricks to play with. A thought strikes me.

"Are there other children coming today?"

"Yes, two. A baby and a pre-school boy."

"Does that mean you won't have enough staff, if Margie doesn't turn up?"

She gives me a curious look. Too late, I realise that I've fallen foul of policeman's wife syndrome again.

"You don't need to concern yourself about that. There's always back-ups I can call on."

"I'm sorry, I wasn't criticising you. You're doing me a big favour by having Sophia today. I wasn't expecting to work, as you know. It's just that you look so worried."

"I'm worried about Margie. It's not like her not to come. She's never missed a day before. And I know she'd have told me if she was ill. I hope that lush of a mother of hers hasn't hurt her in some way."

I think with a pang of my own conversation with Margie the night before. Was her request to work for us a more direct plea for help than I'd realised?

I see Mrs Sims is scrutinising my face and try to smile.

"You think something might have happened to her, too, don't you?"

"I don't know Margie. I only met her yesterday. I'm sure

your opinion that she's reliable is correct, but there are any number of explanations for her failure to show up than that she's come to harm. She may be helping her mother with something, for example."

Mrs Sims looks unconvinced, and so unhappy that I almost tell her about Margie's visit. I stop myself because it would be a betrayal of Margie's trust, and might spoil Mrs Sims' good opinion of her if I tell all the details.

"What do you think I should do? Should I call the police?"

"It's far too early to think of that at the moment. If Margie hasn't either turned up or got in touch by the time I come back this evening, I'll help you contact the police then. They'll want to know if we've talked to the parents and under normal circumstances I'd recommend that you do this first. Given what you've told me about them, though, it's probably best to leave that up to the police, as well. But I honestly don't think it will come to that. There'll be a simple explanation, I'm sure there will."

I put my hand on Mrs Sims' arm. She's clearly sceptical, but she seems to rally.

"Yes, well, I'm grateful to you and I mustn't keep you waiting. Just let me fetch your glass of water, and then you can get off."

I'm first to arrive at the office. Janey's still away and the traffic control rooms are dark and silent. I let myself in with my key, dump my coat and bag, and go to the galley-like kitchen to retrieve mugs from the dishwasher. I set them out on a tray, together with the biscuits I bought for Juliet yesterday which she didn't want to eat. I'm a bit apprehensive about meeting the social services woman. I'm not quite sure what to expect.

I've put the tray down on Janey's desk when the phone rings, making me jump. I hesitate for a moment before answering it. It's taking me a while to get used to taking professional calls again.

"Hi, Katrin, it's Andy. Carstairs, that is. How are things? Glad to be back?"

"Hello, Andy. It's nice to hear your voice again. Yes, great to be back."

"Sophia settling in with the childminder ok?"

I'm surprised that Andy is asking this. Is he implying some sort of criticism? I've always marked him down as a traditionalist, but I didn't think he'd be the mother's-place-is-in-the-home type. Or remotely interested in small children, for that matter.

"Yes," I say cautiously. "Why?"

"No reason, just asking," he says, a little awkwardly. "I'm glad you're back, anyway. Thanks for doing those land registry checks for me. Any idea when they'll be ready?"

"I e-mailed you some preliminary stuff last night. There are a few other checks that I can do, but I need to get in touch with the registry direct for that. I can't make any promises, but if they take their usual sort of time to turn the request round, it should be early next week."

"Magic! Sorry not to have found the e-mail yet. You're as efficient as ever, and one step ahead of me, as usual."

I laugh, but I'm suspicious. It's not like Andy to bandy around the compliments.

"Flattery will get you everywhere!" I say good-humouredly. "Is that all, or do you want something else?"

"No, that's it. But now you mention it, can you tell me when DI Yates will be back? As he's probably told you, he and Superintendent Thornton are thinking of creating a DS post, and there are one or two things I'd like to ask him about it."

"I didn't know about the post. And as far as being able to tell you when Tim's coming home goes, your guess is as good as mine." I realise how curt and brittle I sound even before I've finished speaking. "I'm sorry, Andy," I add. "You know how infuriatingly vague Tim can be about his arrangements. No need for me to take it out on you, though."

"Not to worry. I shouldn't have mentioned it. I'd better get on now. Thanks again."

I hold my forehead in my hands. I mustn't let my problems with Tim sour my professional relationships. Superintendent Thornton will be the first to pick up on it. I know he was dubious about letting us both work for the same police force at first, and just because he relented it doesn't mean he won't change his mind again.

Five minutes after I boot up my computer, the phone rings more. I'm even more reluctant to answer it this time. I hope that it's not Andy again, embarrassing me with a more profuse apology.

"Katrin? Are you ok?" It's Juliet.

"Yes, of course I am. Why do you ask?"

"You seemed to take a long time to answer the phone, that's all. I was worried that you'd had difficulties with the childminder."

"No, everything's fine there. I'm glad you've called, though. Can you tell me a bit more about this woman from social services? I don't even know her name yet and she could turn up at any time."

"That's why I called. I think she'll arrive about 10.30,

as she's going on to Boston afterwards. Her name's Fiona Vickers."

"Mrs Vickers?"

Juliet laughs. "Definitely a Ms, I'd say. I don't know too much about her myself, but I do know that she's in charge of the women in danger unit at Peterborough Social Services. She doesn't deal with just forced marriages. Battered wives and sexually abused minors are part of her remit, too."

"The whole spectrum of female abuse, in fact?"

"You could say that. She's quite tough, I believe. She goes out with the squad cars sometimes when they've been called to domestics, gives abusive men a piece of her mind. She's a bit of an evangelist."

"Sounds as if she may have been a victim herself in the past."

"I've no idea. My understanding is that she's perfectly capable of fighting fire with fire. Not the victim type, really. That's as much as I've found out, except to warn you that you might find her a bit . . . well . . . coarse."

"Fine by me. It goes with the territory, I suppose."

"Yes. Well, good luck with her. Let me know how you get on. And thanks again for doing this; I've got a hunch that it's really going to help us to push forward with the Verma case."

"Thanks. I shall be delighted if I can help. Great to be working at a proper job again. Talking of which, I hope you're going to apply for the new DS post?"

"I didn't know you knew about that. Did Tim tell you?"

"No, it was . . ." I hesitate.

Juliet laughs. "No need to answer. In that case it must have been one of the two other possible internal candidates. Best if I don't know which."

I'm puzzled, until I remember Ricky MacFadyen as well as Andy. Ricky's always struck me as a bit of a nonentity, but that may be the type they're looking for, for all I know.

"Ok, I won't tell you," I say, matching her own light tone.

After Juliet's rung off, I bring up Peterborough Social Services in my web browser and search the site for Fiona Vickers. There's a short potted biography of her: as well as providing a formidable list of the diplomas and awards that she's achieved, it says that she began her career working in London, where she helped to set up a refuge for battered wives and another, more specialised, facility for girls wishing to escape forced marriages. There's a postage-stamp-sized mugshot that doesn't reveal very much. She has a broad face with fleshy features and thick, dark hair which she wears loose and long.

I spend the next forty minutes drafting an e-mail to the land registry. While I'm working, I hear some of the traffic control team and their receptionist arrive. It would help if we could share her. She'd have to be based on our floor, though, and they might not like that. Still, it may be something Janey and I can suggest when we've been here for a while. It's true that we're likely to have fewer visitors than they are.

I've just sent the e-mail when the doorbell rings. I listen for the intercom, but it doesn't buzz. That means it's my visitor, not one of theirs.

A tall, bulky woman is standing on the top step. She's dressed in a heavy black jacket with lime green fluorescent panels and dark trousers. Her long dark hair is windswept and she wears no make-up. I smile and hold out my hand.

"Ms Vickers?"

"Hi," she replies. She doesn't take my hand. "Can I come

in? I'm busting for a pee." Her voice isn't cultured, but it's not rough, either. She has a strong Lincolnshire accent.

"Yes, of course. The toilet's to your left, down the corridor. My office is to the right. I'll wait for you there."

I switch on the kettle while I'm waiting for her. When she appears, she's in the process of divesting herself of the jacket. She flings it on to Janey's chair.

"Too bloody hot in that. Is that a cuppa you're making? I could do with one. I've been out since midnight."

"You mean you haven't been to bed?"

She laughs. "Don't look so surprised! I did get a couple of hours on my office sofa before I left, as a matter of fact. It was one of my nights for doing a police patrol."

"Oh, yes. Juliet – DC Armstrong – did say that you went to 'domestics' sometimes. I hope it wasn't anything too harrowing."

She looks at me curiously.

"It wasn't an incident. Just one of my regular nights out with a patrol car, trying to keep any young girls safe if they're out on the streets."

"Girls that you know, you mean? Ones that you've met through your work?"

"Sometimes. But often the ones who've got on to our radar are the lucky ones. It's the ones who fall through the cracks that are most at risk. They're often cared-for children, though it makes me sad to have to say it."

"From children's homes, you mean?"

"Yes. There are a couple in our area. It's not always the home's fault. These girls are damaged and they can be very sly. And desperately vulnerable. Too willing to believe that anyone who takes an interest in them, perhaps gives them presents, is doing it because they like them. And when a bloke's involved, too willing to believe that he's in love with them until it's too late."

I think of Margie and wonder if I should ask Fiona Vickers for advice. I decide against it: Margie isn't the sort of girl that she's talking about. She hasn't gone off the rails: rather the reverse, in fact. She wants to go places despite the fact that her family has stalled. I don't see her as the type who wants to rely on a boyfriend.

I pass Fiona Vickers her tea. She plonks down heavily on Janey's chair, sitting on her own coat, and gulps the tea noisily, dunking the biscuit that she's also accepted. She's wearing a red plaid man's casual shirt that has seen better days.

"I'm in awe of your work, Ms Vickers. It must take real dedication to do what you do."

She shrugs. "Someone has to do it. And call me Fi, for God's sake. Everyone else does." She looks at her watch. "We've got just over an hour if I'm to be in Boston by 12.30. Is that long enough?"

"I think so. I'm in your hands, really. I'm not sure where to start."

She laughs, revealing uneven, discoloured teeth.

"Well, let's start with what I think it's about, shall we? Your DC Armstrong told me that you're looking into a suspected forced marriage killing. That you'd like to get some idea of what the girls are like who get pushed into forced marriages and perhaps build a profile of the types of people who do the pushing? Profile's the word you use, isn't it?"

"That's it in a nutshell. Profile is a word that we use, though I sometimes think it sounds a bit too cut and dried. I'd like to get a grasp of the kind of mind that thinks honour

140

killings are a good idea. And I'd very much like to speak to some of the girls that have escaped from them, if you are able to introduce me. I promise not to scare them."

"Ok." She looks at me for a long minute. "I'm liking most of what you say. You're right, there isn't a single 'profile', but there are types. From what I've seen, the most typical is the shit-house sadist elder brother, who hides under his religion to persuade his parents to let him bully and terrify his sister or worse. There's no religion that officially allows this kind of behaviour, though often people in authority, such as clerics, are involved. But there's one thing you and I need to get straight: we never talk about 'honour killings', all right? There's no such thing." Her voice has risen shrilly and she's glaring at me now.

"Of course. It's just a figure of speech . . ."

"One that needs knocking on the head. End of story."

"All right. I understand. Do you think you will be able to arrange for me to meet some of these girls?"

"Yes, but I'll want to be there, too. I'm sure you mean it when you say you don't want to scare them, but I won't give you the opportunity. And you won't find out their real names."

"I assure you that the police . . ."

She looks at me mockingly.

"Will guarantee them protection?" she asks fiercely. "How much do you think that's worth, practically speaking?"

Chapter 28

TIM TRUDGED WEARILY out of Surbiton station and up the short steep hill to Ewell Road. The euphoria he'd experienced when escaping from Patti's hotel had deserted him, and he now felt tired, grubby and depressed. Even if his plan to circumnavigate Derry's prying questions was successful, he knew that he should anticipate at least two sticky altercations before the day was over, one with Katrin and one with Freya.

He rounded the corner into Ewell Road and almost collided with a woman hurrying towards him.

"Tim!" Few women could imbue a single short syllable with such complexity of meaning. She made the word sound simultaneously anguished, accusing and outraged.

Christ, he thought to himself, it's bloody Freya. Freya had taken a couple of steps backwards and was scrutinising him intently. Best to get the first word in. He managed a weak smile.

"Hello, Freya. A bit later than usual, aren't you? I thought you'd be at work by now."

Freya's crystal laugh rang out, pure and cold as ice.

"You mean you hoped I would be, don't you, Tim? As a matter of fact, the reason I'm late is that I've been frantically trying to find out your whereabouts. I've only given up now because I've got an important meeting later this morning."

They were standing in the middle of the pavement. Late commuters and early shoppers were staring as they went by, some having to step into the road to pass. Tim saw a woman with a double buggy approaching and drew Freya nearer in to the wall.

"Look, Freya, I'm sorry," Tim muttered, keeping his voice low. "I can explain what happened, but not in a few minutes, and I'd prefer not to have to stand talking here. Is there somewhere we can get a coffee?"

"I've told you, I've got a meeting. I need to go. You can tell me this evening, Tim. I shall be all ears. Where are you going now?"

"Back to yours, to have a shower, if that's ok. I'm not needed at work until later."

"Fine. I'll see you this evening. I'll be back at around seven. I'll cook. Don't be late."

Freya sprang back into the moving throng. She gave Tim a single backward glance as she disappeared. He responded with a half-salute that was intended to be apologetic. She'd turned her head before he could see her reaction.

Tim carried on walking. It took him ten minutes to reach Freya's house; by the time he arrived he was feeling knackered. He slumped down on one of her pristine sofas and immediately fell asleep.

He was startled awake by the bleeping of his mobile. He fished it from his pocket and answered it blearily.

"Hello?"

"Tim, old son, it's Derry. I just wondered if you were all right. I was expecting you to be here first thing again this morning. I wasn't particularly worried when you didn't show up, but I had to go out again and while I was away your sister rang the office. She left a message to say that you hadn't got back last night and weren't answering calls. I thought I'd have a go at calling you myself before I rang her back. I'm glad I've got you now. Where *have* you been?"

Derry sounded genuinely worried, but Tim was sceptical. He knew that when Derry had had time to think about it the teasing and innuendo would kick in. That was the least of his worries, however. If Freya had tried to contact Derry, she'd almost certainly also called Katrin again. He should have thought to ask her. That was the trouble with Freya, she ambushed you with her logic so that you couldn't think straight.

"There's no need to worry about Freya. I've already seen her. I'm sorry she bothered you: it's unlike her to over-react. It's a bit of a complicated story. I'll tell you about it when I get there."

"You are coming in today, then?"

"Yes. I just need to have a shower first, freshen up a bit."

"I see." There was a long pause. Wait for it, thought Tim. But when Derry spoke again he was clearly preoccupied with something other than the previous evening's dinner or finding out where Tim had spent the night.

"Good," he said. "Because I'm working on something you might be interested in."

"What's that?" Tim knew that he sounded wary. He had plenty on his plate with the honour killing enquiry and the mess he appeared to be making of his personal life, without getting embroiled in one of Derry's unorthodox investigations.

"It's connected with the incident I was called to last night. We haven't caught anyone yet, but I'm pretty sure the Khans were responsible for it. They run a string of businesses in the Mile End Road, some of them more or less legal, most of them emphatically not, though it's difficult for us to get a handle on what they do because no-one will shop them. We're pretty sure that they operate some kind of protection racket, but we need a lot more evidence than we've been able to scrape together to charge them. They certainly own a hotel with a casino attached, but the financial accounts of both are clean. We suspect all kinds of goings-on there, but again there's no proof. They're flash joints, attract quite an affluent clientele."

"That's all fascinating, but I'm not sure why you think it would be particularly interesting to me. What was the crime last night, anyway?"

"Give me chance, I'm getting to that. Last night's incident took place in a bar that's well known to us. It's one of the places we think the Khans are 'protecting'."

"Was it a fight?"

"Not exactly. An old guy went in there, apparently in a bit of a state. He'd come in off the street and seemed to be running away from someone. The landlord wouldn't say much, but some of the punters said he seemed frightened. With good cause, it turned out, because three guys came into the bar shortly afterwards and removed him. Forcibly. They dragged him through the back of the bar and out of the kitchen entrance into a side street. When they were out of sight some shots were heard."

"So they shot him?"

"We don't know. At least one of the shots was fired into the ceiling of the kitchen corridor, so possibly not. We've found a bullet which has been sent for analysis. But if they didn't shoot him, they probably did him over."

"Sounds like a gangland brawl to me, but you know more about them than I do."

"It was hardly a brawl: the old guy didn't put up any re-sistance. He seems to have been frozen with terror. Besides, 'brawl' implies a spontaneous fight, and the Khans don't go in for that. If it was them, they'd have had a reason for roughing him up."

"I still don't see that it has anything to do with me."

"It may not have. I can't tell you for sure, because we don't know who the old guy was. But several witnesses described him, and when I was going over their statements it struck me that he sounds like the spitting image of that geezer you told me about. The one you thought you saw at King's Cross."

"You mean Peter Prance?"

"Yes. The only thing was, the witnesses were agreed that he looked a bit down and out, as if he'd fallen on hard times. From what you've said, your guy usually lands on his feet."

"Usually, but not always. It depends on how successful he is at finding someone gullible enough to sponge off."

"He might have discovered that's a bit more difficult in the East End."

"You're right. And if it is him, and he gets away from his attackers, he won't report it, because he's still wanted for questioning about blackmail in the murder case in Spalding I told you about."

"See, I have grabbed your attention now, haven't I? You're sounding a lot less jaded than you did five minutes ago. Bit of a heavy night last night, was it?"

Tim sighed.

Chapter 29

AFTER FIONA VICKERS has left, it occurs to me that Tim doesn't know I'm working today. I turn on my mobile. Immediately, three missed calls flash up on the screen. I'm about to check them when the phone rings again.

"Katrin? Thank God. Where have you been? I've been calling home as well as your mobile and not getting an answer from either."

"I'm the one who's supposed to be asking that question," I say, as drily as I can manage. "I'm working today, as it happens. It wasn't planned, Juliet asked me to because something has come up. Pardon me for asking, Tim, but where the hell were you last night? Freya called late to tell me you hadn't made it back to Surbiton. One of her insufferably gloating calls, but I think she was worried about you."

"Trust Freya to create a drama out of nothing. I'm sorry."

"I don't think it was quite 'out of nothing', was it? Especially after what she described as your odd behaviour on Monday. And you haven't answered my question. Where were you? And where are you now?"

"I'm back at Derry's office. Where's Sophia? Is she with Mrs Sims?"

"Yes. Mrs Sims has a couple of vacancies at the moment, so was able to take her at short notice, despite the fact that one of her helpers – a young girl called Margie – didn't turn up for work this morning. I was going to tell you about it. The parents are estranged and the girl lives with her mother, who apparently's an alcoholic. Mrs Sims was worried about Margie, said it was out of character to let her down. I spoke to her again an hour or so ago and she was all for calling the police. I told her to wait until this evening for that, but I suggested that she try to contact the mother and she hasn't called me back. What do you think?"

"I don't think you should leave it as long as that. If you can't raise the mother, I'd do something about it now. Call Juliet, ask her to investigate."

"All right, I will."

"Do it now," said Tim. I recognise his tone of voice immediately. Earnest Tim, pillar of society, trying to deflect the person he's talking to from raising an uncomfortable issue.

"I *will* do it now, Tim," I say. "In about thirty seconds, at any rate. Just tell me first where you were last night."

"What? Oh, I was at Derry's." I know immediately that he is lying. "It's too long a story to tell you now. I'll call you this evening and explain."

"I shall look forward to it. I can't wait to find out how much explanation it takes to convince me that you had a good reason for not sleeping in the right bed."

"Katrin, I . . ."

"Goodbye, Tim. Call me this evening. After 7.30, when I can be sure that Sophia's in bed."

I push the red button.

Chapter 30

SHIT, THOUGHT TIM, as Katrin ended the call, that's three women who all want to have a serious talk with me: Patti, Freya and Katrin. What have I done to deserve this? He didn't dwell on the question for too long: he knew it wouldn't bear too much scrutiny. But still he felt sorry for himself. He hated conversations about emotions, especially when his own integrity was being called into question. Freya would be the easiest to deal with in that respect, he reflected: at least he hadn't been 'in a relationship' with her. He frowned as soon as the phrase entered his mind. Of course he'd never been romantically entangled with her, but his relationship with Freya was certainly the oldest and most probably the most complicated of the three. And talking to Freya was never easy if she thought she had the upper hand.

He was sitting alone in his borrowed office, drinking yet another cup of coffee, his third or fourth of the day. He'd yet to meet Derry and didn't relish the prospect. A light rapping at the window set in the door made him jump. He thought perhaps this *was* Derry, returning from one of his mysterious errands, but the silhouette in the frosted glass was at once much shorter and chunkier than Derry's. With a sinking heart he recognised the outline of Nancy Chappell. She opened the door.

"Can I come in?"

"Yes, of course. No need to knock."

"You feeling any better today? You looked quite rough yesterday."

"Much better, thanks."

There was a prolonged silence. Looking up at her, Tim thought she'd made more of an effort with her appearance than on the previous day. She was dressed in a plain purple tunic-like dress with short sleeves over thick black tights. She was still shod in the Doc Martens. When she met his eye, he thought her expression more amenable, almost conciliatory.

"Right. Well, I said I'd come back today to see if you wanted anything. You read those reports yet?"

"Most of them. There's a lot I don't understand, but I'm not sure whether anyone can explain it."

"Try me."

"It's partly the idea of 'honour killing', which seems a nonsense to me. DI Hacker's told me to ignore it. He says it only hinders murder investigations if people think there's some kind of acceptable motive attached to them. He's right, but where did it come from in the first place?"

She regarded him steadily.

"What 'as DI 'acker told you about me?"

Tim looked back at her. He could see that trying to fudge the issue with this woman could only earn him contempt.

"He said that you've been a victim of it yourself. And that you've successfully rebuilt your life."

She smiled grimly.

"I don't like being thought of as a victim. Victims are passive. I fought and clawed my way out of my family, though that didn't mean my life wasn't in danger. Still would be, if I 'adn't 'ad help wiv changing my identity completely. I 'ad to 'ave ferapy when I got away from my Dad and bruvvers.

Some of it was about trying to understand them, get inside their 'eads, not so's I could sympafise wiv them, but so I could 'move on', as psychiatrists like to say. I read a lot about so-called honour killings." She almost spat the words. "They go back a long way, back into ancient 'ist'ry. We're supposed to be more civilised now. But the fact that 'honour's' been called on frough the ages to justify striking blind terror into people, mostly women, and killing them is just a scam. It's a cowardly bully's pretence at justifying oppression, coercion, and sometimes depravity. That's all there is to it. Can I sit down?" Her cheeks were burning red; she was breathless with emotion.

"Yes. Sorry, I should have asked you to before."

She hadn't said anything that hadn't occurred to Tim already, but he was shaken by the strength of her passion. She sat silently for a couple of minutes until her chest stopped heaving.

"It wasn't my Mum's fault," she added, talking to herself now. "They'd already broken her. She was too afraid."

Tim thought she was going to cry, but with a supreme effort she managed to regain her composure. She attempted a wan smile.

"What else do you want to know?"

"How many girls succeed in getting away, like you did?"

"Who knows? Some do, obviously. It's 'ard for them unless they change their identity, like me, and you need 'elp wiv that. The real question is 'ow many escape but have someone in their family – more often than not a bruvver – go after them. If they've run away with a man, they're certain to be killed, sometimes the man, too. If they've only defied their parents' choice of 'usband, they might – just – be allowed to live if the 'usband will still marry them. Otherwise, they'll be killed, too. What nobody knows is 'ow many 'disappear' wivout anyone noticing, or at any rate reporting it. If a girl's left school and not been allowed to take a job, not many people are going to know if she vanishes. Or care, in some communities."

"Do you think that Ayesha Verma has been murdered?"

"I don't know enough about the case to 'ave an opinion. You want to tell me a bit more about it?"

"She'd just left school when she disappeared. Wanted to go to university, which her parents agreed with, but said she should be married first, so she deferred taking up her place until next year. The parents wanted her to marry a cousin from India. He came to visit – with a view to marrying her quite quickly, I think – and she disappeared about a week later. He went back to India. The parents are adamant that she wanted to marry him, but he's more than twice her age."

"Sounds unlikely to me. What sort of family does she come from?"

"Her parents are reasonably well-educated. The father works for the local authority. Mother's a florist. The father came from India originally. The mother was born in Sweden."

"Does she have bruvvers?"

"No, just two younger sisters. The father reported her missing."

"'ard for me to say whether I think she's been murdered. From what you say, the family isn't typical of the ones I've worked with. What sort of standing do they 'ave in the local community – the local Asian community, I mean?"

"There isn't really a local Asian community. Only a few people of Indian heritage live around Spalding and they're not all together in the same area."

"What's 'er mother like? Does she seem afraid of her 'usband?"

"Not afraid, but deferential, I'd say."

"And the florist's? Is it a family business? More or less part of the 'ome?"

"No. Mrs Verma doesn't own the shop. It's some way from where they live, in the main shopping centre."

"So the main cause for concern, apart from the girl's disappearance, obviously, is the arranged marriage, especially taken together wiv the fact that she wanted to go to university and the fiancé's age. But there are no bruvvers, no neighbours pressuring them to punish 'er and she 'as a father who's enlightened enough to let 'is wife work away from 'ome and allow 'is daughter to go to university once she's married, though if I was 'er I'd be sceptical about my chances. I fink she's a runaway. If she didn't want to marry the cousin and felt confident that 'er father wouldn't punish 'er if she scarpered and was recaptured, it'd be the logical thing to do."

"But surely, equally logically, she could have been murdered. You've made a lot of assumptions based on what we understand of the family's circumstances, but we know almost nothing about their characters. And if she is a runaway, she's succeeded in covering her tracks amazingly well. She hasn't used her bank account or her rail card since she disappeared and, according to the mother, couldn't have had more than thirty pounds on her."

"I'm not suggesting she may not 'ave come to 'arm. Runaway girls often get into the wrong clutches, as you know. Or someone might be 'elping 'er."

"Do you think I'm wasting my time going to India to talk to the cousin?"

"Not wasting your time – 'e's an obvious line of enquiry. But I fink you should keep an open mind. I fink it's odds on she's either gone to ground or someone is 'olding 'er against 'er will. Or she's been murdered, but not necessarily by someone she knows. There's a lot about this that doesn't strike me as," she sneered, "an 'honour killing'."

"I think I will go to India, then," said Tim. "But you're right. We should keep an open mind on this." He hesitated. "Would you like to interview the Vermas for me?"

"Don't you have a person on the ground who's been talking to them?"

"Yes. Yes, I do: DC Juliet Armstrong. She's very capable, but I thought someone with your . . . perspective . . . might help. Juliet doesn't have your experience, either personal or professional, for this type of crime."

Nancy Chappell shrugged, but she looked pleased. "DI 'acker's my boss. You'd have to ask 'im."

The door burst open at that moment and Derry Hacker bustled noisily in.

"And my name's never out of your conversation, isn't it? What do you want to ask me?" He winked at Nancy. To Tim's surprise, Nancy didn't seem to be affronted by this laddish gesture. Her indebtedness to Derry must run deep.

"DI Yates wondered if you'd let me go to Spalding to interview the family of the girl who's disappeared."

"Really? Your coppers not good enough, Tim?" Derry cast an amused eye in Tim's direction.

"On the contrary, they're excellent. But, like me, they don't have much experience of this type of crime. I think Nancy could help them a lot."

"I'm sure we could spare you for a couple of days, Nancy, if you want to go. You can probably travel back with DI Yates. I think he'll be going home later today, if that's not too short notice. You'd better watch him, though. He can be a bit of a lad, eh, Tim?"

Tim groaned inwardly at the gibe, and would have taken Derry to task if his attention hadn't been arrested by the earlier sentence.

"Going home today?" he said. "Why do you say that? I'd planned on staying until at least tomorrow."

"I know you had, old son, but I've just had a message for you via Thornton from the police chief in Delhi who's been handling the investigation into Ayesha Verma's cousin. As you know, the cousin appears to be being co-operative, but he's just announced that he's working away from next week onwards."

"Where away?"

"I don't know. Wherever it is, it'll complicate matters if you have to question him in some rural outpost, probably with no local police to help. Much better if you see him in Delhi with the policeman present who's familiar with the case: the one who got Verma to say he's willing to be interviewed. You could travel straight from London, I suppose, but you said you wanted to go home first and my guess is you probably don't have the right clobber here?"

"No, I don't; and yes, I must go home first: I promised Katrin that I would." He turned to Nancy. "Are you able to travel with me today, or is it too short notice? I'd like to introduce you to my colleagues in Spalding myself if I can."

"If I can go back to my flat now to pack, I can be ready to leave in less than a couple of hours."

"Off you go, then," said Derry. "But I doubt if DI Yates'll

be ready as soon as that. Won't you have to go back to Surbiton to pick up your stuff?"

"I'm not too worried about that. I didn't bring very much with me. I can leave my things at Freya's until the next time I visit her." The thought crept into the back of Tim's mind that he might be able to get out of the showdown with Freya after all. Then there'd only be Katrin to worry about, for now at least.

"Should I meet you here or at the station? King's Cross, isn't it?" Tim realised that Nancy was speaking to him.

"Uh? Oh, sorry, I was thinking about something else. At the station might be a good idea. It'll save a bit of time. I'll meet you in the Pret-a-Manger café. It's just opposite the departure boards."

"I know it. I'll see you there in two hours from now."

"Out with it, Tim," said Derry, as soon as Nancy closed the door. "What happened last night?" He wasn't smiling now, but fixing Tim with the beady look Tim knew he usually reserved for punters.

Tim briefly put his head in his hands and smoothed back his hair. The bone-deep feeling of weariness returned.

"Trust me, Derry, nothing happened. Nothing at all. But if Katrin should get in touch and ask you if I spent last night at yours, I'd be eternally grateful if you'd say that I did."

There was an uncomfortable silence.

"I see. Well, I've had no reason not to trust you up to now, Tim. And I daresay you'd do the same for me."

Tim nodded, but avoided meeting Derry's eye. He knew that this would not necessarily have been the case in the past. As for the future – he would owe Derry, now.

"All right," Derry continued heavily, "if necessary, I'll do it, though I think we're agreed that it would be much better all round if she doesn't ask. There's just one condition." The beady look returned.

"What's that?"

"Promise me that wherever you were last night, and whatever you were doing, it didn't hurt Patti."

"I promise you," said Tim, not knowing whether even this was true. He'd already hurt Patti, as Derry knew. Had last night made it worse? He didn't think so.

"And I trust that you saw her back to her hotel, before you went off to do whatever it was?"

"Yes, I did."

There was another pause.

"Good," said Derry. "I suppose she's gone home now? She said she would be leaving today."

"Yes," said Tim. "I think she caught the train this morning."

"I don't suppose you had a chance to put in a word with her for me?"

"Not really. But I'll try again next time I see her."

"Did she mention me at all? No? Well, time to get on. We've got ninety minutes before you have to leave to meet Nancy. Enough time to dig out the photo of your Peter Prance character from the files."

Chapter 31

THE SMALL MAN had managed to sleep fitfully, despite his injuries. He'd woken up late in the morning and set about the painful business of bathing his wounds and rubbing ointment into his bruises. His mouth was particularly painful. He screwed up the courage to examine it in his spotty mirror and was horrified at what he saw. His lower lip had burgeoned like a bud bursting from its calyx. It was an exotic but unlovely mixture of red and purple. The small man wanted to cry.

He'd have to get on with the job, and do it today if he could, before they lost patience and came after him again. Distraught, he poked among the bundle of rags on the floor which were all that was left of his clothes. Somehow he'd have to patch them up, dust them down, make himself presentable. He set to work.

Chapter 32

I CALL JULIET as soon as I've put the phone down on Tim. I'm still fizzing with anger and afraid that Juliet will pick up on it, but Tim's got me worried about Margie now. I'm afraid that I gave Mrs Sims bad advice. I don't want to waste any more time.

"Hello, Katrin. Everything ok? I was just going to call you, as a matter of fact, see if you had some time to spare this afternoon. Did the meeting with Fiona Vickers go well?"

"Quite well, thanks, but that's not why I'm calling. I need to speak to you about a girl who's gone missing. She works for my childminder but didn't turn up this morning."

"Doesn't sound like much of a cause for alarm . . ."

"That's what I thought. But Mrs Sims, the childminder, says it's out of character for this girl to let her down; and I've just been speaking to Tim, who said I should call you."

"Ok, I'll be right with you. Or would it be better if you came here? Where does the girl live?"

"I'm not sure. Mrs Sims lives in Haverfield Street. She can't leave her house during the day, obviously, as she's got all the kids she looks after there."

"Why don't you come here first? Then we can go and see her together. If you can get away, that is."

"Yes, that'll be all right. There's nothing urgent here now that I've seen Fiona Vickers."

I quickly gather my things and step outside into the street. I'm greeted by brilliant sunshine, so bright it hurts my eyes. The police station is only a brisk ten minutes' walk away and soon I'm climbing the stairs to the open plan area where Juliet works. As I approach her desk I see that she's talking on the phone. I stand still, not wanting to look as if I'm eavesdropping her conversation, but she waves me over.

"She's here now," she says. She hands me the phone. "It's Tim." I manage to smile. I note that Juliet doesn't respond, but frowns and looks away.

"Thanks."

"Katrin, is that you? Elusive today, aren't you? I've just been trying to get you again at your office."

"As Juliet probably explained, we've decided to go and see Mrs Sims together. I told Juliet what you said about not leaving it any longer before we try to find Margie."

"Yes, she mentioned it. What I wanted to tell you was that I'm coming home today. I'll probably be flying to India tomorrow."

"That's a bit sudden, isn't it?"

"Yes, but it can't be helped. I'll explain when I get there. I'm bringing one of Derry's team with me. I've asked Juliet to meet her today, so that I can introduce her. Will you still be there?"

"When will you be arriving?"

"I'm not sure. Around 4.30, I suppose."

"In that case, the answer's no. I'll be on my way home with Sophia by then."

"Of course, I should have thought of that. I'm really looking forward to seeing you both."

"I'm sure that Sophia is looking forward to seeing you, too." I glance at Juliet, but she has bent her head discreetly over some papers on her desk. If she's noticed my tone, she doesn't show it.

"Ok, well, goodbye," Tim says awkwardly. "I'll see you soon."

"How are you?" I ask Juliet, after I've killed the call and handed back the phone.

"I was going to ask you the same thing. You seem a bit uptight."

I laugh, knowing as I do so that it sounds forced.

"Tim's just pissed me off a bit, that's all," I say. "I expect I'll get over it."

"Yes, well, he seems to have developed a talent for doing that at the moment," she replies.

"Has he done something to upset you?"

She hesitates.

"He's been behaving rather erratically lately," she says slowly. "And like a fool I've let him turn me into a dogsbody. Still, as you say, nothing that I can't deal with."

"I guess neither of us has time to waste at the moment, obsessing about Tim's behaviour," I say.

"You're right. If another girl's disappeared, we need to swing into action, and quickly."

"Another girl . . . are you connecting Margie with Ayesha Verma?"

"It seems an obvious conclusion to draw, doesn't it? Girls don't disappear in Spalding every day of the week."

"You're right. But I think it's unlikely that Margie is the victim of an honour killing. From what I've heard, her parents take no interest in her whatsoever."

"I'm getting a bit tired of all this talk of honour killings," Juliet snaps back. "I'm far from convinced that that's what's happened to Ayesha. As a theory, I think it's got out of hand."

"But you encouraged me to meet Fi Vickers."

"I did, and at least partly because I don't want Tim to make a fool of himself by haring off to India when there's probably a more logical solution staring him in the face."

"What do you mean?"

"When girls do run away, they sometimes do so off their own bat, but often in cahoots with each other. If this girl called Margie really has gone missing, I think we should explore any connections she may have with Ayesha before we jump to more exotic conjectures. And we don't need an 'expert' from London to help us do that."

"You mean the woman that Tim's bringing with him?"

"That's exactly who I mean. No doubt some superior female copper who's done amazing things in the Met and who's now coming here to show us how it's done."

"Steady on! This doesn't sound like you!"

"It may not sound like the me that you know, but it's a side of me that you'll probably be seeing a lot more of in the future! Come on, let's go!"

Juliet heads for the stairs, and uses an unnecessary amount of energy to clatter down them. I follow more slowly. When I join her at the foot of the staircase, she's already contrite.

"I'm sorry, Katrin, you're right: it's not like me to over-react like this, and you certainly don't deserve to have it taken out on you. But sometimes I could kill Tim, I really could."

"That makes two of us." I smile wryly and she smiles back. Unexpectedly, we both burst out laughing.

Chapter 33

WHEN TIM ARRIVED at King's Cross station Nancy was already there, waiting patiently outside Pret-a-Manger. He saw that she'd changed out of the purple tunic and was now wearing black jeans and a black leather jacket festooned with multiple zippers and small chains. The inevitable Doc Martens remained. Her lips and eyelids were painted in deep plum. She was wearing a tiny rucksack that looked incapable of holding much more than a change of underwear and a toothbrush. Tim permitted himself a small mischievous smile as he pictured the likely reactions of his colleagues in Spalding when they met her.

"Sorry to keep you waiting," he said.

She glanced at the station clock.

"You're dead on time," she said. "Pafologically early, that's me. There's a train to Peterborough in ten minutes. I've bought my ticket. You should have time to get yours."

"I bought a return ticket on Monday, so we're good to go. Unless you'd like to grab some tea?"

"Good idea. The platform hasn't been announced yet, so we're ok."

"Black tea?"

She threw him a scornful look.

"I don't like the green stuff, either," he said. "My sister keeps on making it for me."

"Cat's piss," said Nancy dismissively, gazing out across the concourse.

Tim headed for the Pret counter, recalling only too vividly his party trick of a couple of days ago. He hoped none of the staff remembered him. He didn't recognise any of them, but that didn't mean anything: he'd hardly been in a fit state. He took his place in the short queue, returning with two lidded beakers of tea just as the platform announcement was made.

He was handing Nancy her tea when he spotted a woman with short blonde hair walking towards the barriers, and paused in the act. The woman's back was turned to him, but he felt sure it was Patti. He wondered what had kept her in London until this afternoon. If she was intent upon catching the same train as he and Nancy, he hoped fervently that they'd manage to choose different carriages.

Nancy was alert to his hesitation and followed his gaze.

"You know her?"

"I . . . yes. At least, I think it's her: Patti. She's a Scene of Crime Officer. She works for South Lincs, too. We've been on several cases together."

"Want to catch her up?"

"No. No, I don't know her that well. She'd probably rather have the journey to herself."

Nancy didn't reply, but unless Tim was imagining it, the look she shot him was one of disapproval.

"We'd best be getting on the train, anyway."

She led the way, Tim following in silence. He saw the woman he thought was Patti getting into one of the first class carriages and decided he must have been mistaken. Even if he hadn't been, there was no prospect of his running into her if she stayed there.

He and Nancy found a carriage towards the end of the train in which few of the seats had been reserved. She divested herself of her rucksack and tried to heft it into the luggage rack but missed; it rebounded off the tubular steel and hit her in the face.

"Oh, no! Let me do that," said Tim, taking hold of one of the straps. She snatched it back.

"I can manage, thank you."

The brief thaw in her attitude towards him seemed to have hardened again. During the journey, she was uncommunicative, gazing out of the window and barely bothering to reply when he attempted some desultory conversation. When they were within ten miles of Peterborough, Tim decided he'd had enough and confronted her.

"Is something the matter, Nancy? Have I done something to upset you?"

She shrugged.

"Come on, I know you're annoyed about something. I can't try to put it right unless I know what it is."

"You can't put it right, anyway. And in any case, it's none of my business."

"What isn't?"

"I could spot it a mile off. You've had an affair with that woman, haven't you? The one you saw catching the train. You've been cheating on your wife."

"Nancy, I haven't, and that's God's honest truth."

"Yeah, right."

Chapter 34

MRS SIMS OPENS the door as soon as she sees Juliet and me coming down the street. She's holding Sophia. Thomas is clutching at her legs.

"Come in," she says.

"Mrs Sims, this is DC Juliet Armstrong. She's come to ask you some questions about Margie."

"Please, come through." Sophia is holding out her arms. Mrs Sims passes her to me and picks up the boy. She leads us into the room where I first met Margie. The building bricks lie scattered on the floor, but most of the other toys have been tidied away.

"Sophia's the only one I'm expecting to keep until the end of the day," she explains. "Thomas's mother's coming for him shortly. If you don't mind watching them for a few minutes, I'll make some tea."

"Not for me, thanks," Juliet says brusquely. I'm surprised. Juliet's well-known for her calm, polite 'bedside manner' when it comes to dealing with members of the public. Mrs Sims looks at me enquiringly.

"It's kind of you, but we should probably get on with this now," I say.

"Right you are," says Mrs Sims, sitting down on a low armchair. She gestures towards the sofa. Juliet pointedly remains standing. Awkwardly, I scurry past her and perch myself between her and Mrs Sims, dandling Sophia on my knee. Mrs Sims puts Thomas down and he returns to the bricks.

"Do you know Margie's address?" Juliet asks.

"Yes, she lives in Chestnut Avenue. I've got the exact number written down. I'll fetch it for you."

"Thank you. Do you have a telephone number, too? And can you tell me Margie's surname?"

"Her mother's telephone number's on the same piece of paper. Margie has a mobile as well. I bought it for her so she could call me if she had any difficulties when she took the children out. Her surname's Pocklington."

"Thank you. Presumably you've tried to call the mobile?"

"Yes, several times. I think she's switched it off."

"Mrs Yates tells me you suspect that Mrs Pocklington's got a drink problem."

"I more than suspect! The woman's off her face most of the time."

"Have you met her?"

"No, but I've spoken to her on the phone a few times. Or rather tried to make sense of what she's been saying. Margie's embarrassed by her. She tries to keep her out of her life as much as she can."

"I see. What about Mr Pocklington?"

"He walked out last year. I think it was just before Margie came to work here. That was the reason she took the job: to pay her way, because her father won't and her mother can't support her. She'd hoped to go to university this year. She'll have to wait now."

"Have you ever seen any marks on Margie?"

"Marks? What do you mean? She isn't the sort of girl to have tattoos."

"I mean bruises. The sort of marks she might have got if someone had hit her."

"No, nothing like that. The only thing that's unusual about her is that she's very slim. Far too thin, in fact, and I'm sure she's lost weight since she first came here, though she denies it."

"She was here at work yesterday?"

"Yes. She came around eight, as usual in time to have some breakfast. She left a bit later than usual. I suppose it must have been five-thirtyish, perhaps closer to six."

"Did you notice anything different about her behaviour? Did she seem more subdued about anything, or upset? Or the opposite, more giggly and talkative than usual?"

"No, I don't think so. She does get upset sometimes, either because her mother's been drunker than normal or because she's seen her father, but she didn't mention either of them yesterday. She's never giggly or talkative. She's a solemn little lass."

"Have you tried calling either of her parents?"

"I've called her mother. I can't get a reply. I don't have contact details for her father, but I'm sure she wouldn't go there. She's not welcome. Her father's new woman doesn't like her. I think the feeling's mutual: Margie would have more pride than to visit her."

"Do you know her parents' first names?"

"The mother's name is Liz."

"She shouldn't be hard to track down," said Juliet. "There can't be more than one Liz Pocklington living in Chestnut Avenue. I'm going back to the station. I'll get on to it straight away."

She stands up abruptly. "I'll let myself out."

Juliet strides out of the room and has reached the front door before I can pass Sophia to Mrs Sims. I race to catch up with her.

"Juliet, what's the matter?"

Her face is a mask.

"Nothing's the matter. You're worried about this girl, aren't you? You've told me you think her disappearance should be treated as an emergency. Well, I'm treating it as one. Satisfied?"

She turns the catch on the door.

"You'll keep me informed, won't you, as you make progress?"

She sighs.

"Yes, I'll keep you informed. You and Tim and Andy and Ricky and Superintendent Thornton and the policewoman Tim's bringing back with him from London and anyone else who wants to know. You can all share a piece of the credit if we find this girl alive; and I have no doubt that someone will expect me to shoulder the blame if we don't, and I'll probably accept it. How's that for being flexible?"

"Juliet, you know that's not . . ."

She's halfway through the door, but she looks back over her shoulder.

"Not fair?" She says. "Is that what you were going to say? No, it isn't, is it? It isn't bloody fair at all."

The door closes smartly behind her. I see Mrs Sims hovering at the end of the short hall, her eyes alive with curiosity.

Chapter 35

THE SMALL MAN had a shopping list in his pocket. It was the client's list, not his own. Now he was pacing the streets of London, thinking best how to service it.

Railway stations were always a good bet. King's Cross was his favourite. There was a touching naïveté about travellers from the North. From the eastern side of the North, he corrected himself. No flies on people from the North-West, his own homeland.

The digital clock at the station gave the time as 14.30. He scanned the arrivals board and saw that a train from Peterborough was due in at 14.42. He leaned against the barrier, waiting for it to arrive. His head was throbbing and his face felt raw. He hoped that his appearance would not frighten off his prospects. Glancing down at his shoes, he saw that the toecap of one had been so badly scuffed that the leather had almost worn through. He felt desperately sorry for himself. He needed a drink, but his attackers had given him only £20 to 'do the business' and he doubted that'd be enough even if he didn't make unnecessary inroads into it. He resolved never to get himself into this mess again. He should have stuck with picking off individuals like Hedley Atkins and that City wanker, Jennings. They played better to his talents than the Khans. He should not have tried to better himself by mixing himself up with an organisation whose endless tentacles stretched everywhere. Ambition could be a terrible thing: he knew he had no hiding place. He might even have to opt for another stretch inside. He shuddered at the thought, but it might be the lesser of two evils.

A woman walked past him, rattling a collecting bucket. She paused for a moment, looked him up and down and moved on. She thought he looked more like a recipient of charity than a donor, he realised with a sudden access of rage. How dare they reduce him to this!

An announcement rang out over the tannoy. He hadn't been listening, but he guessed that the train he'd been waiting for had arrived. Giving himself a mental shake, he turned to the job in hand. He knew that doing the work he'd been assigned was the first step towards breaking free.

He spotted her almost immediately when the passengers on the train disembarked and streamed out on to the concourse. He knew his prayers had been answered. She was exactly what he was looking for; she fitted the bill to a 't'. Gamine, gauche, slender, fragile, with just a hint of spirit. And dark-haired. And, even more important, he thought she must be 'eighteen years old or less'. Who would have thought it?

He watched as she approached the barrier. She didn't have much luggage - just a rucksack and a large zipped bag - but he could tell that she hadn't come to London as a tourist. He could always spot them, the runaways. Usually they were escaping from some vile relative, or perhaps they'd committed a minor crime and it had blown up out of all proportion in their minds. The odd one was pregnant. He made it his business to sniff that out and ditch them like red-hot irons if they were. He could usually distinguish them, though. There was a pathos, a sense of betrayal, of loss, about the ones who were up the duff. This girl wasn't like that. He saw a muted defiance in her, a willingness to take on the world. Good, because she'd need it.

She was almost level with him now, but she seemed not to have noticed him. She frowned as she took the ticket from her bag and held it against the barrier as if it was an Oyster card. Nothing happened, of course. He glanced around him. There should have been a railway official on duty at the barrier, but there wasn't a uniform in sight. He blessed the inefficiencies of British railways and stepped forward.

"Are you all right, my dear? You're looking a little bit lost." He put on his blandest, most charming voice, ever the friendly old gentleman trying to help. Noblesse oblige, and all that.

She looked up, startled, and recoiled slightly as she met his eye, glinting clear and black as usual, but encased in a puffy mess of swollen flesh. His lip was hideously swollen, too.

"Oh, don't be alarmed," he drawled. "I'm terribly short-sighted and I had an argument with a plate glass door this morning. Nothing serious, I assure you, so please don't worry." He congratulated himself that he'd neatly turned her concern to himself. That usually worked. "Now, what's the problem? Don't you have the right ticket?"

"I'm not sure," she said. She was very pale and seemed close to tears. All the better.

"Let me see."

She handed over the pink ticket, slightly damp and dog-eared from the sweat on her anxious fingers. He smoothed it out, saw that it had been purchased using a student railcard. He looked at her face again. She didn't look old enough to be a student, but appearances could be deceptive.

"This is a valid ticket," he said. "You need to feed it into that slot in the barrier. It's quite simple."

She did as he suggested. The barrier swung open and she managed a wan smile as she passed through. He realised that she felt foolish. He needed to think quickly, find a reason for detaining her before she disappeared into the crowds.

"You look tired," he said. "Would you like a cup of tea?"

She stood and stared at him, undecided.

"Oh, I understand," he said. "You can't be too careful. But I'm quite safe, I promise you. And we don't need to go very far. There's a Pret-a-Manger just over there." He gestured towards the concourse café. "Perhaps I can help you with a bit more advice before you venture out into the city? London can be quite daunting if this is your first visit. Is it your first?" he added, regarding her beadily from beneath the swollen eye.

She nodded.

He took her lightly by the elbow and steered her across towards the tables.

"You sit here and I'll get you something to drink. Would you prefer tea or coffee?"

"Coffee, please. A cappuccino?" she added hopefully.

The small man shuddered inwardly. He might have guessed that she would order something vulgar – 'trendy', he believed the word was – but he'd expected a little better from her. Still, it would help him to harden his heart. She'd seemed almost too much of a waif at the barrier. She'd had a quick tug at his heart strings but he banished it now.

He queued at the counter, returning with a frothing cappuccino and a tall glass cup containing a muslin net filled with green leaves. He fished the latter out and inspected it.

"An apology for a cup of tea," he observed. "But the best on offer."

She was uncertain whether to laugh. She thought from

173

the tone of his voice that he was joking, but it was hard to tell.

"Thank you," she said, removing the coffee from the tray.

"Oh, it's nothing," he said, making a batting-away gesture. "Where do you come from?"

"From Spalding," she said. "You probably haven't heard of it. It's in . . ."

"Oh, believe me, my dear, I've heard of it," he said, incredulous of his good luck. He had some slight misgivings about the coincidence, but it couldn't have been anything else. "I lived there for a short time, some years ago. You'd have been very young then: still at primary school, probably."

"That's amazing!" she said, her eyes widening. "How long ago was it, exactly?"

"Oh, let me see – five years, I think, or was it six?"

"I'd have left primary school by then, but only a year or two before. I've left school altogether now."

"Really? How old are you, then?"

"I'm seventeen, eighteen next week. I passed the eleven plus early, so I'm younger than most of my year."

"Well, I'd never have guessed. You look even younger than that."

She smiled ruefully.

"That's not necessarily a good thing, when you're looking for a job."

"Oh, you're looking for a job, are you? I'd thought perhaps you were on holiday, here to do a bit of sight-seeing."

"I wish. I need to find some work pretty quickly. And somewhere to live."

"I see. Fallen out with your parents, have you?"

"Not exactly. But they've split up, and I don't really belong with either of them anymore. And I need to save some money so that I can go to university."

"Is that so? Well, I'm not making any promises, my dear, but I think I know someone who may be able to help you. There's a job he needs to fill at the moment which would just suit you. If you get it, your accommodation will be provided for as well. How does that sound?"

Chapter 36

JULIET HAD FOUND an address for Mrs Elizabeth Pocklington. She'd also tried calling the number that Mrs Sims had given her, but couldn't get a reply. She was on her way out of the police station when she met Tim coming through the door. He was accompanied by a short, thick-set woman who had jet black hair and was wearing Doc Martens.

"Juliet! Just the person I want to see," said Tim effusively.

"Hi, Tim." She was studiedly off-hand. "I'm sorry, I need to go out right away, to see the mother of the girl that's disappeared."

"Somefing come up, 'as it?" said the short woman.

Juliet looked at her without responding.

"This is DC Chappell, Juliet," said Tim. "Nancy, you'll have guessed that Juliet is DC Armstrong. I've mentioned her to you already. She's been working on the Ayesha Verma case."

Nancy Chappell nodded, evidently unfazed by Juliet's hauteur. Tim, on the other hand, was astonished by her hostility: Juliet was usually so eager to please, to co-operate with everyone.

"So, what's 'appening?" Nancy Chappell pursued. "Some kind of breakfrough?"

Juliet realised her mistake.

"No. Nothing, as far as I know. I'm going to talk to the mother of another girl who's disappeared. Nothing to do with Ayesha Verma. DI Yates knows about it: he discussed it with his . . . with another colleague earlier. But perhaps you've forgotten?" She raised a satirical eyebrow. Tim decided she'd gone far enough.

"No, Juliet, I haven't forgotten. I'd hoped you'd have time to talk to DC Chappell now, while I'm still here, but, if you've got more important things to do, that's fine. Nancy'll be here tomorrow. She'll be able to get some rest this evening now."

His tone wasn't lost on Juliet. She immediately felt uncomfortable: creating difficulties wasn't her style. She flushed and held out her hand.

"Sorry if I seem a bit distracted," she said. "I'm worried about this girl, that's all."

Nancy Chappell took her hand and squeezed it in a vice-like grip.

"That's all right. See you tomorrow."

"And I'll see you next week, Juliet."

"Yes. Take care. And good luck, Tim."

"She doesn't like me," said Nancy Chappell, after Juliet had disappeared. "Not surprising, really. I wouldn't like it if DI 'acker plonked someone down on my patch."

"That's too bad. I'm not in the business of massaging Juliet's ego. We need to find out what's happened to Ayesha Verma as quickly as we can. You've got the experience, Juliet hasn't. End of story."

"And you think that beetlin' off to India will help?"

Tim hesitated. "Yes. The fiancé cousin's the most likely suspect and he's offered to answer questions, but only if I can get there before the end of the week. What do you think?"

"I'm not sure . . ."

"Ah, Yates." A voice came booming down the stairwell. "I'm glad you've got here at last. There are several things I want to go through with you before you set off on your little jaunt."

Tim and Nancy Chappell looked up simultaneously. Superintendent Thornton was peering over the banister.

"Can someone else deal with that good lady?" he asked.

Tim was embarrassed. Obviously Thornton thought that Nancy Chappell was a member of the public. He shot her a sideways glance and was even more disconcerted to see that she was grinning from ear to ear.

Chapter 37

JULIET KNEW CHESTNUT Avenue well: her flat was in Rowan Avenue, the adjoining street. Chestnut Avenue was the road nearest the river on the St Paul's Estate, a large social housing development built in the post-war years partly to accommodate Spalding's burgeoning population, partly to provide decent accommodation for people who'd been living in ancient sub-standard cottages or buildings damaged by bombs. Most of the houses and flats on the estate were well cared-for; many, like her own flat, were now owner-occupied.

There were exceptions, however. Juliet had a hunch which house Number 131 was going to be and once she arrived there she was proved right. The house, a fairly substantial semi, stood in a wilderness of garden strewn with old cardboard boxes and bits of bicycle. The lawn was choked with weeds and two standard roses set in a small circle in the middle of it were struggling to survive. The paint was peeling from the front door and the windows at the front of the house, one of which had been half boarded up. It couldn't have been one of the houses still owned by the council: they would never have let it get into such a state.

Juliet shoved open the rusty gate and picked her way gingerly along the path leading to the porch. She stepped inside it, avoiding a pool of something viscous that was leaking from the doorstep to the paving stones below it. The door had no doorbell, but the letterbox was fitted with a doorknocker, both spotted with verdigris. Juliet lifted it gingerly, sickening as something sticky smeared itself on to her hand, and rapped it several times. There was no reply, but, peering through the thick net curtains, she could see a light shining deep inside the house. She rapped the doorknocker again and waited, listening. She thought that she heard some movement from behind the door, but she couldn't be certain. She banged on the door with her fist.

"Mrs Pocklington? It's DC Armstrong, South Lincs Police. I urgently need to talk to you about your daughter."

There were distinct sounds coming from the house now, of falling furniture, perhaps, or someone bumping carelessly into something solid. Juliet decided to walk round to the back door. She knew the back doors of these houses were protected from the weather by a short passageway, and that the occupants of some of the houses had built a gate across the entrance. Mrs Pocklington had one of these gates, though its base was rotting. Juliet hoped that it wouldn't be locked. Its poor state meant she'd probably be able to force it, but she'd prefer not to have to try. She was relieved when she turned the handle to the gate and, slowly, it yielded.

Beyond there was more filth. Several black sacks lay scattered in the area between the back door of the house and the adjacent wash-house, their contents spilling malodorously. All the houses had wash-houses which had originally been fitted with gas coppers. Most of the inhabitants now used them as garden sheds. A row of council refuse bins was lined up against the wash-house wall. It seemed that Mrs Pocklington didn't have the strength or perhaps the co-ordination to carry her rubbish the extra few feet to the bins.

Stepping over one of the split sacks, Juliet saw that the back door was ajar. She knocked on it loudly.

"Mrs Pocklington? Police. We need to talk to you about your daughter."

She heard more sounds coming from inside the house. Juliet waited. It was clear that no-one would be coming to invite her in.

Juliet hesitated. She knew she shouldn't go into the house without asking for back-up. She doubted that Liz Pocklington would be dangerous to anyone except herself, but it probably wasn't worth taking the chance. She stepped to one side of the door and spoke into her radio.

"DC Armstrong," she informed it, as quietly as possible. "I'm at 131 Chestnut Avenue. Back-up requested."

"Request received," came back the crackly message almost immediately. "Back-up on its way. Do not enter the house until back-up has arrived. Repeat, do not enter."

"Ok. Message understood."

Juliet had no sooner disconnected than she was aware of a presence in front of her. A woman was standing there, holding a kitchen knife. She had greasy hair plastered all over her face and was wearing a track-suit top caked in dried vomit and a pair of knickers. Her legs and feet were bare.

Juliet swallowed.

"Mrs Pocklington?"

"What's it to you?" The woman slurred, the words running into each other. "Who are you? Why are you here?"

"Mrs Pocklington," Juliet said again, her voice steadier now. "Please let me have that knife. You aren't in any trouble. I just need to talk to you about your daughter."

To her relief, the woman let go of the knife. It dropped on to the concrete yard with a clang.

"I suppose the little bitch has got herself into some kind of trouble. You'd better tell me what it's about."

Juliet thought about waiting for the back-up team, but she knew it was no longer an option.

"Ok," she said. "Can we go into the house? It's draughty out here and you probably won't want your neighbours listening."

"I don't give a fuck about the neighbours," the woman shouted belligerently, looking round wildly through the handicap of her hair. "But come in if you want to. Liberty Hall, this is."

Juliet followed her into her witch's cauldron of a kitchen.

Chapter 38

I'M AT HOME with Sophia, waiting impatiently for Tim to come home too. Sophia's eaten some salmon and rice and is now rolling around on her rug with some of her toys, working off her surplus energy before bedtime. I've told her that Daddy's coming home today, but I don't think it's registered with her. Probably just as well: who knows when he'll actually deign to turn up? And tomorrow he'll almost certainly have left for the airport long before she awakes.

She tires suddenly, as I've come to recognise is her way. She'll be engrossed in her toys one minute, the next they're too much trouble: none will do as she asks of them and she loses patience. Then the tears come. I scoop her up.

"Bedtime," I say. She nods vigorously. I know I must make the most of this: the time when she is happy to embrace bedtime is likely to be short.

As I'm carrying her through to the hall, I hear a click in the lock of the front door. The handle turns, and Tim is standing there. I see another figure waiting slightly behind him.

"Daddy!" shouts Sophia. It's one of the few words she knows.

"Tim?" I say.

He rushes towards me to envelop us both in an ostentatious embrace. Normally I'd have loved this, been prepared to forgive him everything, but knowing that the other person's hovering there makes me uneasy. I extricate Sophia and myself as soon as I can.

"Who's this?" I say lightly, trying to sound welcoming.

"It's Nancy Chappell. I think I mentioned her to you. She's an expert on honour killings."

The woman steps forward, holding out her hand. I take it reluctantly.

"Mrs Yates, it's good to meet you. I'm sorry to put you out like this."

"You haven't put me out," I say. "It's good to meet you, too." I try to mean it, thinking that the woman will be gone in a few moments. Then I look at Tim. I see that he's squirming inwardly. This can only mean that he's let me in for more than I know about. I don't need to say anything: he starts talking immediately, though without meeting my eye.

"The thing is, Katrin, Nancy doesn't have anywhere to stay tonight. I thought we could book her into that boarding house we use when people need to stay over for training, but they can't take her tonight. The White Hart's booked up, too."

"So you thought you'd bring her here?"

"If you don't mind. The spare room's made up, isn't it?"

"I wouldn't want to make extra work for you, Mrs Yates," the woman pipes up. Now she's moved into the hall, I see that she's a punk. I could kill Tim. I could actually kill both of them. She doesn't want to make extra work! This would have been my only chance to spend an evening with Tim since last weekend, and tomorrow he'll leave for India. Of course I fucking mind, I'm going to say. When I open my mouth, it seems to process the wrong words.

"I suppose that's ok," I say. "Welcome to Spalding. I'm

sorry the circumstances aren't different." I turn to Tim. "I don't know what you're planning for supper? I doubt if I can cater for three."

Tim's jaw drops. It's as if he's never thought about the fact that guests need providing with food. I enjoy his discomfort for a moment, until the resourceful little policewoman suddenly speaks again.

"We can get a takeaway. I'm sure DI Yates can charge it to expenses. It's the least the force can do."

Tim looks even more alarmed. I'm assaulted by a sense of how ridiculous this all is and have to try hard not to smile. Tim and I both know that Superintendent Thornton's unlikely to sign off a claim for a takeaway under any but the direst circumstances. I don't think that offering a policewoman from another force shelter for the night will qualify.

"Great," I say. "Which do you prefer, Indian or Italian? How about Indian, to get Tim in the mood?"

Nancy Chappell pulls a face.

"If it's all the same to you, I'd like Italian. Indian never seems very aufentic outside London."

"Oh, doesn't it?" I can't help the tinge of sarcasm that creeps into my voice. "Italian it is, then. Or I suppose we could each choose either. Tim, what would you like?"

"Oh . . . either. Anything. Italian's fine."

"I'll find some menus while you give Sophia her bath."

I thrust Sophia at him. He takes her meekly and plods off, carrying her. She's triumphant and waves her arms, looking up ecstatically into Tim's face. I glance at Nancy Chappell again and am smitten with guilt. She's red with embarrassment. I put my hand on her arm.

"I'm sorry," I say. "It is good to meet you. Truly. It's just that Tim can be infuriating with his last-minute arrangements and total disregard for anyone else's plans."

She smiles bravely.

"'E's just like my boss. I'm sure 'e means well."

"I suppose you're right: he probably does. Who's your boss, by the way?"

"DI 'acker."

I grit my teeth again.

Chapter 39

S HE DIDN'T FEEL comfortable walking along the street
with him. There was a familiarity about the way he took
her arm - more than that, a kind of possessiveness - that upset
her. More than once during the five minutes after they'd left
the café, she'd thought about running away from him, turning
and diving into the crowds and escaping. He was limping quite
badly and she knew he wouldn't be able to catch up with her.
She gave him a sidelong look. He noticed it immediately: it
was weird the way his attention was focused on her, the way
he fixed her with his swollen eye. It had begun to look quite
horrible. His hands were grazed, too. How had he managed
that by 'having an argument with a plate glass door'?

While she was still drinking her cappuccino he'd asked
for her name, and on an impulse she'd given him a false one.
'Marisa', she'd said. 'Marisa Price.' She'd read somewhere that
it was easier to keep up pretences with a false name if you
retained your own initials. "What's your name?" she'd added.

"It's really of no consequence, as you won't be seeing me
after today, but since you ask, it's Pedro."

"Really? Isn't that a Spanish name?"

"I've got exotic blood, my dear," he'd drawled. "Appearances
can be deceptive."

"Are you all right?" he was asking now. "Not feeling faint,
are you?" He tightened his grip on her elbow. "We'll be at the
bus stop soon. I would have hailed a cab, but the price from

here would have been extortionate. We can get one nearer our destination if the next bus takes a long time."

"How far are we going?"

"Oh, it's quite a way, but I think you'll find it's worth it. Yes, yes, I'm sure of that." He nodded vigorously.

She wasn't convinced. His cultivated voice was the only reassuring thing about him. She looked across the road at the crowds gathered on the pavement. The traffic lights were just changing. If she sprinted across now, before the waiting cars and vans roared into gear, he'd be unable to follow. She glanced at him again. He was regarding her oddly, as if he could read her thoughts.

She didn't make the break and the moment passed. She reflected that she had no options other than what he'd offered. He'd promised her somewhere to live and a job. If she spurned his kindness, there was no guarantee that she wouldn't fall into worse hands. The prospect of spending the night on the street terrified her.

"Ah, excellent," he said. "I can see a bus approaching. It's a bit hemmed in by traffic at the moment. We'll get to the stop comfortably before it arrives."

She adjusted her rucksack – it was biting into her shoulders and he'd made no attempt to help her carry her belongings – releasing her arm from his grasp as she did so.

"Comfortable now?" he said. He grabbed her again. This time the intent was unmistakeable: he was keeping hold of her rather than guarding her. She gave a false, uneasy little laugh.

"You don't need to hang on to me all the time. I won't get lost."

"Oh, I do hope not, my dear," he said, pushing his damaged

face alarmingly close to her own. "But we don't want to take any chances, do we?"

The bus was just edging into its halting-place as they drew level with it. The doors opened and he shoved her inside.

"Go and find a seat, my darling, while I pay the fares."

He swept her forward into the seating area, first giving her a little push, then waving his arms.

"Go on, dear, before it fills up."

She did as he bid her and looked back to see him touching a card to a yellow reader. There was no way of finding out where they were going.

She found a seat near the back, two steps up on the raised platform over the wheel arch. Taking off the rucksack, she slid into the window seat and put the sack on the seat beside her to save it for him. She peered through the grime at the street she'd just left. People were hurrying past, none taking notice of her. She thought of banging on the window, or running to the front of the bus and jumping off before it started again, but she shrank from making a spectacle of herself. She wouldn't be taken seriously: she knew that. The old man would probably concoct a story about her having been 'released into the community', or some such thing. She looked at her fellow passengers, wondering if there was someone she could confide in in the few seconds she had available. Two stout black women sat side by side, bulging shopping bags planted between wide-apart legs. They were deep in a rowdy conversation. There was an elderly man who looked more disreputable than 'Pedro' by some margin; a sulky-faced girl absorbed in her iPad, trying to ignore the infant that sat on her lap; a bunch of workmen who'd elected to stand so that they could talk to each other, even though some seats were still free; and a gaggle of schoolboys. None of them looked likely to sympathise with her.

He was walking towards her now, trying to be brisk despite his damaged leg. He turned on his avuncular smile, passing the rucksack to her as he took his seat.

"Penny for them," he said.

"I was thinking maybe I've been a bit impulsive," she said. "If I go back and tell my Dad how I feel, perhaps he'll help me to go to university this year. I need to tell him where I am, anyway. I wouldn't want him to worry about me."

He let out a strange sound, a cross between a whinny and a snort of contempt. His face had darkened.

"Oh, really . . ." he began, in a high fast falsetto. The woman with the iPad glanced across at him curiously. He saw her and immediately changed tack.

"Marisa, my dear," he said, emphasising the name loudly, "your soft heart does you credit, but I can assure you that you're mistaken. Quite mistaken. If he'd cared about you he'd have done something for you before now. If you'll take my advice, you'll stick with the plans you've made. You'll do better that way."

"Perhaps you're right. But I still want to speak to him. I could call him now, on my mobile."

"A crowded bus is hardly a good place to have what will probably be a difficult conversation, is it, my dear? Do be sensible. Of course you must talk to him, when we've reached somewhere a little more private."

The woman with the iPad returned to her scrolling.

Suddenly he was pinching her arm, grinding it into the back of the seat. She felt warm breath: his mouth was close to her ear.

"Listen, sweetheart, stop drawing attention to yourself. Do you understand? I'll tell you who you can call and when. Now just sit back and shut up, if you know what's good for you."

His breath was sour and metallic. It filled her with revulsion. She twisted her face away and stared out of the grimy bus window. Tears sprang to her eyes but she didn't brush them away because she didn't want him to see them.

Chapter 40

LIZ POCKLINGTON TRIPPED on an empty carton that was lying on her kitchen floor and stumbled. She fell against the lintel of the door that led to the next room.

Juliet bent over her.

"Are you all right?" she said. "You've given your head quite a crack."

"No more than I'm used to." She stood up unsteadily and flicked on the light. Juliet saw how skinny she was. Her shoulder-length hair was dirty blonde, matted in places and thinning at the crown. She smelt of unwashed clothes and something worse: vomit, probably.

"You'd best go through," she said. She continued to enunciate every word carefully, obviously trying not to slur it. It was a battle she was losing.

"I'll follow you. Are you sure you're quite all right?"

"As I'll ever be." Liz Pocklington laughed crazily, as if she'd said something witty. She pushed open the door she'd fallen against and reached round her arm to turn on the light in that room as well, entering it afterwards. Juliet thought it an odd sequence of actions, but the woman was drunk, after all.

The room they were in was tidy, if a little grubby. The surfaces were free of dust, the magazines neatly piled on the coffee table. Someone had tried to impose some order on it recently, even if the curtains were in need of a wash and dark spillages had blotched the carpet. It contained two mock leather armchairs that had aged without grace. There was a television in one corner. A dining-table stood before the window, covered with an old-fashioned 'day cloth' similar to the ones she remembered in her grandmother's house during her childhood.

"Take a seat." Liz Pocklington gestured grandly at one of the chairs. "Margie's cleaned up. She's a good little worker."

Juliet sat on the edge of one of the chairs.

"Would you like some tea?" said Liz, her voice a parody of the perfect hostess's.

"No, thanks. You mentioned Margie. Where is she?"

"I s'pose she's at school. Or – no. Wait a minute. She's left school, hasn't she? She's probably with that Sims cow."

"She isn't at Mrs Sims'. Mrs Sims has reported her missing, said she didn't turn up for work today, which she says is unlike her. Do you have any idea where she might be?"

"Not a clue." The reply was delivered in a sing-song staccato. "I haven't got a bloody clue!" Liz Pocklington looked up at the ceiling for inspiration.

"Mrs Pocklington, this is serious. If we can't find your daughter, we have to assume that something bad may have happened to her. Could you try to think back to when you last saw her?"

"Yesterday evening, I think. Or it might have been the evening before. The days run into each other a bit at this time of year, don't they? But, yes, I'm pretty sure it was yesterday. She came in late. Seemed a bit upset about something, now I think of it."

"Did she tell you what she was upset about?"

Liz Pocklington giggled.

"Oh, I didn't ask her. Would you have done? They need

their own space at that age, don't they? I thought she'd tell me when she was ready. And if not . . ." she shrugged, abandoning the sentence almost before she'd started it.

Juliet's patience was wearing thin.

"Mrs Pocklington, should I make you some coffee? You need to be taking this a lot more seriously. Do you have any idea where your daughter is? Could she be with her father, for example? And if you think she might be, can you tell me where to find him?"

Again the giggle and silly shrug.

"Bastard's tucked up with his scheming little bitch. Didn't give me his address. Margie may have it. I did hear tell he was living in Bourne."

"Thank you. That's helpful. What's his full name? And can you remember his date of birth?"

"His name's Gerald."

"Gerald Pocklington?"

"No, Gerald Arsehole! What do you think? Oh, my God . . ."

"Mrs Pocklington?"

Liz Pocklington suddenly rose to her feet and scurried, crabwise, across the floor. She disappeared into her kitchen. Juliet could hear her throwing up in the sink.

Chapter 41

IT IS HARD for me not to warm to Nancy. She and Tim and I managed to enjoy our supper together and afterwards she helps me to clear away while Tim goes off to pack his suitcase. I tell her that Juliet has asked me to talk to some women who've been abused by their partners. Immediately she fixes her eyes on mine, her attention rapt.

"I fink that's a good idea. If you need any more 'elp, let me know."

"I will. How long are you going to be here?"

"A few days, probably. I'll be 'elping DC Armstrong." She pulls a wry face.

My loyalty to Juliet won't let this pass.

"She's a fine policewoman and a good friend of mine," I say. I realise straight away I sound a bit pompous.

"I'm sure you're right, but she doesn't like me."

"How do you know that?"

She chuckles.

"Oh, believe me, it wasn't 'ard to find out. She didn't exactly beat about the bush."

"That doesn't sound like Juliet." But I realise as soon as I say it that there's a new Juliet, different from the one I've known for several years, a more strident, less tolerant woman than I've ever thought Juliet could be.

"Oh, I don't blame her. I'd probably 'ave felt the same if I'd been treated like she 'as: 'ad a strange woman dumped on my case when I wanted to solve it myself."

"Strictly speaking, it's Tim's case. Juliet reports to Tim and I'm helping her."

Nancy shrugs.

"You know what I mean. She'll be the one doing the donkey-work. And you. And me, if she'll let me. Does she want you to talk to some abused women to make a stronger case for an 'honour killing', or to prove the opposite?"

"I think probably to prove the opposite. She's not convinced that it was an honour killing, or even that Ayesha Verma's actually dead. What do you think?"

"I'd say the same. It's a pity you couldn't have got a bit further with it before this trip to India."

"I think part of the plan was to use the information to decide whether the trip to India was really necessary. But Tim's had his hand forced by the fiancé now. If he doesn't see him this week, he might lose the opportunity."

"Yes, I know. Still, quite glad to 'ave 'ad 'is 'and forced, isn't 'e?" She grins again. Her combination of perceptiveness and outspokenness is disarming. I close down the conversation.

"The bed in the spare room's made up," I say. "You must be tired. I'll find you some towels."

It's now almost midnight. Tim and I are alone in our bedroom. Nancy Chappell has been installed in the spare room – I can still hear her moving around – and Sophia is asleep. Tim's put his case on the floor on his side of the bed, the lid open, awaiting a few last-minute additions in the morning. He's getting undressed. He looks tired and haggard. I know it's not a good time, but I'm desperate to talk to him.

"How's Freya?" I say conversationally.

"Oh, Freya's Freya. You know what she's like. She doesn't change. You were probably right: I should have stayed in a hotel."

"She was very worried about you when you were taken ill. And then when you didn't go back to hers."

"She made far too much fuss about it. Trying to prove her point, I suppose."

"What do you mean? What *was* her point?"

"That I'm hopelessly feckless and inept. That's always been Freya's point about me, ever since we were kids."

"I think you're being a bit unfair. Freya's too grown-up to pursue childhood squabbles."

"So she'd have you believe. Why are you sticking up for her, anyway? You and she are hardly best mates, are you?"

"I don't think sisters-in-law often get on all that well. But she *was* worried."

"So you keep saying. Let's change the subject, shall we? We're both tired. The last thing we want to talk about is fucking Freya."

"She does know you're all right, doesn't she?"

"Yes, of course she does. I saw her this morning."

"This morning? She said you spent last night somewhere else."

"Yes, I did, but I needed to go back to Freya's for a show . . . for a shirt."

"Couldn't you have borrowed one from Derry?"

"I suppose I could have. But he got up before I did and left early. I didn't like to go poking around."

I can tell when Tim's lying. His irises seem to shrink and his face takes on a pinched, shut-in look.

"Why didn't you just go out and buy another shirt? It's a long trek back to Surbiton from Derry's. It must have taken you most of the morning."

"Look, Katrin, can't you just drop it? I've got to get up in a few hours and I'm dog-tired. I'm pretty sure I felt ill because of the malaria tablets I was taking. I've finished the course now, but I'm still knackered. And having you nagging at me doesn't help. If you must keep on pestering me about what I did in London, I'd appreciate it if you could save it until I come back. Ok?"

He swings his legs into bed and hurriedly turns off his bedside light. I stand in the semi-darkness for a while, drained of all energy. I'm certain that something happened in London that Tim doesn't want me to know about. I'm not sure what it is: I'd suspect him of having an affair, but it's hard to believe that he could have started one in the few days that he's been away, especially as he's been ill. Perhaps he and Derry are up to something? I wouldn't put anything past Derry: he'll sail too close to the law himself one of these days, if he hasn't done so already.

As I undress, I hear something fall to the floor in the spare room, followed by a muffled expletive. I get into bed and lie there quietly, my back to Tim's, as far away as possible from him. I wonder if Nancy Chappell knows more about what Tim's been doing in London for the past three days. I'm immediately annoyed with myself for such an underhand thought until I put up my hand to my face and discover that it's wet with tears. If Tim has betrayed me, he doesn't deserve my loyalty.

Chapter 42

WHEN THEY GOT off the bus, 'Pedro' decided neither to wait for another bus nor to hail a cab. Instead he gripped her arm above the elbow and they began to walk.

"It's quite a way," he said. "Made a rod for your back, now, haven't you, my dear? Not to be trusted on public transport, so we'll have to rely on Shanks's pony."

She allowed him to frog-march her, if that was the correct term for the shuffling half-lope that was all his injured leg would permit him. Every step he took was causing him pain. She wondered what had prompted the determination that drove him on so ruthlessly. He was undoubtedly stronger than he looked: his thumb was digging viciously into her arm. She envisaged the large purple bruise that would be forming there.

She knew she must try to keep calm. She looked around her. She hardly knew London at all, but guessed that the street along which they were hastening was very far from the centre. It was lined at intervals with late Victorian parades of shops built in dark red brick, punctuated with scruffier establishments: greasy spoons, launderettes, repair shops. They passed several pavement stalls selling fruit and flowers. Most of the people they encountered were dressed in Western clothes, but some of the women wore burkas or saris and some of the men also were wearing flowing robes. She couldn't guess at their nationalities, but they were many. As she had on the bus, she thought about calling out to one of these people, imploring them to help her, but she was terrified that they'd ignore her. Perhaps they didn't even speak English. If she failed to escape from Pedro, he'd probably punish her for trying. Many of the people looked strange: aliens preoccupied with their own poverty or misfortune. She tried to catch the eye of a smartly-dressed woman who was walking purposefully towards her, but the woman's eyes swept through her, intent perhaps on reaching a meeting on time or simply desirous of getting out of this mean street as soon as possible.

They arrived at a crossroads. The street they had been walking along was now bisected by another, wider, one. They turned into it. Immediately the buildings were cleaner and more prosperous, some of the people better-clothed. She was aware that she and Pedro appeared more incongruous here. They attracted some curious stares: an elderly down-and-out man who looked as if he'd been in a fight, manhandling a girl young enough to be his granddaughter: he dressed formally but shabbily; she wearing jeans and a thin, short-sleeved T-shirt. But no-one was suspicious enough to challenge him.

Pedro stopped suddenly, as if recollecting himself, and steered her down an alleyway. It led into a courtyard, from which rose up an imposing white building several storeys high.

As they approached the glass doors of the building, she could see its name and function discreetly displayed in embossed white letters: Caspiania. Private Hotel. There was a black doorman wearing dark red livery and a top hat standing guard on the cobbles in front of the entrance. She didn't know what a 'private hotel' was: to her it seemed a contradiction in terms.

The doorman looked askance at Pedro: it was obvious

he both recognised and disapproved of him. Pedro released Margie's arm and prodded her, as if playfully, in the back.

"Get along dear. Go inside. What are you waiting for?"

"Do you need a porter, Miss?" said the doorman.

"A porter? Good Heavens, no, why should she need a porter?" said Pedro. "She travels light, as you can see."

He fussed around her in a pretence of care and hustled her through the glass door.

She found herself in a kind of atrium, a high-ceilinged empty space separated from the deeper interior of the building by an opaque glass partition before which gigantic pots containing young trees had been placed. She tried not to be impressed by its splendour. The cool elegance of the exterior was misleading: inside, ostentatious opulence had been restrained neither by economy nor good taste. Margie suspected that the décor was vulgar, but she didn't care: she was impressed by the cream and gold shimmering beauty of the walls and, above all, their spotlessness. It seemed a magical place, incapable of co-existing in the drab, run-down, forlorn world she customarily inhabited.

"Not bad, is it?" She was jolted back to reality by the sound of Pedro's voice, his usual plummy drawl now restored, obliterating the sibilant viciousness that had frightened her so much. "A little obvious for my liking, but you can't expect them to go in for English Arts and Crafts."

She stared at him, at a loss to understand what he was talking about. He let out one of his high-pitched whinnies.

"But I daresay I'm expecting too much of you. Follow me, now. You need to meet your new boss."

He led her to the glass partition. Another man in uniform

sprang smartly out from behind it. He studied Pedro's ruined face with some curiosity and waved them through.

Margie found herself in a vast area partly filled with long streamlined desks arranged in a fan pattern, each one an island separated from its neighbour by yards of gleaming floor tiles. Two young women stood or perched on stools behind each. They were exotically and identically dressed in sophisticated pale brown and scarlet suits. Each desk had been fitted with a small black screen at the end nearest the centre of the room and some of the young women were sitting behind these screens, talking into telephones. She had no clue what they were engaged in. She wondered if the job Pedro had mentioned meant she would be joining the young women, although most looked older than she was. Her spirits rose.

"What are they doing?"

"They're receptionists, my dear."

"Receptionists? Why does the hotel need so many?"

"They have very important clients. It wouldn't do to keep them waiting," Pedro replied smoothly.

Margie's experience of hotels was limited to being taken for a drink at the White Hart in Spalding, where the reception consisted of a small boxed in area in one corner of the bar that was accessed via a mahogany counter with a flap that could be raised to let the receptionist in and out. She nodded as if she understood, but still wondered how the hotel could possibly need so many people doing the same job, especially as some of the women were just sitting there, with nothing visible to occupy them.

"Will I be working here?"

"I'm not sure," he said, suddenly evasive. "Ah, here's Mrs Ali. She'll tell you what your duties will be. Hello, Moura."

The woman inclined her head very slightly. She was plump but well-proportioned. She was dressed in a fitted costume made of the same light brown material interfaced with red as the receptionists' outfits, but she alone was wearing a floor-length skirt. She either did not hear or chose to ignore Pedro's comment.

"Is this the girl?"

The woman turned to Pedro unsmilingly. She didn't acknowledge Margie.

"Yes. Promising, don't you think?"

"We'll have to see. Name?"

"Marisa Price," said Margie, almost as an aide-mémoire to herself.

"We'll have to see what we can do with that." This time the woman addressed Margie directly. "How old are you?"

"Seventeen."

The woman took her by both shoulders and turned her round slowly in a complete circle.

"She's slim enough," she said to herself. "Can you dance?"

"Not much. I've never really been interested."

"You'll have to make it your business to be interested."

Margie looked across at the gazelle-like brown and scarlet receptionists. None of them was taking the slightest interest in her.

"Can they dance?"

The woman ignored the question. She sighed.

"I suppose she'll have to do. Come with me," she added over her shoulder.

She headed for a door set into the wall beyond the furthermost desk. Margie did as she was told. She was aware that Pedro was close on her heels.

When they reached the door, the woman pressed numbers into a keypad and pushed it slightly ajar before looking back at them. Pedro was standing beside Margie now. The woman gave him a vigorous push in the chest. He flinched, grabbing at his ribcage.

"Not you," she said. "You're not to come any further."

"But I have to see Jas . . ."

"You're perpetually whining about Jas. I should have thought you'd have had enough of him for one week."

"I've done the goods. I deserve to be paid."

"You'll have to take that up with him. He's away at the moment. Amsterdam," she added, as if that explained all Pedro needed to know.

"But he's left me without money again. I haven't got . . ."

"Oh, for God's sake shut up. Here!"

She took a fistful of notes from her pocket and handed them to him.

"There's a hundred. It comes off your fee."

"Thank you. When . . . ?"

"That's enough. I'm going now. Arrange to see Jas when he comes back."

Margie had been observing this scene playing out, dreamy with fatigue, as if she'd been watching a television soap. She suddenly understood that Pedro wasn't coming with her. She was convulsed with panic.

"Don't leave me!" She said to him. "Please don't leave me!"

Still wrapped up in his own concerns, he barely registered her plea.

"That's enough," said the woman sternly, grabbing her arm in the exact place where he had bruised it earlier. "I'm warning you, if you make a scene, you won't last long. We don't allow hysterics here."

She shoved Margie through the door, quickly following and banging it shut behind her. Margie caught a last glimpse of Pedro staring down at the notes in his hand, lost to the world of opulence surrounding him.

Chapter 43

JULIET HAD PERSUADED Liz Pocklington to be taken to hospital. She didn't think the woman was dangerously drunk, but Juliet needed her to sober up quickly. She'd forgotten that she'd called for back-up and was about to request an ambulance when PCs Giash Chakrabati and Verity Tandy appeared. Juliet knew they wouldn't like it if Liz threw up in their car, but they'd take it more philosophically than some of their colleagues. It would be a better option than tying up an ambulance crew for a couple of hours.

She led them into the living room, where Liz Pocklington lay slumped, sleeping, in an ungainly pose on one of the mock-leather chairs. Verity regarded her with distaste.

"Stomach pump job?" she said.

"Probably. Whatever the doctor thinks. I need to get her sober enough to talk to me. He daughter's gone missing."

"Not surprising, is it, if she's been living in this dump with an alkie?"

"There's probably something in that: she may have disappeared because she couldn't stand it any longer. It's where she's disappeared to that I'm worried about."

"How old is she?"

"Seventeen."

"Old enough to get a job and fend for herself. Old enough to go off the rails, for that matter."

"You're right about that, too. But from what I've heard,

she isn't that sort of girl. She wants to go to university and the parents aren't helping. She may have agreed to something stupid to get some money."

"Gone on the game, you mean?"

"I don't think she'd choose to do that if she knew what she was letting herself in for. But she could have been tricked into it."

"I suppose you're right," said Verity doubtfully. "From where I sit, they mostly know exactly what they're doing."

"There's no point in standing here talking about it," said Giash. "I'll need your help to get her into the car. Can you open the front door? It'll be easier than taking her round the side of the house."

He nodded towards the door that led out of the living room. Juliet opened it. Beyond was a tiny hall area with a flight of stairs leading from it. A battered handbag stood at the foot of the stairs and some newspapers had been piled on the first step. Otherwise the whole area was dusty but tidy. Juliet noticed that the carpet on the stairs was dangerously frayed in places. She grabbed the Yale catch and twisted it. It took her some time to get the door to move: evidently this door was not in everyday use. She propped it open and moved the handbag and newspapers into the short passageway that abutted the stairs. A row of coat pegs had been fixed on the passageway wall and a navy-blue school coat was hanging on the peg nearest to where Juliet was standing. She removed it. It might provide a sample of Margie's scent for sniffer dogs, if they had to start an outdoor search. She debated whether she should slip upstairs and try to find something carrying Margie's DNA as well, but decided they'd have to come back for that. She didn't have a warrant, and she couldn't risk being accused of taking advantage of Liz Pocklington's inebriated state.

"Is the door open?" Verity called. "We've got her on her feet. We're coming through now."

"Yes, I've propped it open. Bring her out. You'll need to be careful when you get onto the path – it's covered in all sorts of muck."

Giash and Verity appeared in the living-room doorway, supporting Liz Pocklington from either side. They had each one of her arms slung around their shoulders. The doorway wasn't wide enough for them to go through it three abreast, so Verity tried to disengage Liz's right arm.

"Steady, now," she said. "You just need to get through this space here and the front door. PC Chakrabati will hang on to you. When you're outside we can both help you again."

Liz didn't reply, but suddenly twisted away from Giash and threw up on the stairs.

"Christ!" he said.

"At least it didn't go on either of us," said Verity. "Can you grab her again? Keep going!"

"If you two can manage now, I'm going to secure the back door," said Juliet. "I'll be with you in a minute."

"Are you coming with us to the hospital?"

"Yes, I want to make sure . . . On second thoughts, you go without me. I'll join you there as soon as I can. I want to try to track down her ex-husband. He might know where the daughter is."

"Perhaps she's with him."

"It's possible, though the woman she works for thinks it's unlikely. Apparently she can't stand his new girlfriend."

Giash and Verity had heaved Liz Pocklington into the

porch. She slid away from them again and sat down heavily on the concrete floor. From the light shed from the open door, Juliet saw a thin stream of urine snake its horizontal way along the path and trickle on to the grass.

"Fucking hell!" said Giash.

"There are some foil insulation blankets in the car," said Verity. "I'll wrap one around her and put another on the back seat."

"I'm sorry to have landed you with this," said Juliet. "Good luck. I'll see you later."

Chapter 44

I WAKE WITH a start to find Tim tiptoeing around the bedroom. It is just getting light: it must be about 5 am. Tim lifts his case on to the bed and puts my toilet bag into it. He's borrowed it, because he's left his own at Freya's. He zips up the case carefully, trying to make as little noise as possible, and sits on the end of the bed, beside it. He takes out his wallet, tidies the notes and receipts it contains and checks that he has all his credit cards. It's a little ritual of his: he does it every time he goes away. He puts it back in his pocket and stands up, lifting the case off the bed as he does so. He tiptoes past me towards the bedroom door.

I sit up quickly and fumble for my bedside light. It takes me a moment to find it, while Tim stands there as if turned to stone. He has a strange look on his face: it's his 'I've been caught out' look.

"Tim! You weren't going to go without saying goodbye to me, were you?"

"I thought I ought to let you sleep. You looked pretty worn out last night."

"You should have thought of that before you brought a colleague home with you."

"Keep your voice down! I've explained that. I didn't have an alternative. She'll be gone to the station in a few hours and she'll be able to book into the boarding-house tonight. It wasn't so bad getting a takeaway, was it? And I thought you quite took to her."

I sigh. Having Nancy Chappell stay here for the night isn't the issue, and Tim well knows it.

"Of course I want you to say goodbye. You always do, don't you?"

"Sorry," he says, "I wasn't thinking." He bends and gives me a quick kiss on the lips. "Goodbye, darling. I'm sorry you've been left on your own so much lately. I'll make a point of not going anywhere for a while when I come back from India."

"Don't make promises you can't keep," I say, as lightly as I can. "Stay in touch, won't you? And keep safe." I smile at him.

"I will. And I'll call you every day – well, most days," he adds, smiling back. "I'll just take a quick look at Sophia on my way out." He gives me another kiss. Then he heads briskly for the bedroom door, wincing when it creaks as he opens it. He shuts it behind him. I hear him open Sophia's door very briefly and close it again. He moves soundlessly along the corridor. Then there's the sharp click of the front door and he's gone.

I lie still for a while, but I'm wide awake and know that I shan't sleep again. I'm upset and angry with Tim and I don't want to think about him any longer. I decide to take a shower. My head is aching and I don't want to turn on the light again. Outside, the dawn is rapidly turning into broad day. I get out of bed and draw the curtains. As I turn back towards the en suite, I see a folded piece of flimsy blue paper lying on the carpet. I pick it up, open it out and smooth the creases. It's a restaurant bill for £169 with Tuesday's date on it. There can be no doubt it's Tim's bill and that he paid it: his name is printed on the credit card receipt neatly clipped to the top of it. The bill is itemised line by line: three gins, three tonics, three starters, two main courses and a very expensive bottle of wine. Tim had told me that he was having a working dinner with Derry and someone else that night. He'd said he didn't know who the other person was. If it had really been a working dinner, why hadn't Derry footed the bill? And why did the bill start with three covers and finish with only two? I can think of only two explanations: either he and Derry did meet someone and that person left in a hurry – but then why wouldn't Derry have paid the bill? And why the outrageously costly wine? – or Tim was meeting someone for some kind of assignation and enlisted Derry's help to provide him with an alibi. The more I think about it, the more likely this seems: it would account for Tim's paying the bill, the wine, and, even more, Tim's very odd behaviour since he came home. Nancy Chappell might inadvertently have played a part, too: perhaps Tim made sure she'd have nowhere to stay so that we'd have virtually no time alone. He didn't want me asking awkward questions: he made that clear last night.

If anyone had told me that this was going to happen, I would have expected to be distraught: so stricken with misery that I would have felt paralysed, unable to do anything, unable even to think straight. But I don't feel like that at all: I'm flooded with a white-hot anger that fills me with fierce energy. I toss the bill on to Tim's bedside table and dive into the shower. I wash in warm water, then turn the setting to cold and stand there for long minutes, shivering but cleansed. When I emerge, my headache's cleared and my thoughts are collected, hard, logical. If Tim thinks he can treat me and Sophia like that, I'll make him think again. I tug a comb through my wet hair, dress in my work clothes. It's another

Mrs Sims day for Sophia: I've agreed with Mrs Sims that I'll pay for yesterday, rather than swapping it for today.

I hear sounds coming from the spare room. Nancy Chappell's out of bed and moving around. Perhaps I've woken her: being quiet is the last thing I've had on my mind. I'm briefly repentant: after all, the woman is a guest in my house. There's a lot more to Nancy than I've managed to plumb so far. I think she might be a good ally. I completely understand why Juliet resents her, but I have to admit that Tim's probably right when he says she can help us to solve this case – perhaps even both these cases. My thoughts turn to Margie. Wherever she is, I hope she's safe.

Chapter 45

MRS ALI HAD taken Margie to one of the upper floors in a lift. They'd emerged into a long corridor lined with a dozen doors, all of them firmly closed. Mrs Ali made Margie walk in front of her. They kept on walking until they had almost reached the end of the corridor. Margie had slipped one arm from the straps of the rucksack and began to carry it on her shoulder.

"Stop here."

Margie halted obediently.

Mrs Ali unlocked the nearest door and motioned to Margie to go through it. When they were both inside, she locked it again.

The room that Mrs Ali had taken her to was peculiar. It was a small bedroom with a narrow bed. A tiny shower cubicle had been shoehorned into one corner and an even smaller recess containing a curtained lavatory and basin into another. Margie was familiar with small rooms: her bedroom at home, most of her friends' bedrooms, the cell-like, but to her wonderful, rooms that she'd seen at university halls of residence on open day visits. What all these rooms had in common was that they were modest, if not downright Spartan. This room, despite its midget dimensions, could only be described as luxurious. The floor was carpeted in thick cream-coloured wool. The bedclothes were also cream, the quilt cover embossed with gold. The walls were painted cream and gold.

The shower fittings were gilt. There was a mat in front of the shower cubicle made of fine linen, and another beside the bed. A tall cupboard had been set into the wall. It was decorated with a gold filigree pattern.

"Take off your clothes," Mrs Ali said.

Margie shrank away from her, clutching the rucksack.

"Give me that and take off your clothes," Mrs Ali said again, stretching out her blood-red-taloned hand. "Be quick, girl, I don't have all day."

"But why?" Margie tried not to let the panic creep into her voice. "Why do you want me to get undressed?"

Mrs Ali barked a short laugh.

"Oh, don't worry, I don't have the hots for you," she said. "I just want you to take a shower. Take your clothes off and I'll leave you to it. I'll come back in half an hour. You'll find toiletries in the shower cubicle and clothes and make-up in the closet."

"All right, I'll have a shower if that's what you want. But I'll take my clothes off and shower after you've gone."

The flick of the wrist was so rapid that she didn't see it coming. The blow to the side of her head took her completely by surprise. Despite her vow to hang on to her dignity, the pain was so unexpected that it made her cry. She turned her head away, weeping silently.

Mrs Ali folded her arms. Her expression was bland, as if she'd just given an employee a mild reprimand for some transgression.

"Stop that. Now." She said. "You're no use to me with red eyes. And think yourself lucky that you'd be useless with a bruised face, too. Otherwise I might have taught you a harder lesson. Now, give me the bag and get undressed. There's a dressing-gown on the back of the door if you insist on being prudish, but if I were you I'd save all that for the client. You haven't got anything I haven't seen before."

She reached behind her and grabbed a flimsy garment from the gold hook on the door.

"Here," she said, throwing it at Margie. It fell to the floor. As Margie bent to retrieve it, she removed her cellphone from her pocket and tried to push it under the bed.

"I'll take that, too," said Mrs Ali grimly. "And any more tricks like that, my lady, and you'll wonder what hit you." She grabbed the phone from Margie's hand and checked that it was switched off. She shoved it into the rucksack, which she'd claimed when Margie dived for the floor.

"Now your clothes," she said. She watched impassively as Margie stripped to her pants. "Those, too," she said. She produced a plastic bag and held it out. "Drop them in there. And the rest of your clothes. Thank you. Now wash yourself and your hair thoroughly. Use the gels and lotions that you'll find in the shower. Make sure you spray yourself well with the perfume. And dress in the clothes in the closet. You can put on some make-up if you like, or I'll do it for you. I'll want to inspect it if you do it." She looked at her watch. "You have twenty-five minutes. Then I'll be back. Make sure you use the time well."

Holding the rucksack and the plastic bag in one hand, she unlocked the door and disappeared through it, locking it firmly from the corridor side.

Margie's instinct was to hurl herself at the door and bang on it, crying for help; but she knew she was incarcerated deep within the hotel. To draw attention to herself would probably be futile and would certainly be dangerous. She still didn't know what a 'private hotel' was: it might be that all the people staying there were connected in some way.

She needed to think logically. She felt very weak. She sat on the bed for a couple of minutes and let the tears come. Her mouth felt dry. Standing up, she pushed back the curtain that concealed the toilet and basin. There was a plastic cup standing on the basin, containing a toothbrush and toothpaste. She emptied them out and filled the cup with water, draining it in a few gulps.

Despite her intense fear, she felt drowsy. She wanted to lie down on the bed and sleep. She knew that to do so would be foolish: she could have no doubt now that Mrs Ali would punish her for the slightest disobedience. For the moment, she'd have to go along with Mrs Ali's instructions. If she followed them carefully and stayed vigilant, she'd be bound to find an opportunity to escape. She cheered herself with the thought. She didn't allow herself to think of what might happen to her in the meantime. Both Pedro and Mrs Ali had promised her 'work' and Mrs Ali had suggested that she was preparing her for a task of some kind. Margie knew she was naïve, but she couldn't believe that the female receptionists she'd seen had been put through this kind of initiation. But perhaps they had. Perhaps everyone who worked in this place was a kind of prisoner.

Chapter 46

LIZ POCKLINGTON HAD left her back door key in the lock. Juliet locked the door and kept the key, letting herself out of the front door and dropping the Yale latch. She walked the few hundred yards to her flat and went in briefly to pick up her car keys. She felt grubby after her day at work and the excruciating hour spent in Liz Pocklington's company and would have killed for a shower, but she knew she couldn't spare the time. Quickly she drank a glass of water from the tap and shut the door on her flat again. Another evening sacrificed: and for what? Mostly the greater glory of Tim Yates and the South Lincolnshire police force. She grinned sardonically, mocking herself as well as her male colleagues with her thoughts. She knew that if she'd merely been a member of the public she'd still be doing all in her power to try to find Margie Pocklington. Was Margie's disappearance linked to Ayesha Verma's? Although Juliet couldn't see the connection, she felt convinced there must be one. Only once before had two apparently unrelated teenage girls disappeared from the Spalding area in the space of the same week and, although unaware of it, they'd turned out to be sisters. It was impossible that Margie and Ayesha were blood relations, but she still believed that if she could discover something they had in common, she'd be well on the way to finding them. That would make Tim Yates and his expedition to India to pin an honour killing on a strangely co-operative witness look pretty silly, she reflected with grim satisfaction. This time she didn't feel the need to beat herself up for the thought.

She climbed into her car and called the station to see if Gerald Pocklington's address was on the electoral roll, but wasn't surprised to find that he was still listed as a resident of Chestnut Avenue. She started the engine. She'd had to enlist the help of the staff at the Johnson Community Hospital several times before and knew them to be friendly and helpful, but still she shuddered at the prospect of having to stay there deep into the night. She hoped she'd get some sense out of Liz Pocklington without having to sit with her interminably. Then she'd be able to manage at least a few hours' sleep. She'd have to be at the station bright and early in the morning in order to benefit from Nancy Chappell's superior wisdom. The sooner she got that out of the way, the better: she was determined to get rid of the woman before Tim's return, even before the weekend, if possible. The more she thought about it, the more she was convinced that Tim had brought Chappell to Spalding to undermine her own credibility for the DS job; he could hardly have made a clearer statement that he considered her incapable of handling the Verma case unassisted. She wondered if Katrin had told Tim how Juliet had also involved her in the case. She'd probably ask Katrin about it in the morning, although she'd have to tread carefully: it was clear that the Yates's personal relationship was under pressure at the moment.

Juliet drove out of the estate and down Commercial Road, crossing the river. The Welland cut a deep cleft through the town, bisecting it into two almost equal halves. To Juliet it had always had a mysterious, almost magical quality: a primeval feature of the landscape, for centuries it had played a starring role in the economic and social life of the town. Spalding had once been a busy port, and within living memory sea-going ships had navigated the river, delivering grain to be processed into animal cake at Birch's warehouse and transporting sheep from the Spalding markets to Northern Europe. The higgledy-piggledy row of colourfully-washed eighteenth-century cottages that lined Commercial Road at its eastern end had originally been built for the families of ships' captains and their sailors. The river estuary had silted up now and there were more efficient ways of transporting goods and livestock, so the seafarers were long gone. Their descendants had either left for other ports or been assimilated locally as shopkeepers and farm labourers. Juliet wondered how well the good burghers of Spalding and the yeoman farmers who occupied its hinterland had co-existed with their more exotic seafaring neighbours. Had they welcomed them into their community, or looked at them askance and forced them to maintain their own, separate, society? She supposed that reactions would have varied, just as the townspeople still differed in their attitude to incomers today. It would be interesting to know what kind of reception the Vermas had received from their neighbours and work colleagues when they'd first arrived.

Glancing across at the river, she saw a figure walking along the bank. It was a slightly-built man of medium height, dressed in dark clothes. He was carrying something wrapped in a plastic bag. The street lights were dim in this part of the town and she couldn't see his face, but it struck her that there was something familiar about him. The man glanced around him furtively and, delving into the bag, drew out an armful of what looked like rags and transferred them to a carrier bag. He plucked a piece of something white from the rubble path and stuffed it into the bag. Then he raised his arm and hurled the bag as forcefully as he could into the river. Juliet saw that this cost him some effort, as if his arm was injured. She slowed down the car, intending to get out and confront him, but he disappeared into one of the shadowy alleyways that led away from the bank. She knew that she could spend a long time searching for him there fruitlessly: if he knew the area well, he'd be able to escape into another part of the town without encountering her. She decided to forget it: the river bank wasn't a good place to be on her own after dark: she'd have to call for back-up if she wanted to proceed, and she didn't have sufficient reason to tie up police resources in such a way. Fly-tipping in the river was banned, but people did it all the time: catching a litter pest was hardly her priority at present. She stepped on the accelerator again, but filed the incident away in her mind.

When she arrived at the hospital she walked straight into a ruckus. A tall, very tidy-looking man with thick greying black hair and square black-framed spectacles was standing in the foyer, arguing with Giash Chakrabati. For the hour, he was incongruously dressed in a business suit and immaculate white shirt. The night porter was hovering, his expression belligerent.

"I demand to see my wife," the man was saying. "I insist on talking to the drunken bitch myself."

"I'm afraid that's not . . ." Giash began. The night porter interrupted him.

"Look, mate," he said, addressing the man. "She don't want to see you and she ain't in a fit state in any case. End of. Now either you oppit or I'll make you."

Juliet met Giash's eye. She couldn't help smiling. Giash raised both his eyes to the ceiling, but he was grinning, too.

"Thank you, Mr . . ."

"Barry", supplied the porter. "Just Barry'll do."

"Thanks, Barry, it's good of you to get involved, but we'll deal with this."

"Suit yourselves," said Barry sulkily, "But just make sure that 'e shuts it. There's people ill in 'ere. They don't want waking up. I'll be just round the corner if you need me." He indicated a small enclosed kiosk opposite the reception desk and walked off towards it.

Giash turned back to the man.

"He's absolutely right," he said. "If you cause a disturbance here, we'll have to arrest you."

The man glared at Giash, clearly seething, though when he spoke again he'd lowered his voice.

"I only want to try to find out where my daughter is," he muttered furiously. "That bitch was the last person to see her. I need to get through to her fuckwit brain, find out what she knows."

Gerald Arsehole, thought Juliet. Aloud she said:

"Mr Pocklington? I'm DC Armstrong. I'm in charge of the enquiry into your daughter's disappearance. Would you like to come and sit down?"

She indicated the row of chairs that faced the reception desk. Reluctantly, he chose one and sat on it.

"First of all, how did you know your wife was here?"

"I rang that childminder that Margie's been working for. She told me that Margie had disappeared and she'd involved the police. She said you were going to see her mother. I decided to go round myself, see what was going on, but there was no-one there. Mrs Lewis next door told me she'd seen two cops carting the silly cow off in a police car; that they'd only just gone. She said she'd heard the word 'hospital' mentioned. If that cow has hurt Margie in one of her drunken binges, I'll . . ."

"Mr Pocklington, we have no reason to believe that your wife has done any harm to your daughter."

"No? Where is she, then?"

"That's what we're hoping your wife can help us to find out. And you, as well, sir, now that you're here."

"I don't see how I can help. And stop calling her my wife," he replied, gritting his teeth furiously. "But since 'I'm here', as you say," - he wiggled his fingers to indicate invisible apostrophes - "I don't mind assisting."

"That's very good of you, sir," said Juliet smoothly. She needed the man's co-operation, but what a prat! As if he were doing her a favour by helping to find his own daughter! She wasn't surprised that Liz Pocklington was an emotional and physical wreck. What was more astonishing that she obviously couldn't function without him. Had their relationship been an abusive one? There was an even darker thought lurking in the back of Juliet's mind. What if there was a grain of truth - or more - in his suspicion that Liz Pocklington was mixed up in her daughter's disappearance?

Chapter 47

I'M IN THE kitchen giving Sophia her breakfast when Nancy Chappell appears. Sophia holds out her arms, then looks affronted, probably because Nancy is not Tim. Nancy shoots her a quick glance and looks away. It's clear there'll be no love lost between them on either side. Nancy is wearing the same clothes that she had on yesterday. The only difference in her appearance is that her make-up is slightly more subtle, if that's the correct word for when you exchange plum-ebony lips for scarlet ones.

"Good morning, Nancy. Did you sleep well?"

"Not bad. Tim gone, 'as 'e?"

"Yes. He left before six."

"I fought I 'eard 'im."

"I'm sorry if he woke you."

"That's all right. I was already awake. I don't sleep well in strange places."

I'm embarrassed and search her face for evidence that she means her words to convey more than their surface meaning, but can find none. I don't think she can have overheard our conversation. She's scrabbling disconsolately in the workman's knapsack that she carries. She roots to the bottom of it and scoops something out.

"Fank God for that. I fought I'd lost me fags." She extracts a cigarette from the packet.

"Got any matches?" she asks. She notices the look of horror

on my face. "Don't worry, I'll go outside with it. I wouldn't smoke in front of the kid."

"There are some boxes of matches in that tin by the hob," I say. "Help yourself. I'll get you something for breakfast while you're outside. Toast do you?"

She pulls a face.

"Not for me, fank you. Never touch breakfast. I'll 'ave a cuppa black coffee, if that's all right."

"Of course. Do you want me to bring it out to you?"

"That's good of yer, but you and me probably have a few fings to talk about, don't we, before we go to the office? I presume you still want me to come with you to see those two girls today."

"Yes, please. But it might not be easy to talk while Sophia's here. And I don't know how much she understands."

Nancy stares at Sophia as if she is a small wild animal.

"Yeah," she says. "Whatever. Pr'aps when I've 'ad me coffee I'll go to the station to meet Miss Goody Two Shoes, and you could come on later? Is it far to walk?"

I bristle.

"Look, I'm sorry if she was a bit rude to you yesterday, but she's had a lot on her plate lately. And fine if you want to walk to the station. It'll take you between twenty and twenty-five minutes. Don't let me keep you. I'll tell you how to get there."

"Hey, steady on!" She places a plum-rimmed hand lightly on my arm. "No need to bite me 'ead off! As I said yesterday, I sympafise with 'er. I know what it's like to 'ave an overbearing male boss. I'd 'ave been furious, too, if someone like me 'ad turned up on my patch."

I laugh at the mention of Derry, before I realise she's also referring to Tim. I can't be bothered to defend him.

"I must admit Tim's been behaving strangely just lately," I say, bending down to unfasten the safety straps of Sophia's high chair so that I don't have to look Nancy in the eye. I lift Sophia out and put her down on the floor. It's now or never, I think. I take a deep breath. "I don't suppose you know where he went the night before last, do you?"

I'm still not looking at her. There's a prolonged silence. Eventually I feel compelled to squint sideways at Nancy. I see she's more profoundly distressed than such a question would normally merit.

"Nancy? Have I upset you?"

She rubs her nose vigorously with the heel of her hand.

"No, it's not you. It's me, being silly, probably."

"Are you going to tell me what's wrong?"

"Look, if I tell you, you'll have to take into account that I've got a vivid imagination. I'm probably imagining things 'ere, too. DI Yates wasn't well when 'e came to see DI 'acker, in any case. That may 'ave somefing to do with it."

"Something to do with what?"

"It's nofing, really, just a very trivial fing. But we saw a woman at King's Cross yesterday and I fought 'e was determined to avoid 'er. As if seeing 'er would embarrass 'im in front of me. I 'ad the feeling 'e'd been wiv 'er recently. And I don't like cheating men. That's all." She shrugged. "I 'ave no right to say this to you. Remember that."

"You have every right. I asked you about it. As you say, you may be jumping to conclusions. Can you remember the woman's name?"

"No."

"Really?" She can see that I don't believe her.

"Really. I was just trying to take it all in. Honestly. I can remember what 'e said she did, though. 'E said she was a SOCO."

I pause for a few moments. I'm determined to keep calm.

"I think her name might have been Gardner. Patricia Gardner."

"That sounds about right, but I don't fink that's the exact name 'e called 'er."

"Patti," I supply. "Everyone calls her Patti. Is that the name he gave you?"

Nancy nods miserably and looks down at her Doc Martens.

Chapter 48

THE SMALL MAN was at King's Cross again. He'd stumbled off the early train wearily, clutching in his hand a copy of the Metro that he'd picked up at Peterborough station. He'd managed to elude the staff by moving between the platform, the toilets and the waiting rooms, but it hadn't been a restful way of spending the night and his damaged ribs and knee were aching. Nevertheless, he'd been quite pleased with the previous evening's efforts, congratulating himself on a job well done. Despite the lack of sleep, his mood had been too buoyant to be deflated by his various injuries. Until, that was, he'd begun to work his way through the newspaper and spotted a photograph of the girl on one of the inside pages. Ayesha Verma. So that was her name – if indeed it was the same one. The photograph was blurred, made fuzzy by the cheap newsprint, and for a few moments he scrutinised it and managed to convince himself that the picture was of some other girl. Then he read the short paragraph giving details of the girl's disappearance and knew there could be no mistake.

The policewoman who'd spoken to the reporter was named as DC Juliet Armstrong. He remembered her. He remembered her boss, too. Curious that the cop's face seemed to keep popping up all over the place these days, although the small man knew he had the febrile imagination of the haunted and his sight wasn't what it used to be. Yates, that was the name. A country copper: unlikely to have been let loose in the city.

Still, it was a good thing the Khans had said to avoid Spalding from now on. He doubted if the cops would remember him, but you never knew. Coppers' memories were long when they had unfinished business on their books.

But back to the girl. He felt sorry for her, if not for her family. They were just a bunch of bigots who'd deserved to lose her: if they'd left her alone, she'd never have bumped into him. He wasn't ashamed of having helped her; she'd asked him to, after all. The problem was that Moura had a granite will and no compunction about fitting subject to client. He'd tried to say it was harsh to give her to the sadistic bloody Arab kids, but Moura pointed out that she fitted the profile exactly. End of, as Jas always said when Moura had made a decision. He gave himself a little shake: he mustn't lose his grip. He had no reason to feel remorse and, besides, he hadn't been paid yet. Jas kept doling out the money in dribs and drabs, but only for expenses: yesterday he'd barely given him enough on top of his rail fare to buy a sandwich (he'd resisted the temptation to spend the money on this) and hot drinks. Fingers crossed that the girl would find favour: then he would get Jas's payment and perhaps even a bonus from the Arabs as well.

Passing through the barrier, he thought of the other girl and how he'd met her there. A bit of a madam she'd turned out to be: less submissive than the first one. He wished Moura joy of her, although he knew it wouldn't take long to mould her. He wondered which client she was destined for. Someone he didn't know, probably. She was so skinny she looked more like a boy than a girl: the sort of boy he liked himself, as a matter of fact. Definitely not one for the Arabs. The news still hadn't broken about her; the cops were taking their time, that was for sure.

He wondered why Jas had been so keen on faking the drowning. They hadn't bothered to lay a false trail for the Indian girl and her disappearance had been much better reported. He supposed it was because the police were likely to assume that her family was behind it: she'd told him she was unhappy because they had a husband lined up for her. There was an expression for it, wasn't there, when the relatives did away with them for disobeying? Revenge killing, or some such. No, 'honour killing', that was it. Strange term. 'Rooted in dishonour' was more like it. Now how had that popped into his head? He must have read it somewhere. He shook himself again, an old dog sprucing up its fur. No wonder he felt muzzy in the head after all he had suffered the last few days. What he really needed was a good stiff drink. He drew a handful of coins from his pocket and counted them. He congratulated himself again on not having bought that sandwich.

Chapter 49

JULIET JERKED AWAKE from an exhausted doze and tried to focus her swimming eyes on the woman who lay prone in the bed next to her chair. After vomiting several more times during the early hours of the morning, Liz Pocklington had lapsed into a leaden, stertorous sleep from which Juliet had been advised by the duty doctor not to rouse her until she woke naturally. She was still snoring now, but had shifted her position in the bed. Juliet hoped this was a sign that Liz was gradually waking up. She peered at the clock above the bed and saw that it was almost 7 am. Fuck, she thought to herself, there's no way I'm going to get into the station before Nancy Chappell arrives there this morning. She thought about giving Nancy a call, then decided against it. It wasn't her job to run around after an 'assistant' she hadn't asked for.

She eased herself into a more upright position, wincing as some bone in her back clicked rebelliously. She wondered how Giash was coping with Gerald Arsehole. She and the doctor had barred him from entering the side-ward where Liz was being treated and he'd announced belligerently that he'd be waiting outside, demanding to be told as soon as she woke up.

Juliet stood up slowly and helped herself to a plastic cup of water from the water dispenser. She walked down the short corridor from the ward to the waiting area and peered cautiously round the wall. Giash was alone, seated in the waiting area surrounded by empty banquettes. He looked tired but much more alert than Juliet felt. He grinned at her encouragingly.

"Where's Mr Pocklington?"

"He went home around 3 am. Says he'll be back. That's why I'm still here. I told Verity to try to get a few hours' sleep. She called a taxi to take her home."

"Good. Do you know when he's coming back?"

"He wants us to call him when she wakes up. He's left his mobile number."

"She doesn't have to speak to him, but we do. We need to ask him the same questions we ask her, even if Margie was living with her mother."

"Yes, I know. Do you want me to call him? He's probably getting up by now, if he intends to go to work."

"No. We'll wait until she's awake first. Unless she wants to see him, we'll question him at the station. If they discharge her, she can come to the station, too, but we can make sure they don't meet."

"OK. Do you think there's any chance of getting a cup of tea here?"

"I doubt if the café's open yet, but there's probably a nurses' canteen. The day shift should be coming in any minute. You could ask one of them."

The duty doctor appeared from the same direction that Juliet had come.

"DC Armstrong? Could I have a word?"

"Of course."

Juliet followed him into a small ante-room.

"Mrs Pocklington's beginning to stir now. She'll probably be properly awake in half an hour or so. I think we should keep her in for observation, at least until this afternoon. I'm going off duty now and I'll pass care of her to a colleague, but here's my card if you need to get in touch."

"Thank you. Is it all right to ask her some questions when she comes round?"

"It should be safe enough, but you may not get much sense out of her. She'll have a thumping headache."

"But it's ok to try?"

"Certainly."

Juliet returned to the waiting area in time to see Giash being presented with a mug of tea and a plate of biscuits by a pretty nurse aged about twenty. The nurse had disappeared through the swing doors before Juliet could attract her attention.

"I see you're exercising your charm, as usual. You could have got one for me." Giash looked sheepish. "She's got to stay here for the time being," Juliet continued. "So if you wouldn't mind calling Gerald Pocklington and asking him to go to the station, I'll get someone there to interview him. I'm going to have to stay here."

"Sure thing. Who should I tell him to ask for?"

"Good question." Juliet frowned. She knew that Andy and Ricky were going to be out somewhere together that morning – something to do with the land dispute that Andy was dealing with. In any case, she didn't want to hand over part of the investigation to either of them at the moment: it would put her chances of the job in even more jeopardy than accepting Nancy Chappell's help. Tim would be on his way to India. That left Superintendent Thornton, but as everyone knew he hated what he called 'upwards delegation', besides which he had no detailed knowledge of the case and would be much less likely to listen to a briefing from Juliet than . . . a possible if unpalatable solution came to her. It would be the least of several evils.

Juliet sighed. "Tell him to ask for DC Chappell. I'll try to call her now. It would help if I could speak to her before Lady Jane in there wakes up, but knowing my luck her phone will be switched off."

Chapter 50

MARGIE AWOKE FROM a heavy sleep. For one innocent moment she thought she was in her bed at home,
before reality kicked in and she remembered she was being
held captive in the 'private hotel'. Panic seized her, but she
knew she must keep calm. Her head was pounding so much
she couldn't think properly. She tried to recall what had happened after Moura had made her take the shower.

She knew she'd refused the sandwich that had been brought
to her the previous evening and drunk only the water from
the stoppered bottle on the bedside table, but sleep had come
to her so suddenly and she felt so strange now that she was
convinced it had been spiked. What had happened before
that? She'd explored the room, sifted through the contents of
the wardrobe. It had contained no day clothes, only a tawdry
black dress that was slit to the waist on either side and several
sets of tarty underwear. There were also suspender belts, some
pairs of old-fashioned seamed nylons and pointed-toed black
patent shoes with spiky heels. Quickly she'd slammed shut
the wardrobe door, both outraged and afraid. If she'd ever believed she was going to be employed as one of the downstairs
receptionists, she abandoned that thought now. She grimaced
bleakly, shocked that she could have been so naïve.

She vaguely remembered drinking the water and then collapsing on to the bed, but not climbing into it. She looked
across to where the water bottle had been standing and saw

that it was no longer there. As if pushing her brain through a mirage, she dimly recollected that last night she'd put on the red silk dressing-gown which she'd found hanging on the door, the only garment she'd been provided with that could cover her, but saw that now it was draped neatly over the end of the bed. The quilt was tucked around her, but when she flung it off she noticed that she was dressed in the shiny purple and black camisole and tiny knickers that she'd found in the wardrobe. They'd disgusted her then and she could hardly believe she was wearing them. She must have reasoned that it would be better to sleep in them than naked. She looked down at the knickers and saw that the crotch was askew. There was some dried white substance and small specks of blood on the sheet; and a red mark on her thigh. Suddenly the soreness hit her.

She couldn't control the panic now. She leapt from the bed and ran to the door, shaking the handle to try to force it open. She hammered on it until her knuckles could stand the pain no longer, when she fell, sobbing, to the floor. She lay there for several minutes, her tears and mucus soaking into the carpet, its pile prickling her cheek, until the sound of a key rattling in the lock made her sit up.

Moura entered swiftly and silently, bearing a tray set out with a small china teapot and cup and saucer. She fastened the door behind her and locked it, deftly moving to the table to put down the tray. Before Margie could turn to face her, Moura had cracked her smartly across the back of the head with the flat of her hand.

"Any more of that, Madam, and you'll wonder what hit you! I warned you not to make a noise. This is your one chance, so we'd better have no repeats. And count yourself lucky that I can't afford to mark your face. Some patrons don't mind a few bruises, but yours is a bit more refined."

Margie was weeping quietly now. She shied away from Moura, who promptly moved forward so that she was still standing over her. That searing pain shot through her crotch again.

"Now, calm yourself. I want to speak to you about today's work."

"I've changed my mind. I don't want to work. I want to go. Please just let me go. I won't say a word to anyone." Even to herself she sounded childish and effete.

"Ha!" said Moura. "You made your decision when you agreed to come here with Peter."

"Who's Peter? I thought his name was Pedro."

"He may have told you that. He has more than one name. It doesn't matter to you what he's called, in any case: you won't be seeing him again. I'm going to leave you now to drink that tea. I'll be back in ten minutes. I expect to find you quiet and showered by then. You can put on the dressing-gown. I'll show you what to wear when I come back."

"I don't want the tea. How do I know what you've put in it?"

"Ha!" said Moura again. "You don't think anyone's going to make you dopey in the morning, do you? You've got work to do. Now I suggest you drink the tea, because you won't get anything else. It was a bad move not to eat your supper last night. You'll have to earn your next meal."

"Earn it? How?"

"No more questions. Just do as I say. And use the bath stuff and wear the perfume."

Moura turned around nimbly despite her bulk and left the room, locking the door quickly behind her. Margie picked herself up slowly and sat on the side of the bed. She poured a cup of tea and sipped it. When she felt a little stronger, she removed the camisole top and knickers and dropped them to the floor. As she did so, she thought she heard a slight movement on the other side of the door in the stud wall, but it lasted only a moment and she could have been mistaken. She stepped into the shower and scrubbed at her body ferociously, but still felt defiled and dirty when she emerged. Cowed into obedience, she applied the musky lotion and perfume she'd been given and wrapped herself in the fluffy towel which had been neatly folded on the towel rail, before crossing the room barefoot to the bed. Kicking the soiled underwear to one side, she slid out of the towel and donned the dressing-gown. As she did so she heard the noise again, louder this time. It was as if someone were gasping for air. She took the few steps to the internal door and scrutinised it. Like the rest of the woodwork in the room, it was ornately decorated, which must have been why she hadn't noticed it before. A small round spy-hole had been set into one of the gilded panels.

"Fuck off!" she shouted at it. "Whoever you are, fuck off, you filthy pervert!"

There was no reply. Once again she was enveloped in perfect silence.

Chapter 51

NANCY CHAPPELL'S SUSPICIONS about Tim hang like a dead weight at the back of my mind. I'm miserable and it slows me down. Dropping off Sophia at Mrs Sims' takes longer than on the previous days, because she wants to know about what's being done to find Margie. I tell her that I know very little about the police investigation, but she obviously doesn't believe me. She's upset about Margie and I feel sorry for her. There's someone else helping her today, a woman in her twenties who tries to take Sophia from me. Sophia shrinks away from her. The little boy called Thomas is subdued, too. Either they have already both come to love Margie, or they sense that something is wrong.

Eventually I manage to get away. I'm a bit late reaching the office, but I'm not expecting Fiona Vickers to turn up with her two protégées until around 10.00 am. As I let myself into the building, I see the light's on in the office. It's strange, as I'm sure I didn't switch it on at all yesterday. I open the office door cautiously, ready to shout to the traffic team if there's an intruder, and find Janey sitting at her desk staring into her computer. Her posture is oddly hunched. She looks diminished, somehow.

"Hello! This is a surprise. I thought you weren't coming back until next week."

"I wasn't. Things didn't go according to plan," she says tautly.

"Oh, I'm sorry," I say.

"Well, something's happened, but I just don't want to talk about it. No point in wasting a day's holiday now that I've come home again."

"I won't ask, then." I look at my watch. "I'm afraid I have some visitors coming here soon."

"I can wait in Reception upstairs if I'm in the way," she says huffily.

"Of course you're not in the way. It's lovely to see you. I was thinking more that they might disturb you."

"Sorry, Katrin, I'm not myself, as you can see. I'm not doing anything except checking my e-mails, and I don't need to concentrate very hard to do that. Besides, we're both going to have to get used to working with each other's visitors around. There's no proper interview room here. I did point it out when they were redesigning the building."

"I'm sure we'll cope."

"Who are the visitors? Anyone I know?"

"Not sure if you know Fiona Vickers? She works with women at risk in Peterborough."

"Yes, I do know her," Janey says slowly. "Who else is coming?"

"Two of the women she's been helping. I'm trying to find out more about forced and arranged marriages and so-called honour killings."

"Hefty subjects! Nothing like pitching yourself straight in when you come back to work, is there? Sounds as if you're working on an interesting case."

I see a glimmer of Janey's usual wry humour and am relieved.

"You probably know about it. I'm helping Juliet Armstrong

by doing some background research after the disappearance of an Indian girl. Ayesha Verma. I think she went missing before you left for your holiday."

"Yes, she did. Poor kid. I hope you're wrong about the honour killing. But isn't it Tim's case?"

"Partly. Tim's gone to India to interview the girl's fiancé. He's really grabbed by the honour killing idea. Juliet's asked me to look at it from a different angle, see if the circumstances really fit the pattern. And there's been another development which hasn't been made public yet. Another girl has disappeared now. I know her, as a matter of fact: she works for Sophia's childminder."

"Is she Indian, too?"

"No. A local girl. Parents are separated."

"If the two cases are linked, it seems unlikely that Ayesha Verma was an honour killing victim."

"I agree. But we don't know yet if the other girl – her name's Margie Pocklington – has disappeared, or is just visiting someone or has run away. Her home life is pretty bleak, by all accounts."

"You don't actually know that Ayesha Verma is dead, do you?"

"No. But finding out what happened to both of them is Juliet's job. And Tim's. Tim's asked a DC from the Met who's an expert in honour killings to help Juliet."

"I bet that's gone down well!"

"You've got it in one. Which reminds me, the DC in question's offered to come to this meeting. I don't know what's happened to her. She stayed with us last night. She left for the station first thing but she should have been here by now. I'll give her a call."

"Tim been generous with your hospitality again, has he? You go ahead. I'm going to put the kettle on. It looks as if we're going to be having a tea party very shortly."

"Thanks!" I ignore the jibe at Tim. I really can't be bothered to defend him at the moment, and, like Janey, I seem to have developed some no-go areas. I look at Janey as she gets up. She's always been slender, but now she's positively gaunt. I wonder what can have happened to upset her so much. It's bound to be something to do with Gwillim – his father kicking up about custody again, perhaps. I know there's no point in pressing Janey about it until she's ready to tell me.

I can't get a reply from Nancy Chappell's mobile. I try calling Juliet's extension at the station, but there's no reply from that, either.

Chapter 52

JULIET WAS FEELING better after her call to Nancy Chappell. She found it hard to be annoyed with anyone for any length of time and she was aware that she'd been a bit unjust to Nancy. It wasn't her fault that Tim had involved her in the case. Nancy had seemed to be pleased to be asked to interview Gerald Pocklington. She mentioned that she'd offered to sit in on Katrin's meeting with the two women from the refuge, but she didn't think it would be a big deal if she wasn't there. She'd let Katrin know.

The day staff were on duty at the hospital now. Juliet asked a staff nurse to show her to a bathroom where she could freshen up. After she'd washed and had some toast and tea she was able to grab back a bit of energy.

Giash had already left the hospital. They'd agreed that on balance it would be better if he picked up Gerald Pocklington from the house he was living in in Bourne and drove him to the station to be interviewed. Juliet wanted to keep him away from his ex-wife and she was equally keen to get a proper statement from him about the last time he'd seen his daughter.

Juliet returned to Liz's bedside to find her stirring. The pretty nurse who'd supplied Giash with tea was bending over her, wiping her face with a damp flannel. She looked round at Juliet and wrinkled her nose.

"She's going to need a shower when she's up to it. She stinks."

"I know. I'm sorry."

"It's not your fault! And you've had to put up with it all night. I'll bring some lemon barley for her, see if she can keep it down. Probably best not to try her on tea just yet."

"Thanks."

Juliet sat down in the chair in which she'd spent the night. Liz's headrest had been raised high to stop her choking on vomit if she'd thrown up while no-one was with her, so Juliet was looking up at her when she opened her eyes. They quivered for a moment and closed again. Juliet thought she glimpsed a flicker of recognition, that Liz had now screwed them shut more tightly than someone behaving involuntarily.

"Liz," she said firmly. "Liz, it's DC Armstrong. You need to try to wake up now."

Liz Pocklington groaned theatrically. She pushed rank hair away from her face and sat up.

"God, I feel terrible," she said. "What am I doing here?"

"You're in hospital. I don't know how much you remember about last night, but you were dangerously drunk."

"I expect you're right." She gave a harsh laugh. "Why do you care, though? Why did you bother about me?"

"Quite frankly, I didn't. You can leave here and get rat-arsed again straight away for all I care. But before you do, I need to speak to you about your daughter. I came to see you last night because she's been reported missing."

"Margie?"

"Yes, Margie. Do you have other daughters?"

"No. But what's happened to her? Where is she?"

"That's the point. We don't know. We think she's been missing for twenty-four hours now. When did you last see her? Did she say she was going anywhere – to visit friends, perhaps?"

"No." Liz frowned. "She spends most of her time with that child-minding cow. She puts ideas into Margie's head. Have you tried her?"

"It was Mrs Sims who reported her missing. Can you think back to the day before yesterday? We know that Margie was working with Mrs Sims during the day. Did you see her in the evening?"

"Yes, I think so. She came in late. I don't know where she'd been. She didn't say."

"What do you mean by 'late'?"

"Not very late. The middle of the evening. Late enough for her to have been somewhere else after the nursery closed. But then again, it might have been the night before. Can I have something to drink? I've got a splitting headache." Liz fell back against the pillows and closed her eyes again.

Juliet was losing patience.

"Liz, can you just pull yourself together for a few seconds? Your daughter is missing, probably in danger. Can you try to think of anything at all that might help us to find her?"

Liz Pocklington began to cry. Her performance was noisy and unconvincing. The nurse who'd been there earlier entered the room with a jug of water and a squash bottle. A doctor followed close on her heels.

"You'd better leave it for now," he said to Juliet. He was brisker and less sympathetic than the night doctor had been.

"She'll recover more quickly if you don't harass her. And we need to get more fluids into her now."

Juliet sighed.

"That's fine," she said. "I'll come back later. I don't think there's any use in my staying here longer. I'd be grateful if you'd let me know if you decide to discharge her."

Chapter 53

NANCY HAD HAD to ring the buzzer in order to be admitted to the police station. The desk sergeant had let her in when she'd explained who she was, but didn't know where she was supposed to be going. He called Superintendent Thornton, who came bustling down the stairs to greet Nancy and at the same time show her who was the boss. She saw him react to her clothing and glared ferociously up at him.

"Ah, Derry Hacker's lady! I'm sorry I didn't have time to talk to you much yesterday. No more time today, I'm afraid, but I'll show you where DC Armstrong sits. I'm sure she'll be here shortly. An excellent idea of DI Yates, to ask you to help her. I'm sure you know more about this kind of thing than she does."

Nancy valiantly controlled her fury at the Superintendent's double patronage of herself and Juliet and silently allowed herself to be led up the stairs to the work area outside his office.

"None of the DCs appears to be here at the moment," the Superintendent continued, looking at the floor beneath the desk units as if he might spot someone crouching there, "but I'm sure they'll arrive soon. There's a kitchen through there, if you'd like to make yourself some coffee. A cup of tea for me wouldn't go amiss, either." He gave her a more engaging smile.

"You mean you'd like me to make you some tea?" said Nancy incredulously.

"Well, yes, if it isn't too much trouble, and if you have nothing else to do at the moment." He looked a little abashed, but she recognised the sting in the tail of his last comment. She shrugged inwardly. It wasn't her office, after all. You wouldn't catch her making tea for Derry Hacker.

"All right, then. But I warn you, tea isn't my strong point. People 'ave ended up in 'ospital after drinking my tea."

"Really? Well, I'm sure that won't happen this time." The Superintendent was clearly made of stronger stuff than she'd given him credit for. "My office is just there. Don't bother to knock when you bring it in. And thank you."

He retreated into his office and closed the door. Nancy went to the kitchen and made a half-hearted attempt at locating some clean mugs. She saw there was a dishwasher, but no-one had bothered to stack it the previous evening. Cups and plates that had fallen victim to various stages of fungoid invasion were littered around. In the interests of hygiene, Nancy decided to load the dishwasher. The Superintendent would have to wait for his tea.

She was still tidying up when the call from Juliet came. She was delighted when Juliet asked her to help with Gerald Pocklington, partly because she'd expected nothing but hostility from that quarter and recognised that Juliet had extended an olive branch. She'd intended to call Katrin and explain she could no longer join her, but almost that instant Giash Chakrabati had arrived with the man she'd been asked to interview.

"DC Chappell? Superintendent Thornton said I'd find you in here. This is Mr Gerald Pocklington. DC Armstrong said she'd ask you to take a statement from him."

"She did, and I agreed. I'd expected you to take a bit longer to get here, that's all."

"I saw Mr Pocklington in the hospital car park," said Giash blandly. He didn't know how much Juliet had told Nancy about the events of the previous night. "I can wait in the interview room with him if you're not ready to see him yet."

"No, that's fine," said Nancy. "If you'd just show me the way, we can get started. I'd like you to stay for the interview as well, if you can. Good morning, sir," she added, holding out her hand. "I'm sorry about your daughter. You must be very worried, but she may turn up quite safe. It's better not to jump to conclusions just yet."

The man who was accompanying Giash emerged from behind him. He registered such disapproval when he saw her that it was all she could do not to burst into giggles. Gingerly, he shook hands with her.

"Yes, well my daughter and I aren't very close. But naturally I'm upset," he said stiffly. Nancy took an immediate dislike to him. The guy was a cold-blooded reptile.

"Would you like to come this way, sir?" said Giash. Gerald Pocklington walked out of the kitchen smartly, as if it were contaminated. "I can stay for half an hour," Giash added to Nancy over his shoulder. "I'll need some time to take him back to his car and I'll have to go and meet my partner then. She picked up Mrs Pocklington with me last night, but she's been trying to get a few hours' sleep."

"'alf an hour should be fine," said Nancy. "Fanks."

"We should probably offer him some tea. And I could use a cup myself."

"Don't you start! I've put the dishwasher on. It won't have

finished its cycle until he's gone. If you really need to give him a drink, you'll 'ave to send out for some."

"I'll get some polystyrene cups from the canteen," said Giash. "We could fetch the tea from there as well, but theirs tastes like drains. Don't worry, I'll make it."

"Fanks," said Nancy again. "You might like to take one to the Superintendent, as well."

A few minutes later they had settled in the interview room, fortified with polystyrene cups of hot tea. Unexpectedly, Gerald Pocklington had accepted his gratefully and was gulping it down as if he'd spent the night in the desert.

"Are you ready to start now, sir?" said Nancy. "We won't be taping you, as you're not a suspect, but PC Chakrabati will take notes."

Gerald Pocklington nodded sternly. He looked across at Giash, as if for reassurance. Nancy saw that she made him feel very uncomfortable. It didn't worry her.

"I understand that you're estranged from your wife, and that your daughter lives with her mother?"

"That's correct."

"How long have you and your wife been separated?"

"I really don't see that . . ."

"Please, Mr Pocklin'ton, your personal life is of no interest to me. I'm just tryin' to build up a picture of your daughter's background, try to guess what makes 'er tick. You can only 'elp 'er by telling me what I want to know wivout makin' a fuss."

Gerald Pocklington swallowed and straightened his tie.

"I finally left about three months ago, but we'd pretty much been living separate lives for a long time before that."

"What do you mean by 'separate lives'?"

"I . . . I wasn't there all of the time."

"Where were you when you weren't there?"

"Look, I . . ."

"Mr Pocklin'ton, the more time you waste, the less likely we are to find your daughter alive."

"I resent being threatened."

"I'm not freatening you - I'm just stating a fact. Answer the question, please."

"I've been seeing someone else. I stayed with her sometimes while I was still living with my wife." He had interlocked the fingers of both hands and was staring down at them now.

"Ok. And 'ow did your daughter react to that?"

"She was . . . upset. Of course, she only heard her mother's side - though anyone could see what her mother had become."

"What 'ad 'er mother become?"

"A slatternly drunken lush." He would have shouted the words if he hadn't been speaking through gritted teeth.

"Did your wife's . . . drink problem begin before or after you met your new friend?"

"She would say that I triggered her alcoholism. My own memory is a little more accurate."

"What about Margie? What did she fink?"

"I didn't ask her, not about the drinking, anyway. She and I were close when she was a child, but we've grown apart since then. I believe she took her mother's side, though the drinking probably upset her, or at least the results of it did. She's quite fastidious: I don't think she enjoys living in a tip. But quite honestly, I think she's been more worried about going to university than anything else."

"Did she choose to live with her mother after you'd gone?"

"Yes, I suppose so. She could hardly have found the money to set up on her own."

"No. But what I meant was, did you offer her the chance of coming to live with you?"

"I . . . No."

"Why not?"

"Rosie – my partner – wouldn't have wanted it. And Margie wouldn't have wanted to live with Rosie, in any case."

"I see." Nancy said nothing more for a long moment. Gerald Pocklington darted the odd glance at her, but when she tried to meet his eye he looked down at his hands again. He was clearly disconcerted by the silence. He finally felt compelled to rush in to end it.

"Look, I'm not proud of being part of a broken family, but it takes more than one person to destroy a marriage."

"I'm sure it does. Coming back to Margie, you say she was worried she wouldn't be able to go to university. Was this because the marriage had broken down?"

"Yes. I'd promised to give her some financial support, but I'm a little . . . a little strapped for cash now. And Rosie takes a different view about giving her money. I suppose it wasn't very fair on Margie, when she'd thought she could rely on me. But circumstances change."

"Indeed. When did you last see Margie?"

Nancy shot the question at him staccato-fashion. It seemed to throw him, though he must have been expecting it.

"I'm trying to think. I haven't seen much of her since we . . . since I left. But I've met her for a drink or a coffee once or twice. Yes, I think that was it. I met her in The Punch Bowl a couple of weeks ago. It was when I told her that there definitely wouldn't be any money for university, at least not this year."

"And you haven't seen 'er since?"

"No."

"You're sure of that?"

"Quite sure. If you must know, she stormed out of the pub in tears. I didn't try to follow her."

"Have you heard from 'er since then – by phone or email, say?"

"No. She made it crystal clear that she wanted nothing more to do with me. She called Rosie a tart, which was inexcusable."

"Did you intend to get in touch with 'er again?"

"I suppose so. Eventually, when she'd calmed down. You know what teenage girls are like."

Nancy didn't answer him. She made some notes on her pad and allowed another uncomfortable silence to dawdle through the air.

"Did your daughter have a boyfriend?"

"Not that I know of."

"Close friends? Someone she might turn to if life got difficult?"

"Again, not that I know of. She had some school friends, but she didn't bring people home. It's not surprising. It was a pigsty most of the time."

"My last question, Mr Pocklin'ton. Was your wife ever physically abusive to Margie?"

"No. What makes you ask that?"

"Not even when she was drunk?"

He shrugged.

"I suppose it's possible. I've no reason to believe Liz would have hit her."

"What about you? 'Ave you ever struck Margie in anger?"

Another unexpected question, lightning fast. Giash raised his head from his notes and observed Gerald Pocklington keenly. The man looked flushed.

"Why on earth would you think that?"

"I don't fink it, Mr Pocklington. It's just a question."

"No. No, I haven't."

"Fank you. I don't fink there's anything else we want to ask you at the moment, but please keep trying to remember anyfing that might 'elp us and give us a call if there is somefing. I'll give you DC Armstrong's telephone number, as this is 'er case really. I'm just standing in today. You'll need to keep 'er informed of your whereabouts, too. If you're planning on travelling any distance from 'ome, let 'er know."

"All right."

"I'll take you to get your car, sir," said Giash. He turned to Nancy. "I'll have to go now. I'll come back this afternoon if you need me."

Wow, Giash thought to himself as he followed Gerald Pocklington down the stairs, appearances can be deceptive! That was one of the best interviews he'd ever witnessed; and the bloke wasn't even a suspect – or was he?

Chapter 54

FIONA VICKERS IS looking a bit sleeker than when we first met. She's wearing a smart cotton pea-jacket in startlingly bright turquoise which sets off her dark hair. She sails into the office with her two charges in her wake and does a double-take when she sees Janey.

"Christ, I didn't expect to see *you* here!"

Janey laughs uneasily.

"I wondered if you'd recognise me. It's been quite a while."

"Yes," says Fiona, suddenly serious. "Five or six years. I remember the case well."

Janey ducks her head. It occurs to me that Fiona's words are carefully chosen, meant to protect Janey from something. Had Janey known her as a colleague or as a client?

"But I'm sorry," Fiona continues brightly, "I'm forgetting my manners. This is Rashida and this is Jenny."

The two young women have barely ventured inside the office. They stand awkwardly on the threshold, apart from each other.

"Do come in and sit down," I say. "I'm Katrin and this is Janey. Would you like coffee?"

"I'll make it," says Janey, getting up.

I line up our two spare chairs and pull out my swivel chair from behind my desk.

"I'll perch on the desk," says Fiona. "I don't like chairs much. And you don't want me getting in the way."

I gesture towards the chairs and they edge past me. Rashida is dramatically beautiful: she has flawless olive skin and boldly arched eyebrows. Her eyes are tawny-brown. Her thick wavy black hair has been cut short in a severe style which would be boyish if the hair weren't so luxuriant. She isn't plump but neither is she slender; her breasts are full and she's wide-hipped with a tiny waist: the classic hour-glass figure. She's dressed from head to toe in black: black trousers, black shirt, black jacket, black boots. The shirt is buttoned to her neck. She carries a massive pink tote bag, which she puts on the floor beside her when she sits down. Jenny is petite and pale. She looks under-nourished. I can't see her hair because it's entirely covered by a hijab, but her skin is very fair, her eyes a remarkable translucent blue. She's wearing a very plain long cotton dress. It's light grey and quite shapeless, too big for her so that her body seems to float around inside it without revealing any hint of definition. She could almost be limbless. She also has a large bag, made of the same dull cloth as the dress. I'm a bit surprised by her. She isn't my idea of the sort of victim I thought I'd be talking to. Fiona Vickers seems to read my thoughts.

"Jenny's not Asian," she says. "She married an Asian man. She agreed to convert to Islam."

"So it wasn't an arranged marriage?"

"It was," says Jenny sullenly. "Me Dad made me marry him. He got paid for it."

"What happened to you?"

"Me husband hit me. Not at first, but after we'd been married for a while. We were living with his Mam and Dad and his Mam started hitting me, too. She made me do all the housework and she wouldn't let me go out. I ran away when I got the chance but I daredn't go home. I know my Dad'll send me back to them. He'll have to: they'll threaten him. Tariq will kill me if he catches me now."

"If you don't mind my asking, why are you wearing the hijab?" I don't add that it seems strange that a girl who's trying to hide is wearing a dress that makes her stand out more than if she were dressed anonymously, like Rashida.

"Jenny's in therapy," Fiona says. "She has to unlearn what she's been taught. She's doing very well." She flashes Jenny a bright, encouraging smile. "It's brave of her to come and see you. She hasn't been out much since she came to us."

"I'm very grateful to you," I say to Jenny, "but I wouldn't want you to put yourself at risk for me."

"Jenny's not from round here. She's a long way from where her husband lives. And Jenny isn't her real name. When she's stronger, we'll help her find a job."

"Does that mean you won't be able to see your family again?" I say to Jenny.

"I don't want to," she scowls. "They didn't love me. They just sold me like a pet dog. I'd have been trapped if I'd had a baby."

"I almost had a baby," says Rashida quietly. Although she seems more poised and confident than Jenny, this is the first time she's spoken. I notice she has a soft Scots accent. "I was a student. My parents didn't want me to go to university, but my teachers helped me to persuade them, on condition I lived at home and went straight home after lectures. Then I travelled to France for six months to do a project. They didn't want me to go, but I kept it secret until the last moment so they couldn't stop me. I met my husband while I was there: we got married in secret. He was a Muslim, too, and he understood that it would be hard to persuade my parents to give their permission. I didn't mean to get pregnant, but it happened, and Philippe came back to England with me to explain to them. I knew my father would be furious but I didn't expect the violence. He raged and lashed out as if he'd gone mad. He said he'd arranged for me to marry the son of someone he'd met when he was visiting relatives in Pakistan and now I'd dishonoured him. He punched me so hard in the stomach that I started haemorrhaging. My brother thrashed Philippe until I thought he'd kill him. One of the neighbours called the police and Philippe got away when they came. I was taken to hospital and I lost the baby. My mother came to see me and warned me not to say anything to the police that could help them to prosecute my father or brother. My sister managed to get a note to me, warning me that my brother would kill me when I left the hospital. I was too afraid to ask the police for help, so I discharged myself during the night and got as far away as I could. I made it to a refuge in Edinburgh and they sent me to England. They said I'd be safer here."

"What happened to Philippe?"

"I suppose he went back to France. I haven't seen him since. I tried writing to him while I was in Edinburgh, but the letter was returned. He's probably too afraid to contact me. I suppose he'll get a divorce."

"Don't you think he'd like to see you again?"

She smiles sadly.

"I think he values his life more. We knew each other for less than a year. He probably regrets that he ever met me."

There is a painful silence. It is mercifully broken by Janey, who reappears bearing a tray laden with mugs of coffee.

"Well," says Fiona after everyone is clutching their coffee,

"I'm grateful to you for talking so openly to Katrin. I know it isn't easy for you. Katrin, perhaps you could tell us some details of the case you're working on now, and ask Rashida and Jenny what they think."

I'm taken aback. I hadn't expected her to suggest two-way sharing of information. I try to think rapidly. I mustn't identify anyone in the Verma case, even if Rashida and Jenny haven't heard of it. I'd be committing slander and probably jeopardising any chance of prosecution if a crime is proved to have been committed.

I describe Ayesha Verma's home life and the circumstances of her disappearance as accurately but anonymously as I can.

"So you're thinking her father might have gone after her because she wouldn't marry the cousin?" says Jenny. "It's what my Dad would do. But from what you say her Dad was proud of her. Mine just sees me as a meal ticket."

"My Dad was proud of me, too. He wanted me to be educated, just like hers. But he still turned nasty when I didn't obey him. Her Dad could be like him. I'd say it depends on her mother. And her brothers. My mother agreed with my Dad completely, and my brother was spoiling for a fight. I don't think my Dad would have done it on his own."

"This girl has no brothers, only sisters. Her father wanted her to go to university, but to get married first."

"Sounds iffy to me. What about her Mum? Under the thumb, is she?"

"I don't know," I say. "But it's good advice to find out more about her. Thank you. Can you think of anything else that might help?"

"Are they upset? Her parents, I mean."

"I think so. I haven't met them."

"Find out if they're upset or just faking. You'll know if they're faking it: they'll be more interested in getting her back to punish her than in worrying about what's happening to her. You'll be able to tell by their attitude. And talk to her sisters. They're more likely to tell the truth."

"They're only little kids."

"Even better."

They finish their coffee.

"Do you fancy a look round Spalding while we're here?" Fiona says.

"Yeah, all right," says Rashida; but Jenny hangs back. Her face is even whiter and more pinched than before, if that's possible.

"I don't think I'll come. I'm not that keen on going out," she says. "And I've no money to spend, in any case. You go if you like; I'll wait here, or in the car."

"Don't worry about it," says Fiona, "I just thought we'd make a bit of a trip out of it, that's all. It'll do another time."

"I'd like to thank you both very much," I say.

They nod and stand up. As they prepare to leave, I see that Jenny's shoulders are hunched. She'd been quite animated when she was speaking earlier, but now she looks defeated.

Fiona pauses at the door and turns to Janey. "Are you doing all right?" she asks.

"Fine, thanks, couldn't be better," Janey replies briskly. I hear a slight catch in her voice and I know that Fiona Vickers has noted it, too.

"Good," she says, her eyes still fixed on Janey. "Keep in touch. And let me know if I can do anything to help you."

"Thank you very much for bringing Jenny and Rashida," I say to her.

"That's ok. I hope it was useful."

"Very useful. I'm grateful."

"So was it?" asks Janey penetratingly, after we've heard Fiona's car start.

"Was it what?"

"Useful. Did you really find what those girls told you helpful?"

I have to think about this. At the time I'd found the conversation disappointing. I thought Jenny's and Rashida's accounts of the abuse they'd suffered cliché-ridden and too pat, as if they'd both told their stories many times before in more or less the same words. But the fear they'd shown, and the lengths to which they'd gone to avoid their families, had made a deep impression on me.

"It was useful, though not how I'd expected. I don't think I understood that kind of fear before."

"No, you live in a bit of a cosy domestic bubble most of the time, don't you?"

I know there's something horrible eating away at Janey and I don't retaliate. I'm bursting to ask her how she knows Fiona Vickers, but understand that now isn't the time.

"One thing they're right about: we need to know more about the whole family and how it interacts. I'm sure Juliet will have done some work on this, but she probably hasn't interviewed the children. I'll talk to her about it."

"You have to be careful with child interviews. You may need to find a specialist."

Chapter 55

EVENING WAS FALLING in Delhi. Tim Yates emerged from the cool but by now increasingly smelly cabin of his plane into a haze of heat. It was like standing under a hair-dryer: a blast so intense that it was hard to believe it wouldn't be switched off in a few seconds. Oppressed by their seat-weary muscles, he and the other passengers lumbered stiffly down the steps of the aircraft and hauled themselves on to the waiting shuttle bus. Its driver sped across a tarmac criss-crossed with other crazily-moving vehicles as if on a suicide mission. Tim shut his eyes and waited for the terminal or oblivion.

He arrived at the former and as if on auto-pilot pushed himself through Immigration and picked up his bag from the carousel, exerting the minimum possible expenditure of energy. He found himself in a thronging concourse, at the start of which twenty or so soberly-dressed men were waiting, intent on watching the door through which he had just emerged, each one holding up a piece of card bearing someone's name. Almost immediately he spotted the placard on which the word 'Yates' was spelt out and couldn't believe his luck. He'd had chequered experiences of meeting limousine drivers in the past and had sometimes failed to find them at all.

The driver shook his hand and took the case, leading the way rapidly through the airport to the car park. Tim was impressed by the immaculate shiny black saloon in which he shortly found himself installed. They set off immediately for the police HQ, alternately accelerating and crawling through fantastically congested streets; Tim barely took in the scenes around him as he sipped from the bottle of water with which he had been provided.

His mood was uncharacteristically morose. He had fallen into a loop of obsessive mental replay of certain events and conversations from the past few days, in each case castigating himself for his own bad behaviour. It was a practice in which he'd indulged only infrequently since his adolescence. He knew that agonising over his shortcomings was futile and sternly told himself to snap out of it. At Zayed Verma's own request, he was going to interview the 'fiancé' immediately and it was vital that he made himself concentrate.

He felt as grubby as everyone does after a long haul flight and mildly sick – a residue, perhaps, of whatever had been afflicting him earlier in the week, but more probably because the highly-spiced airline food and reheated rice had disagreed with him. Towards the end of the flight, he'd managed to change his shirt, but this lent only the bare veneer of cleanness to his appearance. He hoped that his no doubt dapper Indian colleagues wouldn't be too judgmental.

He was welcomed by Sanjay Banerjee, the detective whom he'd already talked to several times on Skype. Whatever his opinion of how Tim looked, Sanjay had greeted him with the utmost politeness and overwhelmed him with hospitality. There were certainly plenty of people to provide the latter: Tim had never seen so many ancillary employees working in a police building. The HQ seemed to be staffed with a host of men and women: not only clerks and secretaries, but people whose jobs consisted exclusively of opening doors, making tea, running errands or fetching refreshments. There was a bewildering number of faces for Tim to get used to; Sanjay Banerjee seemed to know them all.

"Isn't it very expensive, employing all these people?" Tim asked him conversationally.

"Not very expensive, no. And everyone is very proud to work." Tim recognised that this was as close to a rebuff as Indian courtesy would allow and changed the subject.

"I'm very grateful to you for negotiating this interview with Mr Verma."

Sanjay bowed. "It is an honour to help you. I hope it will help him, too."

"What is your impression of him?"

"To me he seems like a gentleman. The family is a very good one."

Evidently Tim wouldn't get very far with that line of questioning, either. Circumspectly, he concentrated on the tea which had just been brought to him. After a minute or so, he became aware that Sanjay was hovering uneasily.

"DI Yates, when you are ready, Mr Verma is here."

His anxious tone made Tim feel ashamed. He genuinely hadn't known that Verma had already arrived, but at home he'd have had no compunction about making a witness wait to be interviewed. He leapt to his feet.

"Oh, I'm sorry; I won't keep him waiting."

"No hurry, no hurry. Please, be seated again. Unless you would like to take your tea with you?"

"Yes, yes, of course I'll do that. And could Mr Verma have some tea, too?"

"That is already taken care of."

It would be, Tim thought. Superintendent Thornton would be in clover here: an endless supply of tea, made no doubt exactly to his taste, without having to press unwilling colleagues into producing it. Still, he might blench at the size of the payroll, however reasonable the cost of labour. Headcount was likely to perturb Thornton almost as much as the financial totals. Tim smiled to himself. Sanjay immediately smiled back at him, though evidently puzzled by the joke.

"Would you like to sit in on the interview?" asked Tim.

"Only if I can be of use."

Tim took that as a 'yes'.

"Thank you. I shall feel happier if you're there. Could you take me to Mr Verma now? I'll bring the tea."

"Of course. And no need, no need." Sanjay made a very slight gesture. The man who had served the tea appeared with a tray as if from nowhere. Tim was uncomfortable about being waited on like this but decided it would be unwise to protest. He walked beside Sanjay through serried rows of desks, the servant, a stocky man in his forties, close behind.

The interview room was one of a suite of apparently identical rooms, each one square and functional like the ones at the station in Spalding, but rather better furnished.

He was again surprised when Sanjay knocked on the door before entering. A tall, formally-dressed man who had been examining a poster stuck on the wall turned to face them as they went in. He held out his hand to Tim. Tim stepped forward quickly and shook it. Mr Verma had a firm grip. Tim took a step back and looked at the man as he motioned him to take a chair. He was about six feet tall and slim, but muscular, as if he worked out. He was wearing a beautifully-cut pale grey business suit and a dazzling white shirt. There was a chunky signet ring on his little finger. Tim's first impression was one of opulence, rather than ostentation. Mr Verma had rather fine features and thick jet black hair that had been clipped short but had not thinned. He looked much younger than his years: Tim would have put him at thirty-five, maybe, not much older than he was himself. Still too old for a teenage bride, but he and Ayesha wouldn't have seemed incongruous as a couple.

"Mr Verma, thank you for agreeing to see me," said Tim, as they took opposite seats at the square table. "I've asked Police Chief Banerjee to sit in on the interview, unless you have objections?"

"If he wishes to stay, of course he may." The voice was grave and cultured. Mr Verma sounded like a man who was used to being obeyed. Sanjay joined them at the table and sat down next to Tim.

"I understand you're planning to leave the country very shortly?"

Mr Verma gave him an amused smile.

"Not leaving the country. I'm travelling to a remote area of Uttar Pradesh. I assumed that you wouldn't want to meet me there."

Sanjay was fidgeting nervously.

"Mr Verma is a benefactor," he said. "He has a foundation that helps people in poor rural areas."

"Is that how you make a living?"

The smile broadened.

"Of course not. I'm a chemist by profession. I own a chemical company. I'm trying to 'put something back'. Isn't that how you usually put it?"

"Yes," said Tim. Privately he was wondering why Bahir

Verma was living in the UK, and in modest circumstances, if he had such a wealthy relative in India. Quickly he revised his hunch that Ayesha Verma's 'cousin' had wanted to marry her so that he could obtain work in England.

"But you're not here to quiz me about my business," said Mr Verma, his tone suddenly steely. "You want to ask me about Ayesha."

"Yes," said Tim. "I understand that her parents had arranged for you to marry her?"

"They thought it would be a good idea."

"What about you, Mr Verma? What made you agree to it?"

"I lost my wife some years ago. It hadn't been my intention to remarry – I had a young son – but tragically my son died last year. Bahir came to the funeral and he saw how desolate I was. He said the pain would pass if I had more children and suggested that Ayesha would make a good bride. I wasn't entirely convinced, but I agreed to it."

"Why do you say you weren't convinced?"

"My first marriage was arranged. It's a system that Bahir and I grew up with, that we both accepted. And I loved my wife and I think Bahir loves his. But I've come to realise the danger that arranged marriages place young girls in; it's easy for an arranged marriage to be a forced marriage. My charity is trying to help lift young women out of poverty, make them more independent. You could say that an arranged marriage, even if the bride agrees to it, doesn't fit very well with my beliefs."

"But you still wanted to marry Ayesha?"

"Her family wanted me to marry her. I accepted that Bahir was right when he said I needed a wife, and, to be honest, I was indifferent about who she was as long as she was presentable and intelligent. I knew I'd be able to help Ayesha and her family a great deal if she accepted me. But I stressed to Bahir that it was she who had to make the decision."

"So you went to the UK to meet her?"

"Yes. Only just over two weeks ago. It seems a long way away already. I've been keeping in touch with Bahir, of course. They are all suffering terribly."

"How did Ayesha seem when you met her? What was her first reaction when you were introduced?"

"We first met at an airport. I find that all airport meetings are odd – they're forced, artificial – and the whole family was there. She seemed pleased enough to see me, but I couldn't really tell what she was thinking."

"What did you think of her?"

"I found her beautiful and charming. Intelligent, obviously. And mature beyond her years."

"A fitting bride for you?"

"Yes, a fitting bride for me, certainly a woman I could be proud to stand beside. But only if she wanted it."

"And did she?"

"She said she did. Her mother had some bizarre ideas about chaperoning her and I'd already chosen not to stay at Bahir's house, so we only had a limited time on our own. I managed to take her for several walks. I told her that she didn't have to marry me, that I wanted what was best for her. I said she could attend university as she'd planned, though it would have to be an Indian university and she wouldn't be able to enrol until next year. I'm not 'progressive' enough to want my wife to live apart from me for three years."

"So you intended her to come to India with you?"

"Of course. What else might I have intended?"

"Has she ever visited India?"

"I believe so, when she was a small child. I talked to her about it, briefly. She said she didn't remember."

"Did she say what she thought about living here now?"

"She seemed easy about it. She didn't say much about it; didn't ask me many questions."

"Didn't you find that odd?"

"Yes, Mr Yates, I did. Ayesha was always perfectly polite to me and never said anything to make me think she wanted to reject me. But the more I thought about it, the more I thought her perpetual brightness – almost as if she'd been programmed – combined with her failure to discuss with me anything at all about the sort of life we might be going to lead together was proof that she was just acting on her father's wishes. I was going to confront her with this on the day she disappeared, say that although I would be very happy to marry her, I doubted that she felt the same way about me."

"But you didn't have this conversation?"

"No."

"Did her parents know what you intended?"

"I don't know. It didn't happen and if it had it would have been between me and her. I saw no reason to complicate matters by telling them. Besides, it would have been a betrayal of trust and there was still a chance that I was wrong and she wanted to accept me after all."

"Even after she disappeared?"

Mr Verma paused. For the first time, Tim sensed that he'd exposed a weakness in the man's story. Mr Verma swallowed and looked Tim in the eye very intently, a little too intently, perhaps.

"I don't see what bearing a conversation that never happened could have had on her disappearance."

"Did she seem afraid of her father?"

"I don't think so. I think she respected . . . respects both her parents very deeply. That is quite admirable and becoming more unusual in the young, even in this country."

"What sort of mood was she in when you last saw her?"

"Quite giggly, actually. During most of the time that I spent with her she was very serious; I suppose demure is the correct word. I don't know if she thought that was how she should behave with me, or whether her mother had coached her. But on that day her mood was lighter, more frivolous. I was pleased to see it. She said she needed to buy some things for her hair. I offered to walk with her, but she said she'd go alone. I didn't argue with her and neither did her mother."

"Was there any tension between her and either of her parents?"

"Not that I could detect. Certainly not on that day. We'd just had a family picnic. It was a happy occasion."

"And you didn't see her again?"

Again Tim thought he detected some infinitesimally small hesitation before he received a reply.

"No."

"You left the UK very quickly afterwards."

"That had always been my plan. I've had important work to do for my charity, preparations to make before I go to Uttar Pradesh. And although I feel hugely sorry for my cousin and his wife, there was nothing I could do to help them. To be honest, I thought they'd be able to cope better without the added burden of having to look after me."

"Did you leave the day after Ayesha disappeared?"

"No, the day after that."

"How was her father behaving?"

"He was distraught. The whole family was. By then they realised she hadn't just gone to stay with a friend on a whim – which would have been entirely out of character – but that she really was missing. They were frustrated by the time it took for you and your colleagues to become worried about Ayesha. I think you only really began to look for her that same day that I left."

"You're probably right about the timing. You have to understand that many people are reported missing every day. They usually turn up again quite safely; sometimes we find them and they don't want their families to know where they are. We have to take a balanced view on what type of action to take."

"Even when a young girl is involved?"

"Ayesha is nearly eighteen; almost an adult."

"The delay is perhaps forgivable. Suspecting her family of killing her for the sake of their honour is not. My cousin would never do such a thing."

"How do you know that is a possible line of enquiry?"

"Anni told me. She said it was making Bahir's life unbearable, that coping with being a suspect as well as his grief would have driven him insane if he hadn't returned to work. And still Ayesha is missing. You must have realised by now that such ideas are leading nowhere. In the meantime, she might be in terrible danger, or worse."

Tim noticed that Sanjay Banerjee had begun to twitch again. He realised that this time the police chief's discomfort was caused by the perceived discourtesy to Tim himself. Tim was more impressed by the vehemence with which Mr Verma had expressed opinion than his actual words. Did he believe his criticism of the police in Spalding was just, or was he perhaps protesting too much? Tim realised that he would get no further with this interview, but neither was he satisfied that he'd got to the bottom of Verma's relationship with Ayesha. He would need to interview the businessman at least once more.

"Mr Verma, how long do you plan to stay in Uttar Pradesh?"

"Until next Tuesday. Then I have business back here in Delhi."

"I see. I'd thought you were going to be away for longer."

"No, but I understood the urgency of seeing you before I went. Even though I doubt that I can offer any information that will help you, of course I want to do everything in my power to give Ayesha back to her family."

To give Ayesha back to her family, Tim repeated to himself silently. It was a strange way of putting it.

"I'd like to see you one more time, next Tuesday, when you return. My colleagues may have found out more by then."

"Very well. As I've said, I'm very happy to help."

When Tim stood up the other two men followed suit with alacrity. Verma held out his hand again. Tim noted that although the room was air-conditioned and the man's palm had been cool and dry when they'd first greeted each other, it was now clammy with sweat. Despite or maybe because of Verma's upright and somewhat admonishing stance, Tim wasn't convinced of his innocence.

"What did you make of that?" he asked Sanjay, after Verma had been escorted to the door.

Sanjay seemed startled by the question.

"It was as I expected," he said. "Mr Verma is a very hon-ourable man. Highly respected. I thought that came across. He was a little discourteous to you, but that is understandable in the circumstances. He is grieved by the loss of his cousin's daughter, who might have become his wife."

"I expect you're right," said Tim. "Nevertheless, I'd be grateful if you could do some background checks on him. I'd like to know more about both his business and the charity. And anything you can find out about his dead wife and son might be useful, too."

"Of course," said Sanjay.

Tim couldn't tell whether his Indian colleague thought the request was sensible or outrageous. He registered no surprise and his expression was one of inscrutable professionalism.

Chapter 56

PC VERITY TANDY had had only a few hours' sleep and was still feeling a bit dazed as she walked from her flat in High Street towards the town centre. Giash had arranged to meet her in the Cattle Market so they could begin their shift together. She didn't know what the day would bring. She thought Juliet might ask them to go back to the house in Chestnut Avenue to see if everything was secure.

She looked at her watch and quickened her pace, realising she was late. A couple of bleeps from her phone told her she'd received a text message. It was Giash, probably demanding to know where she was, but when she looked she saw instead a more apologetic message. 'Am taking Gerald Pocklington to pick up his car. Will be ten minutes late. Sorry!' 'No worries', she texted back. She was level with the bridge and as she now had more time decided to cross the road to stare into the depths of the Welland. Since she'd moved from Boston to Spalding, she'd been fascinated by the deep and narrow river which had had such a profound influence on the town's history and livelihood. It always looked murky, though that was because it was so deep; it was a favourite with anglers, so fish must thrive in it, despite the fact that it was used as a persistent dumping-ground for rubbish. South Lincs Police had tried to tighten up on the fly-tippers recently, but with only limited success.

As she peered into the blackish depths, Verity caught sight

of something in the lapping waters at the side of the bank. It looked like a floating cotton carrier bag. Verity thought this was strange: she'd have expected the sodden fabric to sink, particularly as the bag appeared to be stuffed with something. She leaned over the side of the bridge to get a better look and saw that a white trainer had become detached from the other contents of the bag and was wedged in the reeds at the side of the bank.

She walked round to the fence designed to stop people straying on to the bank so close to the bridge and climbed over it. The bank was particularly steep here, but she scrambled down it. She lifted out the trainer easily. The bag presented more of a problem. It was further out, and sluggishly moving away from her. Verity looked around and discovered a half-rotten cane lying in the grass. After sustaining a wet foot and some nettle stings, she managed to hook the good end of the cane around the bag's handle and pull it towards her. Triumphantly she lifted it out of the water. It was a green Harrods carrier bag.

It contained the other trainer and a full set of women's clothing, as well as a large piece of polystyrene. Verity had been given the description Juliet had obtained from Mrs Sims of what Margie Pocklington had last been seen wearing. She separated out the items and spread them on the bank, then brought Mrs Sims' statement up on her phone. Black clothes were common, of course, but Verity saw the contents of the bag matched the list of items on her phone exactly. She was especially convinced by the unusually small size 3 trainers included in the list, each one decorated with a silver star, just like the trainers she'd retrieved. Verity called Giash.

He answered immediately. "I'm nearly with you," he said.

"Sorry, I had to make sure that Pocklington didn't try to get back into the hospital to pester his ex-wife."

"I'm not calling to check up on you. Do you have any plastic evidence bags on you? Large ones?"

"I'm not sure. There's probably a roll of bin liners in the boot. If not, I can stop and buy some. Why?"

"Bin liners would be great. I'm on High Bridge – or rather, almost under it at the moment. Can you meet me here? With the bin liners?"

"Sure, but . . ." Verity cut off his question.

"I think I've found Margie Pocklington's clothes."

"Oh God! Do you think she's in the river?"

"It's possible, but the clothes had been crammed together in a Harrod's bag and there's a big bit of polystyrene with them. They were floating."

"You mean someone wanted us to find them?"

"I don't know. But that's what it looks like to me."

"I'll pick you up and we'll take the stuff you've found back to the station. DC Armstrong's already on her way there."

Chapter 57

MRS SIMS PICKED through the sodden garments that had been spread out on a table in the interview room.

"These look like Margie's," she said. "And I'm pretty certain the trainers are hers, with those silver stars. She's got such small feet; there can't be many pairs of trainers like that in Spalding. And she always wore white underwear. I asked her about it once, when her bra straps were showing: it seemed odd in a girl who nearly always dressed in black. She said she thought black underwear was tarty." She met Juliet's eye, her lip trembling slightly. "Does this mean she's drowned?"

"Not necessarily," said Juliet. "I can't pretend it's looking good – there has to be a reason why these clothes have been dumped – but it could be because someone wants us to think she's drowned."

"Why would they do that?"

"I don't know. If someone's holding her, perhaps to throw us off the trail, so that we think she's killed herself."

"That doesn't make much sense to me," said Mrs Sims. "I'm going to have to go back to the nursery. My friend can only help out for an hour. But you'll let me know if anything happens?"

"Yes, of course I will."

"What's that?" said Nancy Chappell suddenly, moving forward from the other side of the table.

Juliet followed her gaze. One of the items from the bag had slipped from the table and was hooked up on a chair, dripping pungent water on to the ground. Juliet retrieved it and laid it on the table, smoothing it out as much as possible.

"It looks like a long scarf," she said. "It's black as well, or dark blue. There's a fine metallic thread woven through it. Have you seen Margie wearing this?"

"No, never. I don't think it's hers. She isn't the floaty scarf type. She's always very neat and quite – I suppose conservative's the word. She dresses plainly. I don't think that's her type of thing."

"It could be hers, though?"

"I suppose so," said Mrs Sims doubtfully. "But I don't think so. I do need to get back now. You'll let me know if you make any progress?"

"Of course."

"I need to check what Ayesha Verma was wearing when she went missing," said Juliet after Mrs Sims had gone and they'd moved back to the office area. She started to boot up her computer. "I'm pretty certain her mother said there was a scarf."

"If you're right, it looks as if we can scrap the idea of an honour killing."

"If I'm right, we're looking for someone who is kidnapping young girls. It may be a serial killer. We'll have to tell Superintendent Thornton straight away."

"Check the mother's statement first."

"I'm going to . . .here it is. Ayesha was wearing a blue and white top and dark blue trousers. And a scarf. A dark blue scarf with a silver thread."

Nancy whistled.

"We'll still need to show the scarf to Mrs Verma, ask her to identify it."

"You're right. But I don't fink there can be much doubt about it, do you?"

"No. And I've just remembered something else."

"Go on."

"Last night, when I was driving to the hospital to try to talk to Liz Pocklington, I saw a man behaving strangely on the river bank. He was on the other side of the bridge from where Verity found the clothes. He definitely threw something into the water. I'd say that I saw the person who dumped them."

"So you fink it's a local crime? That the girls haven't travelled anywhere, but are being 'eld somewhere round 'ere?"

"It's possible, but I'm not convinced. Whoever dumped those clothes wanted someone to find them. Otherwise, why put them in the bag to keep them all together and why the polystyrene? They may be being held round here, but it's just as possible they're somewhere else altogether and the clothes are meant to put us off looking further away. There's something else bothering me, too. Somehow the man looked familiar – there was something about him that made me think I'd seen him before, although it was too dark to make out much more than his shape. He was limping slightly. And his arm movement, when he threw whatever it was, was awkward, as if the arm had been injured."

"Keep on finking about it. Do you want me to take the scarf to show Mrs Verma?"

"Thanks, but I'd better do it myself. She's going to be very upset. And we ought to see Superintendent Thornton first. He won't want to waste any time getting out a description of Margie Pocklington now."

Chapter 58

SUPERINTENDENT THORNTON WAS in a strange mood as he set in train a nationwide search for Margie Pocklington. He'd agreed with Juliet that, given the circumstances in which the clothes were discovered, it was too risky to assume that Margie (or her body, but he wasn't going to be the first to suggest that) was being held locally. He was recognising belatedly the wisdom of not jumping to conclusions: it was going to be tricky to extricate himself from the predicament he'd landed himself in by assuming too precipitately that Ayesha Verma had been the victim of an honour killing, and, worse, giving Tim Yates permission to go gallivanting off to India even after the Superintendent himself had begun to harbour serious doubts about that particular line of enquiry. Yates could have interviewed the Verma fiancé by video link, for God's sake. As it was, they'd probably wasted valuable time and equally valuable public money by barking up the wrong tree. He hoped that Yates and Armstrong hadn't been too specific when voicing their suspicions to the Vermas. The last thing he wanted to be landed with was some kind of racial prejudice enquiry.

He'd decided, and Juliet had agreed, that they wouldn't disclose the discovery of the clothes just yet. To do so would be playing into the perpetrator's hands and it would be giving far too much away if they were to announce that they thought Margie's disappearance was linked to Ayesha's. He didn't want the Press to start voicing that idea just yet, even though they were bound to jump to that conclusion eventually and would probably question him about it at the press conference he'd agreed to later in the day.

He ordered CCTV footage to be checked at the most likely stations: Peterborough, London King's Cross, Nottingham, Leicester. A similar initiative had drawn a blank after the disappearance of Ayesha Verma, but it was important to show willing and there was always the chance they might strike lucky this time.

Once all police forces had been alerted and Margie's description and photograph circulated, he turned his attention to the evidence they had gathered already. Patti Gardner was summoned to carry out forensic tests on the clothes. Juliet and Nancy were told to type up the interviews that had taken place with Liz and Gerald Pocklington. He doubted that either would be of much use, but he was determined to do everything by the book this time.

"What's Katrin Yates doing today?" he demanded peremptorily of Juliet as she handed over a print copy of her report. "Is this one of her working days?"

"Yes, sir," said Juliet. "She's been talking to a couple of victims of domestic abuse – women whose families would have almost certainly have killed them 'for honour' if they hadn't managed to escape."

"That's a bit of a waste of time, isn't it? We don't think it is an honour killing now, do we?"

"No, sir," said Juliet patiently. "But if you remember, you asked her to do some background work on honour killings, see if the profile fitted the Verma case."

"Did I? Well, it would have been more useful if she'd come

to her conclusions before Yates left for India, wouldn't it? Anyway, that can't be helped. Call her now and tell her to waste no more time on it. I want her here, now. She can do some background checks on Gerald Pocklington and see if there's anything we should know about him. And Liz Pocklington, for that matter. And call in Chakrabati and Tandy. I want them to make door-to-door enquiries in the High Bridge area: perhaps someone else saw your mystery man last night. Pity you didn't apprehend him, wasn't it?"

Juliet's heart sank. She'd been thinking the same thing herself.

"Yes, sir. I thought he was just a fly-tipper. It seemed more important to interview Mrs Pocklington at the time. Besides, I'd have needed back-up and he'd have gone by the time they arrived."

"Yes, well, you weren't able to interview the Pocklington woman until this morning anyway, were you?" the Superintendent retaliated tetchily, ignoring Juliet's latter observation.

"Steady on," said Nancy. "She's not a clairvoyant."

Juliet held her breath for a moment, but when she dared to look at Thornton she realised he seemed quite pleased by the rebuke.

"That's what we need, a bit of spirit around here," he said sotto voce, almost to himself. "Now," – in a louder voice, to Juliet – "what are the chances of picking up your friend the fly-tipper on CCTV? Is there any in that part of the town?"

"Some of the shops are fitted with CCTV cameras, but I don't know if any of them point towards the river. I'll check."

"Good. And when you've done that and got Katrin Yates and Chakrabati and Tandy back at the station, perhaps you could take that scarf to show to Mrs Verma. Or do you think that Gardner will want to sprinkle her potions on it first?"

"I doubt if she's going to find much evidence on the clothes now they've been in the river all night, but it's probably best to give her the chance to find out."

"Agreed. Well, you can wait for a bit, then, and brief Katrin when she gets here. You might like to get on with writing a press briefing for me."

Chapter 59

ALTHOUGH JULIET DOESN'T tell me much when she calls, I surmise from what she says that I shall be at the station for the rest of the day. I say goodbye to Janey and wish her a happy weekend before leaving to pick up my car at the station car park.

"Thanks," Janey says, her voice heavy with irony, "you, too."

I drive the short distance to the station and am just getting out of the car when I see Patti Gardner getting out of her white van. Awkward as a schoolgirl, I begin to tremble and wonder if I can avoid her by sitting here until she's safely inside. But it's obvious that I'm bound to bump into her inside and in any case I haven't done her any wrong: rather the opposite. Slowly I climb out of the car and see that she's standing motionless beside the van. I approach her at a snail's pace, but I can see she's determined to wait for me.

"Patti!" I say as breezily as I can. "What brings you here?" I realise how foolish the question is as soon as I've said it.

"I work here," she says crisply. "Perhaps you've forgotten. Sometimes I'd like to forget it myself. How are you? I don't think I've seen you since the baby was born."

"Of course I haven't forgotten. It was a really silly question. I'm fine," I gush. Patti's like Freya - she brings out the worst in me. Something to do with how close they've both been to Tim, I suppose.

"You're back at work?"

"Yes. This week."

"Great. Tim said . . ."

She pauses. She's suddenly confused.

"What did Tim say, Patti? Do tell me. And when did you last get the chance to talk to him? I've barely seen him myself for the last couple of months."

Patti looks down at the ground. She's frowning and her mouth is working. I make no attempt to help her.

"Look, Katrin," she says at length, trying to fix me with her guileless blue eyes, "I don't know what Tim's told you, but I hate concealing the truth, especially as it's nothing like you think it is. But this isn't the time and place . . ."

"Oh, I think it is."

"I've got an emergency job to do. Juliet thinks they've found something belonging to Ayesha Verma in the river."

The news electrifies me, but I won't be put off.

"Fine," I say. "We can go in together. You can tell me as we walk."

"But we'll be inside in a couple of minutes. Someone might overhear . . ."

"Overhear what?"

"All right, Katrin, you win. I'll tell you the details later if you want to hear them, but basically Tim spent the night before last in my hotel room because he was too ill to get back to his sister's. He wasn't drunk, either: it was something to do with the medication he'd been taking. Nothing happened, nor did either of us have any intention that it should. He was passed out on the floor until he woke up and left in the early hours."

It's my turn to be speechless.

"Satisfied?" Patti says. "You should know Tim better than

to think he would cheat on you. He's one of the most principled men I know."

She turns her back on me quickly and stalks off towards the station doors. As she takes out her swipe card, I see her brush the back of her hand across her face. I'm miserable, but in no mood for tears.

Chapter 60

MARGIE SURVIVED THE day second by second, convulsed with terror. Her fear took a physical form, as if someone were clutching at her throat. There was no release from it; it incapacitated her, making it hard for her to concentrate on the sordid little acts she was ordered to perform. The rituals that she was forced to play out were tedious and demeaning. Moura came back at intervals and barked commands, making her change into yet more outlandish outfits. Moura brought these with her and took them away again: Margie wasn't allowed to keep them. Margie was banned from using the dressing-gown for modesty when she was taking her clothes off: Moura threatened to take it away if she tried. It sickened her that she was stripping naked for her unknown watcher. She knew he was ogling her from the other side of the door, and the indelible image that insinuated itself of a vile old man sitting there, depraved and gloating, made her flesh creep.

Progressively, the outfits became scantier and more bizarre. Some consisted only of feathers held together with strips of lace. The colours were garish: purple, orange, lime green and gaudy yellow in hideous combinations, a madman's designs. Ridiculous in one of these concoctions, Margie was made to parade around the small room and instructed to adopt obscene or provocative postures, often for half hours together, until suddenly Moura would tell her to stop and take off the clothes. Moura would seize them and disappear for a while, but when she came back the whole charade started up again. Sometimes Margie thought she heard voices when Moura opened the door, but when it closed again she was trapped in a weird silence, a soundlessness made eerier because she knew she was not alone.

She heard no more sounds from beyond the connecting door. She inspected it several times when Moura was out of the room, once moving close to the spy-hole so that he could see her fear. She hoped perhaps that he would take pity on her, see how young and inexperienced she was, or, if that was too much to expect, see how hopelessly unsuitable she was for whatever he wanted to do next. She could not imagine what that might be.

She sat on the floor with her back to the door for a while, thinking that he couldn't see her there, but when she lifted her head from her knees she spotted a camera set high in the wall opposite her. It moved at intervals. The whole room was under surveillance. Terrified that he might suddenly burst through the door and grab her, Margie lay down on the bed and hoped that Moura would reappear.

Chapter 61

SHAKING AFTER MY spat with Patti, I climb the stairs to the open plan office area. I can't decide how I feel about Patti's explanation. Do I believe her? I don't know her well enough to be able to tell whether she's a good liar. She seems genuine, but she was very keen to give information I didn't ask for, and if she's telling the truth why couldn't Tim tell me the story himself instead of being so evasive? And why did he pay all of that outrageous restaurant bill, if it was just for a dinner shared between friends? Patti didn't mention the dinner: I should have asked her if Derry was there. I'm too much of a coward to try now. And I'm still furious with Tim.

Juliet and Nancy are sitting together, both staring at a computer screen. I'm not surprised at Juliet's professionalism in co-operating with Nancy, but I don't detect the tension between them I would have expected.

Juliet turns round.

"Hello, Katrin. Goodness, you look annoyed."

"Sorry, I didn't mean to frown. I was just thinking about something."

"We need your help. Verity Tandy found some clothes in the river and they've been identified as Margie Pocklington's."

"Oh, God. Does that mean she's drowned?"

"We're sending divers down, but there's no proof that she jumped in. The clothes were packed into a bag with a floating device, as if someone wanted us to find them. And there was a scarf with them that almost certainly belongs to Ayesha Verma."

"So the two cases are linked?"

"It appears so."

"But that means . . ."

"Yes, I know. We can't completely discount the honour killing theory, but it makes it much less likely. Did the women that Fiona Vickers brought to see you give you any more clues?"

"Not directly. They showed me what it's like to live in perpetual fear, and they suggested that we should talk to Ayesha Verma's sisters. They said if we did that we'd know then if Ayesha was being coerced. But what about Margie?"

"Superintendent Thornton's started a nationwide search for her. He wants you to help with it – I'll explain in a minute. It's not a bad idea to talk to the Verma daughters, although they're very young and the mother's protective. You'll probably be better at getting her to let me talk to them than I will. I'm going to take the scarf to Mrs Verma for identification when Patti Gardner's finished with it. Will you come with me?"

"Yes, but I don't think we can talk to the daughters until we've got a child interview specialist with us. We'll get into trouble if there isn't an expert there and something goes wrong. You can still show Mrs Verma the scarf today."

"I've worked wiv a good a child interviewer in London," Nancy says. I realise I've not spoken to her since I arrived and try to smile at her. I wonder if Juliet has introduced her to Patti. "I could go and brief 'er. She doesn't normally work at weekends, but I know how to get 'old of 'er."

"But doesn't Juliet need you here? You're welcome to stay with me for the weekend," I say, guilty again.

"Fanks, but I don't fink you do need me 'ere at the moment. Margie's your priority, before the trail goes cold. You don't need my 'elp wiv 'honour killing' just now. And I fink Juliet's 'unch is right: Margie's probably not in the river or anywhere near 'ere at all. Best thing I can do to 'elp is wiv the CCTV footage."

"You mean for King's Cross?" says Juliet.

"Yes. If she ran away, she could 'ave planted those clothes 'erself. And fink about it, if you was running away from 'ere, where would you go? London's the obvious answer and King's Cross would be the station you'd arrive at."

"That doesn't explain the scarf."

"No, it doesn't. But it's the best I can do. We 'aven't got any answers and we 'ave to start somewhere. I've got a feeling about King's Cross and I can tell you that footage won't get prioritised unless someone makes it 'appen. We get dozens of runaways every week."

"I'll have to okay it with Superintendent Thornton," Juliet says. "But if that's what you want to do, as you say, it may help."

I try to read Juliet's expression. If she's relieved at getting rid of Nancy so easily, she isn't showing it.

The animated look on Nancy's face freezes at the same time as Juliet smiles politely. I turn to see Patti standing at my elbow.

"I've done all I can with the clothes now," she says. "You can take the scarf wrapped in a plastic bag for identification purposes, but I'd like you to bring it back as soon as you can. I'm not hopeful, but there's an outside chance there's DNA on it."

"Have you found anything on the other stuff?"

"Nothing on the fabrics. I didn't really expect it: they'd been submerged for several hours. As I've said, DNA's still a possibility, though I doubt it. But there is a partial fingerprint on one of the trainers. One of them wasn't as wet as the other."

"That's right. Verity said one was lodged in the side of the river bank. Is the fingerprint good enough for a match?"

"I'm not sure, but I think so. I'll get it checked out straight away. The weekend's coming, but presumably Superintendent Thornton won't mind paying extra for a quick result?"

"I'm sure he won't," said Juliet. "He's talking to the Press at the moment, but don't hang around until he comes back. I'll authorise it myself."

Juliet gives me a quick look. I know what she's thinking; but even Superintendent Thornton couldn't be comfortable with putting his budget before finding Margie.

"Right, I'm on my way, then," says Patti. "I'm going to take the other things to the lab. Do you want me to sign for them?"

"I'll get you a chitty. What shall we do with the scarf when we've finished with it?"

"Bring it back here. I'll send someone to pick it up. It's on the desk through there. Remember, don't take it out of the plastic. I've spread it out so the fabric can be examined."

Patti is speaking only to Juliet. She ignores Nancy and me. She signs the paper slip that Juliet gives to her and walks away.

Chapter 62

I ACCOMPANY JULIET to the Vermas' house, even though we've agreed I can't talk to the children. Juliet wants me to be with her and, after all the work I've done on honour killings, I'm curious about the Verma household. I wonder if I'll pick up on any bad vibes there.

Bahir Verma opens the door.

"Good afternoon, Mr Verma," says Juliet. "May we come in? I'd like to speak to your wife."

He's a short, almost gaunt, man with haunted bloodshot eyes and greying, wiry hair.

"Anni's upstairs," he says. "She's not well. That's why I'm home early. She won't be able to see you. Is it about Ayesha?"

Juliet has told me she'd found him courteous, if reserved, precise and dapper when they'd met previously. To me he seems unkempt and broken, as if he's losing life's struggle. His shirt is grubby at the collar and his tie has been loosened so that it hangs askew.

"This is Katrin Yates. She's a police research officer. I asked her to come with me." He looks at me as if he doesn't understand what she is saying. "Yes, it is about Ayesha. Perhaps you can help us instead of your wife. May we come in?" Juliet repeats.

He hesitates and then collects himself. He opens the door wider and motions us into his sitting-room.

The room is not untidy, but it has a neglected look. The

bright sofa cushions have been piled in an untidy heap. The petals of the roses in a vase of flowers on the table have turned brown at the edges.

"Please, sit," he says. "She's been ill since you were here the other day. She's much worse today. She coped so well at first but now she can't take the strain."

He sinks on to the sofa himself and sits on the edge of it, his hands clasped. His bloodshot eyes wander around the room, lingering on Juliet as they take us both in. "Please tell me you don't have bad news."

Juliet is brisk.

"It's neither bad nor good news, Mr Verma. We'd just like you to take a look at this and tell us if you think it might be your daughter's. I'm sorry that it's wet, but the plastic should prevent it from dripping on your furniture. It was pulled from the river, with some other items that we know were not hers."

"From the river? My God!"

"There's no need to jump to conclusions. There are many possible explanations for that. Now, would you just look at it carefully and see if it could be the scarf that Ayesha was wearing? Don't remove the plastic, please."

He takes the plastic package in both hands, holding it draped across them reverently as if it's a religious artefact.

"Yes," he says. "Yes, I'm sure it's hers. She loves the silver stripes. Many of her things have those stripes, with dark colours so that the stripes stand out more." He captures Juliet's gaze. I see her flinch from his silent stricken appeal.

"You tell me not to jump to conclusions. What does this mean? What should I tell my wife?"

Juliet struggles to give him an answer.

"The scarf may have been thrown into the river deliberately.

Because it was with other items, there is reason to believe that this might be the case. But we won't make any assumptions until the river has been searched."

Bahir Verma tilts his head forward and weeps. He appears to shrink before our eyes. His shoulders shake as if in rhythm to his grief, but he makes no sound. His tears fall on to the plastic in which the scarf is sheathed; it's still dangling over his arms.

It may be naïve of me, but I can't believe that this man has killed his daughter.

Chapter 63

A S SOON AS he could after the interview with Zayed Verma, Tim extricated himself from the solicitous ministrations of Sanjay Banerjee and took a taxi to his hotel. After he'd checked in, he looked at his watch. It would be 6.30 p.m. at home. Katrin would be there with Sophia and probably hadn't yet put her to bed. He debated whether to Skype her and decided against it. He told himself that he was too tired to have a proper conversation with them and, in any case, he needed to speak to Katrin when she was alone, but deep down he had to admit that he was shunning her out of cowardice. He'd have to tell her about the encounter with Patti, but he needed to be with her when he did it. If he tried to discuss it over the phone, she'd probably get upset and cut him off.

Yet again he cursed his own stupidity at allowing such a ridiculous chain of events to happen while he was in London. Why had he decided to stay with Freya when a hotel in the city itself would have been more convenient? Why had he allowed Derry to persuade him to have dinner with Patti when he was feeling seedy? And above all, why had he ended up spending the night in Patti's room? He could have asked at Patti's hotel for a separate room, found one in a different hotel or paid for a cab back to Freya's. He could have left Patti at the restaurant when they'd eaten and made it back to Waterloo before he began to feel ill. Why had he insisted on walking her back to St Giles? A persistent nagging voice told

Tim that it was because he had been enjoying Patti's company, that although he didn't really want 'anything to happen' he had deliberately been tempting providence.

He'd got what he deserved, then, and he would be lucky if there were no worse repercussions than he'd suffered already. He'd have to be philosophical about it now and try to get a decent night's sleep. He intended to spend the weekend going over all the case notes. He'd also had to accept an invitation to dinner with Sanjay's family on the following day.

He was too tired to shower. He gave his face a cursory rinse before shedding his clothes on the floor and climbing into bed. He lay there for a long half hour, sweaty and uncomfortable, listening to the loud hum of the air conditioning, until at last he cooled down enough to feel drowsy and finally fell into a troubled slumber.

He was rudely awakened by the trill of his mobile phone close to his ear. He'd plugged it into the socket next to his bedside table. He moved across the bed, as far away from it as possible, and burrowed down beneath the quilt. He listened to the phone as it worked through its scheduled twelve rings and then stopped. He heard it click to message and felt relieved, but no sooner had he crammed shut his eyes than it began to ring again.

"For God's sake!" he muttered. He flung himself back across the bed and seized the phone.

"Yes?"

"Ah, Yates. I hope I didn't wake you up?"

"What time is it there?" Tim countered. A quick glance at the phone's display screen told him it was midnight in Delhi. It must be about 7.30 in the evening. "Good evening, sir," he added belatedly.

"Good evening, Yates. Yes, it is late here. I suspect we'll be working all night. Katrin's been helping us. She's gone home now."

"What's happened? And how is Katrin involved?"

"You remember that she told you a local girl had gone missing? Margery Pocklington. She worked at your child-minder's, I believe. We've found her garments in the river, in a bag with a float."

"Christ. You're sending divers into the river?"

"Yes, of course we are, Yates. And hoping that we don't find the worst, obviously. But there's something else: along with Margery's clothes, we found a scarf that belongs to Ayesha Verma."

"You're sure?"

"Ayesha's father has identified it. And it fits the description her mother gave of the scarf she was wearing when she disappeared."

"God. Let me get my head around this for a minute." Tim put his hands in his chin, which was scratchy with stubble.

"There *is* quite a lot to get your head around, isn't there, Yates? For example, wouldn't you say that this looks more like the handiwork of a serial killer – or at any rate a serial kidnapper – than an 'honour killer'?"

"Yes, but . . ."

"But what?"

"Nothing. Have you had a Press conference yet?"

"Of course. The trail may have gone cold on Ayesha Verma, but we need to pull the stops out for Margery Pocklington now. You know as well as I do, Yates, that if we haven't found her by the end of the weekend at the latest, she's not likely to be found alive."

"Did you tell the Press that we think the two cases are linked?"

"No. I didn't tell them about the clothes at all. I thought it best to keep the perpetrator guessing. We simply issued a statement about Margery Pocklington's disappearance, what she was wearing when last seen, that kind of thing."

"I think you should put out another statement about the clothes. It'll let whoever it is know that we haven't been fooled into thinking that Ayesha was the victim of her family."

"Ah, yes, the honour killing theory. It's looking a little tawdry now, isn't it?"

"With respect, you were as convinced about it as I was, sir."

"At first, maybe. Not latterly. You'll agree that it was a mistake for you to go to India? Did you get any joy at all out of the fiancé, by the way?"

"Not much. There were one or two things I didn't like about him, but he seems to be a pillar of society here. I must admit there was little about him that persuaded me he'd killed Ayesha. I had planned to interview him again on Tuesday, when he returns from his business trip, to see what kind of second impression I'd get."

"But you won't be doing that now, will you, Yates? You'll be coming back here as soon as you can get on a plane."

"Yes, of course, it's my case and I must be there now the main line of enquiry's shifted back to the UK. There may be a plane I can catch in the middle of the night here, if I can get a seat booked. But, even if there is, that still means I won't be home until your tomorrow evening. You'll have had another Press conference by then."

"I'm glad that you mentioned it's your case, but you're re-ferring presumably to Ayesha Verma. Margery Pocklington is

Armstrong's case. She's taken all the initiatives so far. I suggest you share leading officer status with her now that we think the two cases are linked. Let's see how Armstrong shapes up, shall we?" The Superintendent paused. Tim didn't reply, but he got Thornton's drift. "So you think I should give the Press information about the clothes and make it clear they belonged to both girls, do you? Give me your reasons."

"I've hardly had time to think this through, but in my book there are two possibilities: either they've been kidnapped by an out-and-out nutter, in which case we're fucked - they were probably killed very shortly after they were last seen and the bodies have been dumped somewhere. Alternatively, they were taken for a purpose. Probably something nasty, but if that's the case, they may very well still be alive. And the fact that you say those clothes were packed into a bag with a float, as if someone intended them to be found, suggests to me that we're still in with a chance of finding them before it's too late."

"All right, Yates. The argument's a bit subtle for me, though I think I understand something of what you're driving at. And as you say, it's your case, your decision: I'll follow your advice. You'd better get on, now. Let me know when you're on the plane."

"Christ," said Tim again when he'd terminated the call. So much for professional solidarity. It was abundantly clear from the call that Thornton would a) play no official part in justifying Tim's trip to Delhi and b) pass the buck to the 'officer leading the case' if revealing the information about the clothes proved to be a mistake.

No point in dwelling on any of that now. He had a flight and a taxi to organise, a hotel bill to pay, and somehow in the next half hour he was going to have to fit in taking a shower.

Chapter 64

MARGIE WAS SICKENED by the knowledge that she had spent the whole day in the company of her unseen spy. He made her feel filthy, diseased. The flesh in every part of her body was crawling, as if vile insects were creeping across her skin. It took all of her self-control not to hammer on the door, demand to be let out, shout obscenities at him, anything to change the situation, release her from this torture. It crossed her mind that perhaps he wanted her to lose it completely. She could try faking that, see what happened next, but, if she'd been trapped in some kind of kinky gratification ritual, moving on to the next stage could be more terrifying. Was he going to come out of his hiding place? What plans did he have for her then? She had no idea how she might be punished if she misinterpreted his intentions and she was scared of Moura. She knew that Moura would have no compunction about beating her up if she got it wrong.

True to her word, Moura had brought no drink or food until Margie had asked for it. She'd tried drinking the water from the washbasin tap, but it tasted disgusting: salty and heavily chlorinated, it had made her thirstier and nauseated. She was desperate enough to plead with Moura on her third or fourth visit. The woman pulled a bottle of water from her pocket but didn't hand it over.

"You will drink all of this?"

"I . . . yes, I'll drink it all."

"No hissy fits? You won't try anything?"

"No, I'll just drink the water."

"There it is then." Moura placed the bottle on the table. "If you work hard you'll get supper this evening."

"Isn't it evening yet?" Moura looked at her steadily without replying.

"What do I have to do? How will I know if I'm working hard?"

"You'll know. When you've drunk the water I want you to take a shower."

"I've had a shower today."

"Well, I want you to take another one. Is that a problem?"

"No. No, of course not."

"Good. And when you've had the shower I want you to put this on."

Moura produced a silky, sleeveless nightdress from the bag she was carrying. It was pure white. It had a lace bodice and tiny straps.

"You can drink the water after you've had the shower. I'll wait for you."

Moura plumped herself down on the edge of the bed. She smoothed out the nightdress and laid it beside her.

"Get on with it," she said to Margie. "You've got ten minutes."

Margie had already forgotten to feel humiliated when Moura watched her undress. The woman wasn't remotely interested in her except as a performing doll. But she hesitated because she knew he would be ogling her through the spy-hole.

"Get on with it!" Moura repeated in a harsher voice. "What are you waiting for?" She began to lever herself off the bed. Afraid she'd strike her again, Margie slid out of the bizarre bikini she was wearing and plunged quickly into the shower.

She was allowed to drink the water only after she'd smothered herself with body lotion once more and donned the nightdress.

"Drink it all," Moura instructed her. "It'll be gone when you come back."

"Come back? Am I going somewhere?"

"You'll see. Drink the water now."

Margie unscrewed the cap and put the bottle to her lips. The first few gulps tasted wonderful: cold and slightly effervescent, it soothed her parched lips and furred tongue; but when the worst of her thirst had been slaked, she thought she detected some impurity, a kind of bitter undertow in the liquid. She held up the bottle. She'd drunk barely half of it.

"Drink it all. As you promised," said Moura.

"Why? Why do you want me to drink all of it? What difference does it make to you if I pour the rest away?"

Moura's broad hand came swinging round the back of her head. There was a sharp crack as the woman's ring clipped at her skull.

Tears of pain sprang into Margie's eyes. She put the bottle to her lips again and upended it, swallowing rapidly until it was drained.

"Good," said Moura. "It would have been easier if you'd done that straight off, wouldn't it?"

Now that Margie had got herself ready, Moura didn't seem in any hurry to leave the room. She patted the bed next to her and told Margie to sit down. Obediently Margie perched on the edge of the bed. After some minutes she began to feel strange: spaced out, as if she wasn't really present, and, although she knew it was absurd, drowsily happy.

"Are you Ok?" asked Moura.

"I think I'm a bit dizzy."

"Nonsense, you're fine. It's time to go now."

Margie hoped against hope that she was going to be taken out of the room the way she'd come in, back into the long corridor and out to where Pedro had been left behind. She wasn't too addled to make a run for it if she got the slightest opportunity. She was disappointed when Moura stood up and tapped softly on the internal door. It swung open. Moura pushed Margie through it and followed her.

The room they entered was dimly lit. The lack of clear light increased Margie's feeling of dissociation. Her head was swimming. Underlying her bogus euphoria was the nagging conviction that her molester would soon emerge from the shadows and pounce on her. Swaying, she tried to take in every part of the room. Gradually it became apparent that she and Moura were there alone.

The room itself was a miracle of baroque ostentation. It was decorated in the same cream and gold as the one she had been occupying, with similar overblown ormolu decoration, but there the similarity ended. 'Her' room was luxurious enough, but this one, which was three times the size, could have been plucked from a dictator's palace. A massive bed occupied its centre. It resembled a four-poster, except that instead of being obscured by heavy curtains hanging from a supporting frame it was partially swathed in gossamer-light drapes that fell from a kind of inverted dais set in the ceiling. Huge mirrors had been fastened on each of the walls. The pile of the cream-coloured carpet was so deep that it half-buried her bare toes. A black and gold lacquered cabinet stood against the far wall. She could make out the gilded handles of dozens of small drawers. There was a door beyond that which she guessed led to a bathroom.

A smooth mechanical whisper coming from behind told her that the connecting door to 'her' room was closing. She turned round to see it snap shut and noticed an exuberantly upholstered red velvet chair standing close beside it. She shuddered. That must be where he sat when he was watching her during her long hours of pretend solitude.

"Are you Ok?" Moura asked again, this time wheedlingly. Margie knew she had no interest in getting a reply. "Perhaps you should lie down for a while."

"Not in that bed," said Margie, aware that she was slurring the words.

"Yes, in that bed." Moura's tone was threatening again. "Get into it."

She felt headachey, drunk. The pseudo-happiness had evaporated. She was terrified of what would happen to her if she got into the bed, but she was powerless to resist.

Moura turned back the coverlet. There was no quilt beneath it, just a silk sheet. She gave Margie a push. Margie fell across the bed.

"Draw up your knees and get under the sheet."

Again she was forced to obey. Moura pulled the sheet and the coverlet across her and walked away. After some seconds, although she had heard no door open or close, Margie knew she had been left alone again.

She tried to sit up, but the room was spinning now and she had to collapse back against the pillows, telling herself it was just to catch her breath, to get back a bit of strength, but she could feel herself slipping into unconsciousness. The walls were closing in on her. Suddenly there was a sharp acrid smell, male sweat, the stench of an unwashed body. As she lost the fight to remain awake, the smell grew stronger. The mattress moved: someone had climbed into the bed beside her. She tried to turn away, but was overcome by the paralysis of an involuntary desire to sleep. As she was on the point of drifting away, she thought she heard a terrified scream echoing through the stillness.

Chapter 65

IT WAS SATURDAY morning and Nancy Chappell was on her way in to the office. She had texted Derry Hacker from the train back to London the previous evening to tell him that she'd like to meet today. He'd replied that he'd be in the office as he was planning to work over the weekend. Progress with his investigation into the Khans was going more slowly than he'd hoped, but one of his network of informers had agreed to meet him that afternoon and there were a few things he needed to check out beforehand.

Nancy was an unlikely champion of Derry's. She knew that to most female colleagues he came across as laddish and a bit of a male chauvinist pig, but she had a lot of time for Derry. He'd given her a chance when others had been dubious about her capabilities and he'd never shown the slightest prejudice of her otherness. He was the only one of her colleagues who knew her true identity; she had no qualms about that, even though it meant she had literally entrusted him with her life. Another great thing about Derry was that as a subordinate you could argue the toss with him and he'd always listen and often agree; and even if he didn't agree, he wouldn't hold it against you.

Nancy intended to challenge him now. She knew that Derry's sole present objective was to catch enough of the senior Khans to break up their criminal empire. Although he'd replied favourably to Juliet's request to search CCTV footage for images of Margie Pocklington, he certainly wouldn't be making it a priority without a lot of encouragement. Nancy wanted to impress on him how urgent it was and she knew she could achieve it only by spelling out the probable link between Margie's disappearance and Ayesha Verma's.

Derry was looking careworn and in need of sleep, but his greeting was as jaunty as usual.

"Great to see you. Couldn't they find enough for you to do in the boggy lands, or did the fact that nothing much happens there just give you the screaming abdabs?"

"Quite a lot 'appened, as a matter of fact, but I fought I could be more 'elp 'ere. As you know, another girl 'as disappeared from Spalding. Margie Pocklington. Juliet Armstrong told you about 'er. What she didn't tell you and Superintendent Fornton didn't tell the media is that clothes belonging to bofe girls were dumped in the River Welland. I fink the clothes was planted deliberately so the police would find them. It's just a feeling, but I wouldn't mind betting that bofe those girls are 'ere in London somewhere."

"Woman's intuition?" said Derry mischievously.

Nany didn't rise to it.

"If you like," she replied. "Fank you for agreeing wiv Juliet to 'ave the King's Cross CCTV footage checked for images of Margie Pocklington. If I'm right, looking at it would be more than a routine elimination of one line of enquiry. It could be an enormous 'elp in finding 'er. And it may be that we 'aven't got very long."

Derry shifted around on his seat and made a great show of squaring up the papers on his desk.

"Yes. Happy to help, of course. I've got all available hands checking footage for the Khan enquiry this weekend, but I'll make sure someone gets on to it next week."

"It's urgent," said Nancy flatly. "It needs doing now."

"We spent quite a lot of time checking King's Cross footage for Ayesha Verma. We didn't find anything. What makes you so sure that this time it'll be different?"

"I'm not sure. It's just a feeling, as I said, but I don't want to give up on it. Ayesha Verma may already be dead: you know as well as I do that the odds are stacked against finding 'er alive now that it's ten days since she disappeared. But we're still in wiv a chance with Margie Pocklington."

"I still don't see why you think she's more likely to be in London than anywhere else, including lovely Lincolnshire."

"It's lovely Lincolnshire that's the problem. It's not a place I'd associate with 'honour killings', for a start. That was a red 'erring, though probably one started by the police themselves."

"Ah, yes. Poor old Tim. I expect he's got a red face now. He's going to have some explaining to do about his little jolly to India."

"But what if they were abducted and someone wanted to encourage the idea of an honour killing?"

"Doesn't make sense. Margie Pocklington's an unlikely honour killing victim and the police have had no contact with the perpetrator, have they?"

"No. But the fact that clothes belonging to bofe girls were found together shows there was a perpetrator. They didn't bofe just run away. And if the perpetrator's a serial killer, why dump the clothes so they could be found?"

"You tell me. Stranger things have happened."

"Agreed. But if we aren't looking at honour killings or a serial killer, the fird possibility is that someone is taking girls for a purpose. If that's so, London is the likeliest destination, especially from Spalding. It's only a 'undred miles away."

"So remind me why you think the clothes were dumped in Spalding?"

"I've fought a lot about that. Putting us off the scent is an obvious explanation. But perhaps someone was trying to tell us somefing else as well."

"You're getting a bit deep for me there. I hear what you say and, while you haven't convinced me, I can see a sort of logic in it. But honestly, Nancy, I really don't have anyone to put on inspecting that footage this weekend. You know how time-consuming it is."

"Let me do it."

"You can't do it on your own."

"I'll get a team of students to 'elp me. You know I keep a list of law and criminology students who are keen on getting involved in police work. I'm always on the look-out for somefing suitable for them."

"I'm not a big fan of unpaid work."

"Well, pay them then. Minimum wage. They'll be over the moon."

"OK, Nancy, you win. I wasn't expecting you to come back until next week, so it's up to you what you do this weekend. You can recruit four students to help you. You're only checking a few days' footage, so that should be enough. If you haven't found anything by close of play on Monday, we'll assume that's because there's nothing to find. Ok?"

"Ok. Fanks. I knew you'd want to 'elp."

"Probably against my better judgment," said Derry. "But good luck with it."

Chapter 66

JULIET WOKE IN the night. Some process deep within her brain invaded her slumber and told her why the slightly-built man she'd spotted loitering on the river bank was familiar. She hadn't been able to place him previously because his pronounced limp had disguised what she recalled had once been a very distinctive gait. The visceral power of recognition that jerked her from her sleep left her in no doubt at all: she was certain the man she had seen was Peter Prance. How strange that Tim had also recently claimed to have seen him in London. It would be even stranger if Prance were involved in the disappearances of Ayesha Verma and Margie Pocklington. There was some cause for optimism, if that was the case: she doubted that Prance was capable of murder. Exploitation was his speciality, which meant that he preferred his victims to be living. If she could work out how he might be exploiting those two girls, she'd probably be considerably closer to finding them. She hoped her colleagues would believe in her identification of Prance. She'd talk to Superintendent Thornton in the morning, and to Tim himself as soon as he got back.

Chapter 67

I WAKE SUDDENLY in the night. Outside, the dawn is just beginning to break. I thought at first I'd heard a sound, Sophia stirring perhaps, but I listen carefully and hear only birdsong. I lie very still and try to recreate the thoughts of sleep. I know I've been dreaming and I try to summon the dream again. It was about Margie. Margie's visit, when she put Sophia to bed. What had she said when I was hesitant about her idea of working as our nanny? "Don't bother. There's other things I can do."

What did she mean by that?

I realise with a shock that I haven't told Juliet that I saw Margie that evening. I meant to tell her. How could it have slipped my mind? I was annoyed with Tim when I met Juliet afterwards, but that's no excuse. Juliet told me that Margie's mother saw her late that evening, but the woman's unreliable. Perhaps I was the last person to see her; almost certainly, the last to have a coherent conversation with her.

God, was it because of me that she ran away? Did she really go home that evening?

I look at the clock. It's 5 am. Despite the early hour I know I can't wait longer. I call Juliet straight away.

Chapter 68

B Y CHANCE, PETER Prance was also watching the news. He didn't like television, but until Jas paid him he had nothing else to do and he needed something to take his mind off that last girl. There was something about her pinched little features and slight figure that kept on haunting him. He chided himself yet again for being too soft. That girl meant nothing to him, after all. Why couldn't he forget about her, as he had almost forgotten the Indian girl?

Despite these stirrings of compunction, when Superintendent Thornton first appeared on the screen, Peter was delighted. His delight increased when Thornton began to describe how the clothes had been found and said they were certainly Margie's. Now that Jas would have proof that he'd followed instructions and dumped the clothes in the Welland so they would be discovered, perhaps he'd pay him what he was owed, or at least give him a reasonable sum on account. But then Thornton started talking about a scarf, a garment he said he was equally certain belonged to Ayesha Verma.

Peter was immediately terrified. He jumped to his feet, opened the door of his flat and listened. There were no sounds of echoing footsteps in the stairwell, but he knew it would be only a matter of time. He closed the door again and leaned back against it. He felt sick and giddy. He turned to the tiny sink and retched several times, but could not vomit.

How could he have made such a stupid mistake? He had

put Ayesha Verma's clothes one by one into an incinerator at a rubbish tip, again exactly as instructed. How could he have missed the scarf? It must have stuck to the bottom of the Harrods bag, or been rolled into such a little ball that he hadn't noticed it. Subsequently, he had used the bag for Margie's clothes, removing them from the clear plastic bag that Moura had given him before he'd left the hotel. The scarf was sheer – he remembered she'd had it folded loosely around her neck – and almost weightless. That must have been why he hadn't spotted that it was still in the bag. But how could he have been so stupid? Jas would be furious. The whole elaborate exercise had been planned to make the police believe the disappearances of the two girls were totally unconnected. Jas would come after him now. This time he knew he'd get the mother of all thrashings. Never mind the money any more, he'd be lucky if he escaped with his life.

If he stayed in the flat he'd be like a rat in a trap: there was only one way down to the street and Jas's men knew exactly where to find him. He had to leave, now. There was no time to collect together his few possessions. He snatched up a coat and hat from the peg behind the door and ran out of the flat. He didn't bother to lock the door: even the few seconds saved by that might be invaluable.

Chapter 69

NANCY AND HER team of helpers had begun to examine the CCTV footage. Each of them had a photo of Margie Pocklington pinned to the side of their computer screens and a typed description of what she had been wearing. The photo was two years old and supplied by her school. Nancy knew it probably wasn't a very good likeness. Margie looked quite plump, for one thing, whereas everyone who knew her now described her as very slender. But it was the best they could do and Nancy was determined not to give up. She'd told the students to consult her if they were in any doubts at all about the images of young women they spotted.

Derry brought her a cup of tea.

"Don't look so surprised!" he said. "I can be a gentleman sometimes."

"Only if you want somefing."

"Well, now you mention it, I've had an idea. When DI Yates was here, he mentioned that he thought he'd seen an old lag he knew a couple of times – a bloke who'd done a runner before he could be charged. Here's his picture. It's a long shot, but I've been thinking all along he could be the guy who was done over by the Khans on Tuesday night. The description fits and he's just the sort of character who'd be working for them. Tim first thought he saw him at King's Cross. Do you think you could keep a look-out for him?" He handed Nancy the mugshot that Tim had downloaded for him.

"Sure, but we've already started now. If we've missed him already we won't have time to go back over the footage again."

Derry shrugged.

"Thanks. I'll have to take a chance on it. I'll get this copied for all of you. He's quite distinctive, so not too difficult to pick out."

Nancy grinned sardonically.

"Not difficult after an hour perhaps. You should try sitting 'ere all day."

Derry knew better than to argue with her.

Chapter 70

PETER PRANCE HAD boarded the first bus that he saw. He didn't care where it was heading. He chose the seat nearest the central exit doors and hunched down low in it. He'd decided not to put on the hat because it made him conspicuous on such a warm day. He'd crammed it into the pocket of the jacket, which he was wearing despite the heat because he didn't think the Khans would recognise it.

He delved into his pocket and brought out a fistful of change, which he counted: he had £10.59 left. Besides the clothes he stood up in, his only other possessions were the cheap mobile phone and Visitor Oyster cards that Jas had given him for the abduction and a fake passport, also courtesy of Jas. He checked to see that the mobile was turned off. He didn't understand technology, but he knew enough about Jas to be certain that if it was trackable Jas would be tracking it.

He had to get out of London, and fast. He needed money, also fast.

Looking out of the bus window, he saw it had reached Tottenham Court Road. It was a good place to get off: a long way from both his flat and Jas and close to several railway stations.

He decided to risk the hat, pulling it on surreptitiously and jamming it low over his forehead. He thrust his hands into the pockets of his coat and tried to disguise his limp by feigning to slouch. He kept his head down, his shoulders knotted back. He would have considered his own behaviour risible if he weren't consumed by panic. He knew that whether or not he managed to vanish would dictate whether he continued to exist. The irony that the two girls he had captured had no future precisely because they had vanished did not escape him.

He was still haunted by his memory of the skinny one. There was something about her that had appealed to him, a defiance, a pluckiness that he believed mirrored the character of his younger self, a resilience which, sadly, he acknowledged he'd long since lost.

He paused to examine his reflection in a shop window. The marks on his face were still livid: he resembled a drunkard who'd been scrapping in a pub brawl. His clothes were dirty as well as shabby and the hat looked ridiculous. He snatched it from his head and put it back in his pocket. He could weep for the beautiful young man he'd once been, or even the urbane middle-aged Peter Prance who, though he might on the odd occasion have been detained at Her Majesty's pleasure, had always presented a decent façade to the world. He'd kept up appearances, had cut a figure of substance and, although he said it himself, had not been devoid of a certain witty sang froid. How had he come from being a person of bearing to this? He hadn't deserved to be the victim of such penury; he felt quite indignant about it. And the barbarisms that Jas was subjecting him to, just because he was poor, were outrageous. He squared his shoulders a little. He'd have to stand up for himself more. But he'd always hated violence, and had no answer for it except flight or abject submissiveness.

Were they being violent to that girl?

Try as he might, he couldn't get her out of his head.

He stared into the shop window, past his reflection, to

the goods inside. It was a television shop. The half-dozen televisions in the window had all been switched on and were all projecting the same image. He peered at one of them. It was that policewoman, the one he'd met when they were after poor Hedley. Yates's sidekick. What was her name? It was impossible to hear what she was saying through the plate glass, but he understood immediately when she was replaced by a photo of Margie Pocklington. It wasn't a very good photo, but even if it hadn't been labelled, he'd have recognised that uncompromising look.

After a long minute the policewoman was back again, talking animatedly, almost certainly asking for help. Then two numbers flashed up on the screen: a mobile number with her name below it (Juliet Armstrong, that was it!) and a Crimestoppers number. Crimestoppers was offering a reward of £5,000 for information that led to Margie's safe return to her family. For a wild moment, he wondered what his chances might be of claiming it, but he knew the idea was ludicrous. After some hesitation he took out the mobile and programmed the policewoman's number into its memory.

One of the shop assistants came outside for a smoke.

"You going to stand there all day?" he said, good-naturedly enough, but Peter realised he was drawing attention to himself and quickly moved on.

The best way to escape would be to board a train. Peter liked trains and in the past had ridden on them buckshee many times. It was such a bore that the arrangement of barriers and programmed tickets they had these days made free-loading almost impossible. King's Cross was his favourite station – he preferred it to Euston, which had no character – so although he'd have to be careful, because Jas knew it was one of his stamping-grounds, he decided he'd go there. He crossed Tottenham Court Road and cut through one of the many side streets leading off it. Walking briskly, he soon reached Gower Street.

Gower Street was the home of his favourite bookshop. He'd spent many hours browsing in there and even paid for the odd tome on occasion: he'd always considered stealing books to be too grubby a pursuit for someone of his calibre. But needs must, and he entered the shop with the purpose of acquiring a little reading matter for the journey ahead. He'd work out how he was going to accomplish the practicalities of the journey while he loitered among the shelves: he was safer in the shop than out on the streets.

He'd picked up a book on rococo art and was just leafing through it when he noticed that the woman operating the till nearest the door was a novice. An older woman from an adjacent till had to keep coming across to help her. Peter watched them. The novice was very slow and clearly embarrassed she needed so much assistance, especially as the colleague's patience was becoming frayed.

Peter continued to watch them for a while. At length, during a period when the novice had no customers, the colleague disappeared, perhaps to take a break. The novice was left glancing anxiously up and down her part of the shop, which luckily was deserted. Peter moved in.

"I'd like to buy this," he said, giving her a winning smile and handing over the art book.

"Thank you." She scanned the bar code on the back of it. "That's twenty-five pounds, please." She pressed some buttons and the till drawer opened.

"Oh, I've just remembered," said Peter, "I have a book

token that I'd like to use. It won't cover the whole amount: I think it's for ten pounds. It is all right to pay part in cash, part by voucher, isn't it?"

"Yes, yes, I think so." The novice bookseller craned her neck across the counter and scanned the shop floor with a wild eye. "I'm not quite sure how to do it. Just let me ask one of my colleagues to help."

"Of course," said Peter. "No hurry." He stepped back a little and folded his hands patiently in front of him.

He was a little alarmed when the woman rang a bell under the counter, but when this produced no effect she said, "Excuse me," to Peter and, to his great delight, emerged from her station to go in quest of aid. He'd expected to have to snatch the money from under her nose, but as it was he was able to empty the drawer of twenties, tens, fives and even a single fifty quite casually before he sauntered out of the shop. He didn't start running until he was in the street. He carried on running until he reached Fitzroy Square. He looked over his shoulder. No one appeared to be following him. There was a pub on the corner. He really needed a drink, but made himself press on. He wasn't out of the wood yet: the police would be after him now, as well as Jas's henchmen. There was no need to kill himself, even so: his heart was hammering away and his injured leg throbbed. He slowed his pace to a fast walk.

This unexpectedly large windfall would allow him to change his plans. He didn't know how much money he'd lifted from the till, but it was way more than he'd expected: enough to take him to France and keep him for a few days until he decided on what to do next.

The girl popped up in his imagination again. There was no

other remedy, he was going to have to help her. He found the number that he'd saved in his phone and pressed 'call'.

"DC Armstrong," said a woman's voice. He hesitated. Was this really such a good idea?

"DC Armstrong. Who's calling?" She sounded impatient now. She'd probably ring off if he didn't speak soon.

"The girl you're looking for," he said, trying to disguise his voice by making it deeper and more monotonous than natural. "Margery Pocklington. She's being held at a private hotel in the Mile End Road. It's called Caspiania. Be careful. The people there are armed."

"Thank you for the information," said the woman. "Who are you? Please identify yourself."

She'll trace the phone, thought Peter. And Jas will trace it, he panicked. He pressed the red button and hurled the phone into the road. Immediately it was flattened by a passing lorry.

Peter Prance allowed himself the smallest puckering of a grin. His conscience was salved. Weary, but walking more jauntily despite his injuries, he continued steadfastly on his way.

Chapter 71

"FUCK ME!" SAID one of the students.

Nancy raised her head and smiled. The student's name was Gus. Nancy liked him, but he'd already been in trouble more than once for using colourful language in the office.

"Now, Gus," she said. "You know what I've told you."

"Sorry. But I think that's 'im – the old geezer."

Nancy shot up from her desk.

"Show me."

Gus turned the footage back for a few seconds. Nancy pushed her face close up to the screen.

She saw a grainy picture of an elderly man loitering near the barriers. There was a break in the footage, but when the picture returned he was still there. The next time round he could be seen walking across the concourse with a slightly-built woman carrying a rucksack. The quality of the film was poor: the images of the woman were blurred and shadowy. Because the man had been caught twice on camera while he was standing motionless, his features were better delineated; although Nancy had never seen him in the flesh, she was convinced it was Peter Prance. She couldn't be sure the girl was Margie, but she was sure enough not to want to wait for forensics to take stills and point up the definition.

"Well done, Gus!" she said. "Can you fetch DI 'acker?"

"He's gone out."

"Damn!" said Nancy. She called Derry on her mobile.

"Nancy? I'm busy at the moment. I'm with a colleague."

Nancy remembered that Derry had told her he would be meeting one of his grasses.

"Sorry," she said. "But it's urgent. We fink we've found your Mr Prance on the CCTVs. And it looks as if Margie Pocklington's wiv 'im."

"I'm coming back," said Derry. "I'll be with you in twenty minutes."

Chapter 72

SATURDAY PROMISES TO be a very long day. After my confession to Juliet, I ask her if there's anything I can do to help her, but she says there isn't. She's forgiving about not having known before about my conversation with Margie: she says that it doesn't even prove that Margie intended to run away. Teenage girls hint at desperate actions when they're not getting their own way and the police already knew she was unhappy at home. Margie didn't really tell me anything that would help the investigation or change its focus.

I think that Juliet's just being kind, until it occurs to me that these days she's much sterner and unyielding than she used to be. Not kind any more, in fact. I can see that she feels she's not getting anywhere with her life. I hope that Superintendent Thornton and Tim will have the sense to give her the DS job.

After I've spoken to Juliet I notice that Tim has texted me from Delhi to say he is waiting for a flight back to Heathrow. He sent it around 1.30 am my time. He should be home by this afternoon. I'm looking forward to seeing him even though I know we have some straight talking to do. I've decided that I believe Patti's story, but that doesn't let Tim off the hook. He's been inconsiderate and foolish, but I'm sorry for him, too. This trip to Delhi was certainly not his finest hour. It may even have damaged his career. I know that Superintendent Thornton encouraged it, but he's not going to admit that, is he?

I try to focus on playing with Sophia, but she's irritable and restless. I decide that the only way to get some peace is to take her for a walk in the buggy. She falls asleep immediately.

Chapter 73

JULIET'S FIRST IMPULSE after listening to the mystery caller's abrupt message was to call Nancy Chappell. She was surprised at herself, but she had good reason: it had been Nancy's hunch that Margie had gone to London and she knew that it was because of Nancy's tenacity that the CCTV request was being actioned. Juliet knew she should tell Superintendent Thornton first, but he'd gone home and when she called his wife said he was taking a shower. Juliet said she'd ring back.

She found Nancy's number and called her just as Derry Hacker had finished examining the CCTV footage.

"Juliet, 'ow amazing! I was just going to call you. DI 'acker's 'ere. I'll put you on speak."

"I've had a call from someone who claims they know where Margie is. They said she was at a private hotel in the Mile End Road."

"Did they give you the name?"

"It was an odd name. Caspeena, or something like that."

"Caspeena?"

Derry Hacker seized the phone.

"Juliet? It's Derry. Could the name of the hotel have been Caspiania?"

"The man who called was speaking in an odd way. It could have been that."

"What else did he say?"

"Nothing."

"Nothing at all?"

"No."

"You know Tim asked me to keep a look out for a bloke with form, a con man who lived in Spalding a few years ago?"

"I didn't know that, but while he was with you in London he told me he'd seen Peter Prance again. Is that who you mean?"

"Yes. You knew Prance, then? Could the guy on the phone have been him?"

Chapter 74

TIM CURSED HIS luck as the plane touched down at Gatwick. At some point when it was flying over Eastern Europe, for a reason not adequately explained by the captain's announcement, it had been diverted to the other airport. The passengers had been advised to collect their luggage and catch the bus. Dog tired and desperate to get home, Tim had queued dispiritedly for a voucher to cover the cost of the bus ticket, incensed by the airline's smug assumption that such largesse offered adequate recompense for 'any inconvenience'.

Having obtained the ticket and a bus timetable, he established that the next bus wouldn't arrive for another fifty minutes. This would seem like an eternity if he just hung around, so despite his weariness he headed for the nearest W.H. Smith, thinking that he might as well make good use of the time by buying a couple of newspapers and reading the press accounts of the search for Margie Pocklington.

At the newsagent's, he joined, with a very bad grace, yet another queue. Belatedly, he realised that he was probably dehydrated and scanned the shelves on either side of the queue to see if he would be able to reach for a bottle of water without losing his place. He spotted a wire basket of bottled water near to the cash desk and his spirits lifted a little.

The queue shuffled forward. As Tim moved along, his eye fell randomly on a 'true crime' magazine. He had nothing but contempt for such publications: the accounts of the cases they covered were anything but 'true', and invariably painted the police officers involved as blackly as possible. Descendants of the Victorian 'penny dreadful', they shrieked sensationalism. This one was no exception: on its cover was the luridly tinted silhouette of a woman's body hanging from a gibbet.

Tim looked again. He must have exclaimed aloud, because the woman standing ahead of him in the queue turned round and glared.

"I'm sorry," he said. "I just saw something I recognised."

The woman raised her eyebrows and faced forward again. Tim seized the magazine and scrutinised the picture. There could be no doubt: it was the same disturbing outline that he'd seen in the upstairs window of the house in Ilford. Had he been suffering from some kind of psychotic episode or was there a simpler explanation? He opened the magazine and began to read avidly.

"Move along," muttered a voice behind him.

"Sorry," Tim said. He was nearly at the checkout desk now. He closed the magazine and added it to his pile of newspapers, just remembering to grab a bottle of water before it was his turn to pay.

Once outside the shop, he hurriedly found a bench where he'd be able to read the magazine in relative comfort. He'd just sat down when his mobile rang. He was surprised to see Derry Hacker's number flashing up on the screen.

"Derry? I didn't expect to hear from you today."

"I've just been talking to Superintendent Thornton. He said he thought you'd be back in the UK later this afternoon. I take it you're here already. Are you at Heathrow?"

"No. I was supposed to be, but the plane was diverted

to Gatwick. I'm waiting for the bloody bus to take me to Heathrow."

Derry chuckled briefly before becoming businesslike again.

"I reckon I can save you from that bus. I think I've got enough information to bust the Khans. I've had permission to deploy an armed officer unit and I'm waiting for them to arrive. Then we're going to arrest the Khans at the hotel they run. Do you want to come?"

"What? I guess I'd love to at any other time, but I have to put my own case first. That's why I've come back from India early: to join the search for Margie Pocklington."

Derry's voice when it came again was grave.

"I think we may have found her. That's why I called you. We think she's being held prisoner by the Khans."

"Why would you think that?"

"A tip-off. Probably from the guy you told us about, Peter Prance. And we're pretty certain we have CCTV footage of him with Margie, too."

"I'll be with you as soon as I can get out of here."

"Stay put. I'll send a car for you. I'll give them your mobile number, get them to call you when they're ten minutes away."

Chapter 75

MARGIE WAS HAULED from a bruised and febrile sleep by a loud bang. Half delirious with pain, she tried to concentrate. She was now back in her own room: how had that happened? She heard the sound of wood splintering and guttural shouts delivered staccato, like machine-gun fire, followed by the din of many pairs of boots running. The noises were coming from another part of the building, but getting closer. There were more angry shouts and a bellowed command, then the firing of a gun. A brief silence, another command, then the running boots moved yet nearer.

More scared even than when she had been abandoned by Moura in the strange bedroom, with her heart hammering in her chest, Margie tried to climb out of her bed, wildly hoping that she'd be able to hide under it until this new danger passed. Again she was stricken by the searing pain, but she tried to ignore it. Her legs betrayed her: they were lumps of lead that refused to do her bidding. She panicked as she discovered that she couldn't move them at all. She allowed her head to sink back on the pillow and wept.

The door in the panel that led to the larger room suddenly burst open. Margie opened her eyes. She saw a thick-set man hastening towards the other door, the one that led to the corridor. He paused for a few moments, his back against the door, listening. For a second his eyes met hers. He motioned to her to keep quiet, his forefinger crossing his neck in a cutting gesture to indicate what would happen to her if she disobeyed. She nodded mutely. He turned to listen again, then wrenched the door open and thrust himself into the corridor. She heard his running footsteps receding. There was another shout. This time she could hear the speaker clearly. "Armed police, get down!" A split second pause, then: "Armed police, get down on the ground and put your hands behind your back!" A shot was fired. She heard rapid talking, someone enunciating very clearly, spelling out an address; a crackling reply accompanied by static, as if the respondent was at the other end of a poor telephone line.

The actions now became less frenzied. She heard doors being forced open along the corridor. They were getting very close to her now. Since she'd heard the word 'police', she'd understood that help was coming. Too weak and still too afraid to call out, she waited.

A door was being pounded. "It's double-locked", said a man's voice, "and stronger than the others. We'll need the ram."

Margie waited. A couple of minutes limped by. There were more footsteps. "One, two, three, go!" shouted the same voice. She heard wood splintering, the crack of a door being ripped apart.

"Oh, Christ!" The man's voice again.

"Sweet God!" said another voice. "Poor kid. How could they have done that to her?"

"Check for vital signs."

"I can see that she's dead . . ."

"Check, all the same."

"She's dead, sir. The body's cold and stiffening."

"Where's DI Yates?"

"DI Hacker made him wait outside."

"Somebody fetch him."

There was another pause. The men in the room were silent for a while. Then the first voice spoke again.

"Carry on checking the rooms. There are two left. We haven't found the other girl yet."

"The door to that one's been left ajar."

"Be careful, then. Shout a warning."

"Armed police! If there's anyone in there, come out with your hands above your head. I'm going to count to three. Then we're coming in. One, two, three."

"Please help me!" Margie called, as loudly as she could.

"Did you hear that? Sounded like a girl's voice."

"Could be a trap. Someone might be holding her in there."

There was another silence. Then Margie could just discern some low whispering. Two men burst into the room, the second covering the first with gun poised. He turned to look behind the door, then crossed to where the panel gaped wide open.

The first man walked up to the bed. He was still holding his gun, but he'd pointed it downwards. He knelt down on the floor so that his face was level with Margie's. He spoke gently.

"Are you Margie Pocklington?"

It was all she could do to nod before she was overcome by a paroxysm of sobbing.

The man turned and looked over his shoulder as someone else entered the room.

"DI Yates, we've found Margie."

Tim nodded. He, too, approached the bed. The armed policeman stood up. Tim took Margie's hand.

"Are you hurt?" he said.

"Yes. I can't move my legs."

"There's an ambulance waiting outside. I'll ask the paramedics to come in right away. You're safe, Margie, you're safe. Everything's going to be ok."

Tim grimaced inwardly as he tried to comfort her with what to his own ears sounded like hollow platitudes. Of course he was glad that they'd found Margie alive, but God knew what horrible injuries she had suffered. Even if her physical condition was not as bad as it looked, the mental scars she bore would probably never heal.

Tim himself had just sustained a raw mental wound that he knew could not be healed. As long as he lived, he would never be able to forget seeing the poor broken body of Ayesha Verma as it lay sprawled on the bed in a room identical to the one from which Margie Pocklington was about to be rescued.

Chapter 76

BAHIR VERMA LED Juliet and Verity Tandy into his sitting-room. Juliet had asked Verity to accompany her because Tim would now be delayed in London while he and Derry established as accurately as they could what had been going on at the Caspiania Hotel.

"How is your wife, Mr Verma?" Juliet asked.

"Anni is still not well. She needs some good news about Ayesha. But I can see from your face that you have not brought any."

"No," said Juliet, casting down her eyes. "Mr Verma, would you like me to ask anyone to sit with you? A neighbour, say? I'm afraid I do have some very bad news."

He shrugged. "If you say you have very bad news, that leads me to expect the worst. Is Ayesha dead? If so, it is not possible for a neighbour to offer me any comfort. But please tell me your news. It is a torture to be kept waiting."

"I'm sorry. Police in London have discovered the body of a young woman who fits Ayesha's description. DI Yates was present when she was found and, although he never met Ayesha, he is satisfied from photographs that the body is hers. She will have to be formally identified, of course. Preferably by you or Mrs Verma."

"I will do it. It is out of the question to ask Anni. Where did you find the body? Had she been dumped somewhere?"

"She was being held against her will by a gang in London. At a hotel for private clients. She died there."

"Why did they want Ayesha? What could she possibly have done to them?"

"There's a great deal we don't know at the moment, Mr Verma, but it seems the hotel was being used as a cover for . . . deviant practices."

"Do you mean they tried to turn her into a prostitute? Was she killed in a struggle trying to resist?"

"I really don't know, Mr Verma. If I had more information I would give it to you."

Maintaining his dignity, Bahir Verma wiped away a tear.

"I'm sorry to have to ask you this, but how soon might you be able to go to London to identify her? We'll take you in a police car, of course. Will someone be able to look after your wife and the children while you're gone?"

"I'm sure the neighbours will be falling over themselves to help, when they find out that I didn't murder her." It was the first time Juliet had heard Bahir Verma allow bitterness to creep into his voice. "May I ask you a question?" he continued.

"Of course."

"If DI Yates hadn't decided so soon that Ayesha was probably the victim of her own family and that, absurdly, I'd had some idea of killing her 'for honour', do you think she might have been found earlier, while she was still alive?"

His question smote Juliet's heart. She swallowed while she considered her reply.

"That was only one line of enquiry, Mr Verma. I assure you that we pursued others. And although the police in London knew of the gang that kidnapped her, they had no idea that Ayesha had become one of their victims."

"How did you find out, then?"

"It was a tip-off," said Juliet. "One of the crooks who'd been working with them had second thoughts."

Chapter 77

I T IS MONDAY morning. Tim is coming home at last. It is actually only a week since he left on the journey to King's Cross and stayed the night with Freya, but it seems like an eternity. Giash Chakrabati has been sent by Superintendent Thornton to pick him up from the station. Showing unusual tact and consideration, the Superintendent has suggested he might like to come home for a couple of hours before returning to the police station for a debriefing.

Mrs Sims is looking after Sophia, as planned, but I haven't left for work myself. Instead I am waiting for Tim, standing at the hall window so that I can see the car when it appears. I open the front door as Tim is saying goodbye to Giash and walk out to meet him. He enfolds me in an embrace. I don't try to resist.

"Come inside, Tim," I say. "You look absolutely bushed."

He is very pale and doesn't smile. We go into the house and he sinks down on to the sofa as if he has no energy left.

"Where's Sophia?" he says.

"At Mrs Sims'. I'm supposed to be at work today."

"I'm sorry."

"Don't worry. Even the Superintendent expected you to want to see me first. Tell me about Margie."

"When we found her she'd been sexually assaulted in a particularly horrible way. Damaged internally. From what I can gather, the Khans ran a sex business that catered for the

339

perversions of very rich clients. The girls were subjected to greater and greater acts of violence. Only Ayesha Verma's body and Margie were there when we busted them, but Derry is certain he'll be able to link other mispers to the Khans now. There have probably been other deaths. Or some of the women may have been released once they'd served their purpose and told to keep their mouths shut. If so, maybe they'll be brave enough to contact us when they find we've arrested Jas Khan and one of his brothers and the woman called Moura who acted as his Madam. Unfortunately, we haven't got the third brother yet. He's rumoured to be travelling in Eastern Europe, which may make catching him difficult. We have arrested the man who was abusing Margie. Unlike most of the Khans' clients, he was British. A wealthy businessman, no-one I'd heard of."

"Will Margie be all right?"

"She'll need an operation. She's in University College Hospital. The surgeon in charge of her thinks she can make a complete recovery, physically at least. Let's hope the experience doesn't turn her into a basket case."

"What will happen to her when she comes out of hospital?"

"I don't know. Nancy Chappell has suggested that she sets up a crowdfunding website for Margie. Apparently she's done this for other victims of sex crimes in the past and it's turned out quite successful. The idea is to collect enough money for her to go to university next year. She won't be well enough when the first semester begins this year."

"She can't go back to that mother of hers. And her father doesn't want her."

"I suppose social services will sort something out. Katrin, I need to talk to you about what happened when I was in London."

I look at Tim. He wears the most wretched expression I've ever seen on him.

"I think we have quite a lot of talking to do, but not about when you were in London. I bumped into Patti when I was helping Juliet and she told me what happened the night you spent in her room. I believe her. I just can't understand how you managed to be so stupid as to get yourself into that situation and, having got into it, why you couldn't just explain it to me in a straightforward way."

Tim holds out both hands in a gesture of helplessness.

"Believe me, I've been thinking about that myself. I'm sure it was something to do with the malaria tablets. Patti told me they could have strange effects, including hallucinations."

"Hallucinations? You didn't tell me about those."

"No. I didn't tell anyone. Freya was so determined to get at me that I decided no-one would understand. But the reason I was late back to hers last Monday was that somehow I managed to take a train to Ilford. I was walking down a street called Belgrave Road and I saw the shadow of a woman's corpse swinging in one of the windows of a house there."

"What made you go to Ilford?"

"I'm coming to that. The next day my computer seemed to go berserk. I saw vivid colours bleeding into each other. And I dreamt some horrible dreams of violent acts that I couldn't have imagined before."

"Sounds like a premonition rather than a hallucination."

"You mean the Khans and their vile business? I hadn't thought of that." Tim pauses. "I guess you may be right. But I think I've got to the bottom of the Ilford thing. There was a girl sitting near me on the train to London reading one of those true crime magazines. I'd forgotten about it until I saw the magazine again in a newsagent's at Gatwick. There was a silhouette of a woman being hanged on the cover, just like the one I saw in the window. Apparently someone called Edith Thompson lived in Belgrave Road in the 1920s. She was convicted of the murder of her husband and hanged."

I'm dubious.

"Do you really think you could store all that in your subconscious?"

"Not normally. As I said, I think it was the effect of the pills."

"If you say so. Coming back to Margie . . ."

Tim looks up sharply.

"You're about to ask me something, aren't you?"

"I think I deserve a couple of favours from you." I say it as lightly as possible, but I know there is a tautness in my voice and I know Tim hears it, too.

"She came here the night before she vanished. She asked me if she could come to work as our nanny so that she could save for university."

"Why do you want a nanny? Aren't you happy with the arrangement with Mrs Sims?"

"Yes, but it was mainly Margie who was looking after Sophia. And I think Sophia's too young to go out of the house every day, whereas . . ."

"Whereas?"

"If she was being cared for at home, I could go back to work full time."

"Is that what you want to do?"

"If you agree, I think it is. I've enjoyed the last few days at work so much. I'm just not cut out for staying at home."

"You know what I think about people who employ servants.

Besides, even with you working full-time, we probably can't afford it."

"She wouldn't be a servant. We could ask her to consider working on an au pair's contract. She'd have fewer duties than a proper nanny – we'd just ask her to mind Sophia, not do any housework or laundry. If the crowdfunding project is a success, she'd still have the money for university. We might be able to contribute a bit to it, too. And she'd be a lot happier with us than staying with either of her parents."

"Won't you mind having someone else living with us all the time?"

"It'd only be for a year. I think we could cope with that."

"She'd have to take the spare room. What would we do when we have visitors?"

I laugh.

"You mean, Nancy Chappell wouldn't be able to come here on spec?"

For the first time since he walked through the door, Tim laughs, too.

"Neither would Freya! Come to think of it, that could be quite an advantage."

"So you'll give it a go?"

"If she still wants to do it when she comes out of hospital. You'll have to ask her."

The phone starts ringing before I can say anything else.

"Superintendent Thornton. Good morning. I'll be with you in an hour."

"Put him on speak," I mouth at Tim. The Superintendent's voice comes booming out, ebullient, as if he's feeling pleased with himself.

"Take your time, Yates. No need to hurry. I just wanted

Chapter 79

PETER PRANCE, EMERGING from the cheap boarding house he'd found in Lille, decided he would splash out on an English newspaper and bought the international edition of *The Times*. When he saw that Jas Khan had been taken into custody, his delight knew no bounds. Virtue could be rewarded, after all, even if it was rooted in dishonour.

Acknowledgements

I T'S DIFFICULT TO express how much I owe to Chris and Jen Hamilton-Emery for their unbounded enthusiasm for and faith in the DI Yates novels, and also to Chris for the beautiful jacket and distinguished typesetting that have become the hallmark of my and indeed all Salt novels. I'd also like to thank the other members of the wonderful new Salt team: Hannah Corbett, whose inspired PR is second to none; Adrian Weston, who works tirelessly to sell the rights; and Medwyn Hughes and Julian Ball, of PGUK, and their amazing representatives who work with booksellers right across the UK to get the books into the shops.

As always, the novels would be as nothing without the readers, and from the bottom of my heart I'd like to thank all of you, including those whom I've actually met, those of you who have taken the trouble to 'meet' me or review my books on my blog or through social networks and everyone who has bought or borrowed my books to read. You are a constant source of inspiration to me.

There are many other people whom I ought to thank here, but as much as I'd like to it's impossible to mention everyone. I feel I must especially single out four friends, all of whom have provided unstinting support and hospitality when I've been out promoting the books: Sally, who has always been a staunch supporter and whose house I've taken the liberty to 'borrow' for Freya; Madelaine and Marc, who are my chief champions in Lincolnshire; and Pamela and Robert, who as well as believing in the books have provided unrepayable moral and practical support in what began as a very difficult year. Once again, I'd like to record my appreciation for the talented Alison Cassels at Wakefield One and her generous and lively reading groups and for Sam Buckley and her reading groups at Bookmark in Spalding, who have followed DI Yates from 'birth'. I'd also like to include Tim Walker and Jenny Pugh, of Walkers Bookshops in Stamford, and Charlie, the events manager at Waterstones Covent Garden. Finally, I must mention Harry, a young man whom I met at Charlie's event at Covent Garden, whose high praise for *The Crossing* and subsequent impatience to read all past and future DI Yates novels exceeded all the accolades I could ever have hoped for.

My inimitable family continues to make its unique contribution. Once again, James and Annika have worked meticulously through the final draft, picking up grammatical inaccuracies and other minor inconsistencies with hawk-like precision. Emma has taught me afresh the power of language and how words may be discovered and combined in new ways by each succeeding generation. Chris has yet to read *Rooted in Dishonour*, but when he does I'm certain will pronounce judgement with his usual pithy and succinct charm.

My very sincere thanks to you all.

CHRISTINA JAMES

NEW FICTION FROM SALT

GERRI BRIGHTWELL
Dead of Winter (978-1-78463-049-2)

NEIL CAMPBELL
Sky Hooks (978-1-78463-037-9)

SUE GEE
Trio (978-1-78463-061-4)

V. H. LESLIE
Bodies of Water (978-1-78463-071-3)

WYL MENMUIR
The Many (978-1-78463-048-5)

STEFAN MOHAMED
Ace of Spiders (978-1-78463-067-6)

ANNA STOTHARD
The Museum of Cathy (978-1-78463-082-9)

STEPHANIE VICTOIRE
The Other World, It Whispers (978-1-78463-085-0)

RECENT FICTION FROM SALT

KERRY HADLEY-PRYCE
The Black Country (978-1-78463-034-8)

CHRISTINA JAMES
The Crossing (978-1-78463-041-6)

IAN PARKINSON
The Beginning of the End (978-1-78463-026-3)

CHRISTOPHER PRENDERGAST
Septembers (978-1-907773-78-5)

MATTHEW PRITCHARD
Broken Arrow (978-1-78463-040-9)

JONATHAN TAYLOR
Melissa (978-1-78463-035-5)

GUY WARE
The Fat of Fed Beasts (978-1-78463-024-9)

ALSO AVAILABLE FROM SALT

ELIZABETH BAINES
Too Many Magpies (978-1-84471-721-7)
The Birth Machine (978-1-907773-02-0)

LESLEY GLAISTER
Little Egypt (978-1-907773-72-3)

ALISON MOORE
The Lighthouse (978-1-907773-17-4)
The Pre-War House and Other Stories (978-1-907773-50-1)
He Wants (978-1-907773-81-5)

ALICE THOMPSON
Justine (978-1-78463-031-7)
The Falconer (978-1-78463-009-6)
The Existential Detective (978-1-78463-011-9)
Burnt Island (978-1-907773-48-8)

This book has been typeset by
SALT PUBLISHING LIMITED
using Neacademia, a font designed by Sergei Egorov
for the Rosetta Type Foundry in the Czech Republic.
It is manufactured using Creamy 70gsm, a Forest
Stewardship Council™ certified paper from Stora Enso's
Anjala Mill in Finland. It was printed and bound by
Clays Limited in Bungay, Suffolk, Great Britain.

CROMER, NORFOLK
GREAT BRITAIN
MMXVI